D1475887

Books by William Stevens

The Peddler
The Gunner
The Cannibal Isle
The Best of Our Time

the
Best of
Our Time

Random House

New York

William Stevens

the
Best of
Our Time

Library of Congress Cataloging in Publication Data
Stevens, William, 1925–
The best of our time.
I. Title.
PZ4.S84563Be [PS3569.T454]   813'.5'4   72–13926
ISBN 0-394-47977-7

Manufactured in the United States of America
First Edition

To true believers Fella Cecilio,
Fran Haas,
Nels Lofstedt
. . . and my mother

We have seen the best of our time:
machinations, hollowness, treachery and
all ruinous disorders follow us quietly to
our graves.

—*King Lear,* Act I, Scene 2

Assembled underground, we wait for
    trains
That move through darkness like the
    track of time;
We, cripples, negatives of promise, lean
Our crutch of bones upon a scribbled
    beam;
While the loud year beats impartially,
    like rain
On eloquent marble, we await our
    trains.

—*The Marginal Dark,*
John Malcolm Brinnin

the
Best of
Our Time

ONE

Eliot Scanlyn had one foot in contact with the briefcase under his seat and felt foolish, as though he
were a courier in an old movie where men wore
thin mustaches and snap-brim fedoras. He was too old for
games, too old even to see himself as a knight in worn and
slightly dented armor riding out on a last grand quest.

Scanlyn asked the stewardess for a second pillow to tuck
into the small of his back. As the girl moved up the aisle showing
a remarkable length of leg each time she bent to distribute one
of her bundles of fluff, Scanlyn longed for the days when short
skirts first came out and a careless slouch or fortuitous gust of
wind revealed all sorts of trimmings. Now it was the all-in-one
of tights or body stockings. When the plane lurched and the
girl's skirt twitched, the view was more architectural than car-
nal, a rounded cornice balanced on impersonal shafts. He
sighed; there was something almost necrophilic in the unwrapping necessary to get at a modern woman.

Scanlyn was aware that the dampening effect might be due
less to the day's styles than to his own chemistry, the accumula-
tion of decaying cells slowly insulating his nerves and fibers. He
was nearly gray and nearly fifty and his stomach hung over his
belt when he ate too much. In an earlier time he would certainly have been pressing conversation on the woman next to
him. She had an interesting and slightly worn face in graceful

transition between thirty and forty, and there was every possibility that with a few words they might have created a way stop among the clouds, a promise to be picked up later. But her rings put him off. He avoided married women because of the complications, and he'd come to distrust women who had been married and who flaunted their rings as a symbolic seam in broken lives.

The lady shifted in her seat and cleared her throat as though she was going to speak. Scanlyn let his head loll toward the window, pretending to be asleep. He opened a cautious eye on that side and saw the moon, tiny and rimless, its light a pale wash on the clouds below. Judith had been the last of Scanlyn's ladies with rings, and she was his moon memory, always busy scratching cabalistic signs on an astrological chart. She calculated the swing of dead planets but paid no attention at all to the moon's effect on her body, Scanlyn's first experience in plugging a seeping cleft. She'd found that cute, sweet; it was sometimes difficult to remember he was a married man. Scanlyn had protested that it was a strictly legal condition, bumbling and fumbling his fidelity to love rather than to a wife.

Tears crept from under her lids. He was so explicit, so full of declarations and explanations, she wasn't allowed even for a minute to forget that he belonged to someone else. And then Scanlyn would feel compelled to say even more, bringing on fresh tears until he wondered who the hell he could talk to if not to her. What was new in the zodiac? Maybe they could talk about that without fighting. And she, snuffling, would tell him they hadn't been fighting, but the moon was in Taurus, a very fiery conjunction with her rising sign. It was also filling, tremendously goatish stuff. Scanlyn offered to run get his pipes and her eyes dried and so did his mouth. Judith made more scratches on her chart and told him she was also filling and it might be messy. But when she looked at him her eyes were round and clear and she raised both hands to the clasp of her necklace, Scanlyn growling something about never never while the watch and the bracelet and the damned rings dropped one by one on the night table . . . never never never.

5
The Best of Our Time

"I beg your pardon?" the woman next to him said.

Scanlyn tried to make his starting look like one of the jerks of sleep, tried to swallow that remembered growl in a glottal sound. He closed the other eye, put his foot on the briefcase. The plane hummed and the image of Judith thinned. Wine washed gently over his dinner until the reflection of the moon flared like a pinprick on his iris and then was gone.

Eliot Scanlyn sat in a whistling silver bolt, guarding ten thousand dollars, because he no longer had a desk of his own to sit at in the Capitol, and because he'd never held a teaching job long enough to qualify for tenure.

During three years of wartime service in a stateside intelligence unit he'd had enough free time to take courses which accumulated into a master's degree, but when he tried to apply it in the postwar rush to education he found himself facing veterans of experience he couldn't hope to synthesize, men more interested in opportunity than knowledge. Their struggle to break out of a mold created in part by the very things Scanlyn was teaching gave him his first real glimpse of the System, and as his focus became more clear he worked it into a Ph. D. thesis which was nearly radical in an atmosphere so recently filled with the snap of flags.

Scanlyn's new vision happened to match a national mood. People were beginning to tire of standing with their hands over their hearts while they strained toward the impossible notes of the Anthem. Except for token handouts, the spoils seemed to have been used up in securing the victory, and the future which arrived didn't much resemble the one which had been promised. There was enough of a rumbling protest to make the situation political, and enough politicians looking to extract what juice they could out of it. Scanlyn and a number of other bright young men who'd attracted attention were invited into government. Like all the others he was grim and hopeful, working long hours over projects which were enthusiastically received even though they disappeared into the dense jelly of legislation. The struggle itself seemed worth the effort.

6

And then the winds changed, blowing cold and red until they stirred and finally stretched nationalistic banners. In the violent corrective measure applied to the Republic's leftward lurch, Scanlyn's people were easily identified as a segment of the worm working from within. When dispute became throttled under a new tricolor of red and black and gray lists, many of his colleagues were ridden out of town on directives or quit in disgust. Scanlyn stayed on. He had no real alternative; acadame clucking at the outrages committed in the name of security managed to be looking the other way whenever one of the victims came begging for sanctuary. But Scanlyn also wanted very much to stay. The more he saw of the inner working of government, the worse it looked, and the more he thought something should and could be done. He held what little position he had until he was actually at the lip of the undertow, one of the subpoenaed blinking and sweating to make his own points of order.

And then it seemed as though the nation awoke from a nightmare and by simply punching the pillows and straightening the sheets, changed the whole landscape. The inquisitors went out of favor, and after their departure there were pious words about a lesson learned—but not so completely that there wasn't an aftermath filled with apprehension, a fear that some new avenging angel might appear flourishing a crooked sword. When Scanlyn pressed for action heads shook warily, suggested another, better time. He worked in limbo; the better times never came to the capital, and outside it the clamor for overdue change increased. Scanlyn was more and more caught up by those voices, by the blight which corroded every promise and mild reform—the urban poor.

He applied for a grant, resigned, began a book and took a wife. His work carried him into city byways no one had paid much attention to before, and he shaped his data into a humanitarian plea couched in sociological and economic and demographic terms. *Masses* had an impressive reception and even made a little money. Scanlyn received honorary degrees, became a guest lecturer, chaired seminars. He was very nearly an

The Best of Our Time

influential figure, and when the administration changed again he was among those chosen to settle along the New Frontier.

By that time Scanlyn was no longer really a young man, but he was as bright as ever and was far more professional than any of the whiz kids he worked with. There were conflicts and pressures, but he followed the twists of his conscience and had more to say than was politic. He was the odd man close to being on his way out when Kennedy's death broke up the power combinations. When the palace guard changed, Scanlyn was kept on, an independent voice in the long transition while new images were being hammered out. The legislation which was finally enacted dealt with realities already past, and Scanlyn had the small satisfaction of seeing some of his ideas adopted too late. But then there was a reaction against the little progress made, and a period of consolidation followed. Reports containing some of Scanlyn's best work were solemnly received and totally suppressed, and his juices were gradually blotted up by the reams of paper which passed from hand to hand in conference rooms dominated by one great seal or another.

He was kept on through a fourth change in administration, a sort of showpiece link in a communications system which didn't exist. Scanlyn earned more than ever but was listened to less, and he began to see himself as a glorified archivist, an expert in a field he'd actually lost touch with. He let it be known on the outside that his talents were being wasted, that he'd be better used in some liberal foundation or as a university department head—and was astonished to learn his person was not in demand, his reputation already in the cool edge of eclipse. There were new theories with more relevance, theorists with more glitter. Out of habit and need he continued to wander from committee to committee, his confidence dwindling until he became a muffled ingratiating presence looking for a place where he could be useful. As he grew more afflicted and less charitable toward himself he began to understand that what he called his work mattered more to him than to either government or society.

By the time Project Flipover took shape Scanlyn was verging on sentimental and nearly sniveling gratitude whenever anyone found something in him worth using. He recognized the project as a bald jiggle, the strategy of some opportunistic high council, but no matter how mean the reasons for it he saw the move itself as desirable. And he thought he was the man to sell it, to cap his decline with a last fine gesture which might in fact be the beginning of a new upward spiral. He jumped at the opportunity.

Now, as he flew westward, he didn't actually tell himself that all things were possible, but he took comfort in knowing he was moving so rapidly in the wake of the sun that he almost caught the clock; he was passing through nearly dead time as he fled absolutely dead ends.

Scanlyn stirred at a shift in altitude and came fully awake at the first warning chimes. They were below the clouds, falling through the predawn morning toward a blazing grid which bled away into filaments crossing enormous stretches of darkness. The plane tilted and dipped until the grid became an electric bonfire raging in all the colors of sea-stained wood. Runway lamps blinked under the slat of the wing. He waited patiently buckled until the plane rolled to a stop. His neighbor wasn't getting off, and he smiled apologetically when he woke her brushing past. A web of lines had settled on her face while she slept, and for a moment she looked haggard and guilty, as though she'd been roused by an unexpected knock on a motel-room door.

Scanlyn's experience in the West was limited to guest appearances at coastal universities. He'd never been in the desert country. The cool dry air of Las Vegas seemed to burn the creases at the corners of his eyes. There were passengers at the loading gate waiting for the vacated seats on the final leg of the flight into the Pacific morning. Those who'd gotten off went through a bleak room where people sat red-eyed or dozing before a board posted with a flight to Chicago. A thunderous takeoff rattled the windows and the fluorescent light on the glass turned oily. The file dipped into a tunnel filled with the whine of a taxiing plane and came out in the main concourse where music blared, slot machines jangled and bars and restaurants were still open.

Scanlyn surrendered his stubs and waited while luggage accumulated along the rim of the baggage wheel. Every airport he'd been in at that hour had had a tomblike atmosphere, a collection point for dead souls who'd missed all their connections, but this one gave no sign of closing down. He watched a man and a woman clutching an assortment of bags and a baby go by arguing furiously. A fresh group of travelers gathered at an adjoining wheel as it began to spin out luggage. A tense couple hurried after a porter jogging behind a hand truck; a man in a Stetson limped past, the heel of one boot broken.

Scanlyn's porter collected him and they marched along the concourse. At a coffee bar a girl with dangling legs took a cup from her mouth and gave him a professional smile. The cab rank was busy. He stood aside while four apparent drunks got out of a taxi and left it smelling of perfume and gin. The driver drawled unintelligibly as they whipped through a corridor of billboards. And then they turned the corner and were in the heart of the bonfire. Scanlyn had seen it in films and on television but he wasn't prepared for the brilliance, the madhouse of colored light. It marched in waves, in pillars and pennons, flew off in wings to bleach the night sky, so intense it might have been a burn-off of gas erupting from the earth. He nearly flinched.

There was a steady stream of cabs in the hotel driveway, nearly identical people entering and leaving. The lobby was piled with luggage, filled with charged faces. As Scanlyn waited at the desk he could hear clicks and whispers and cries from the casino at the end of the corridor, all underscored by a beat of frantic revue music. The bellboy's smile was warm and calculating. They whizzed up the hotel's tower to a room done in tasteful neo-Spanish, one wall a quarter-circle of glass overlooking both desert and city. The bellboy performed his little ceremony of attendance and then told Scanlyn anything he might need, *anything,* was no more distant than a call to the number thirty-eight on the badge he fingered like a corrupt sheriff. Scanlyn tipped him goodbye.

He found a small balcony beyond the window. The automobile sounds which drifted up weren't the brakes and horns of traffic, but the steady hum of tires and engines, beneath them a sort of restrained crackling which might have been the electric beast feeding. Scanlyn thought of the black man he'd never met, but whose voice he'd heard and whose picture he'd seen, hiding in that dazzling wilderness. He heard a rustle of cloth from one of the balconies below. A woman gave a throaty laugh.

Scanlyn gripped the railing and shook his head. That four o'clock in the morning supposed to be the dark midnight of the soul was evidently happening somewhere else.

TWO

The Bureau was housed within the carefully arranged building blocks of a major Department, but
it was an orphan agency. Created as an adjunct of
business regulation during Roosevelt's first administration, its
direction was so often shifted to meet different contingencies it
eventually lost all definition and became an Executive catch-all,
a gypsy operation hidden in different budgets as well as in
different buildings.

Although the clerical staff was structured under Civil Service, management often changed with each administration, and
the Bureau became a way stop for amateurs doing a tour in
government and for professionals marking time until better
opportunities arrived. In its present form it had title to Social
Stability, and Frank Prippet was its director. His office was
furnished with solid well-kept pieces which had been passed
down and would never look as though they really belonged to
anyone, their lines rubbed nearly invisible by the hands of too
many owners. He had an issue rug and issue ashtrays and a clock
which kept official time. The only thing distinguishing the office
from any other in the same civil grade was the framed photographs on the wall.

Prippet was a professional bureaucrat with a broken career. The earliest pictures covered the first twelve years, his
flying hair and button-bright eyes moving gradually from the

outer edge of groups toward their centers. The period cul-
minated in a photograph where the only two subjects were
Prippet and Eisenhower, the President shaking his hand and
bent slightly away, as though he were looking at someone outside the picture. Shortly afterward the party went out of power
and Prippet went with it.

The next grouping covered his eight years in exile, Prippet's action reversed as he moved toward the edge of crowds
around Goldwater and Romney and Rockefeller. His hair was
groomed and his smile more exact, but the camera often caught
an expression of doglike longing toward the centers of attention. Then there was a resurrection of sorts, a new cycle beginning with minor campaign jubilations, Prippet finally taking an
oath to some federal god and going on to pose with faces entirely different from those in the earlier pictures.

Lewis Allenstein had been studying the display for three
years. It had a solid uniform fatuousness, a toothy implication
that good fellowship equaled good government, but the latest
photographs lacked the suggestion of progress, the sidling toward power, which those covering Prippet's first stay revealed.
He seemed to be in a fixed and slightly distant orbit. The most
recent picture showed him at a departmental picnic, grinning
at a forkful of potato salad while surrounded by no one of any
consequence.

Allenstein had formed a parabola theory of government
careers. There were no plateaus; if you weren't going up, you
were going down. The Bureau seemed to be suffering from a
severe and perhaps fatal lack of clout. As things stood, it was in
the double jeopardy not only of being wiped clean if the administration changed, but of being recycled if it survived, the
hive and the workers the same under a new title and new
management.

Allenstein was administrative assistant to the deputy
bureau chief and the least of the floating executives. He'd been
an amateur party activist and associate professor of political
science when the administration recruited him, and he was
happy to take a leave of absence from increasingly woolly uni-

versity crowds who waved little red books in his classroom and who once, in a remarkable demonstration of either production or restraint, left an individually shaped and colored turd in each of his desk drawers. He wasn't anxious to get back to that life. More, he'd been bitten early by the sense of being among the movers rather than the moved, and he was sure that among the shifting planes of power in the city, there were opportunities for a clever and dedicated man. The career Allenstein hoped for did not include posing, after fifteen years of service, in mawkish appreciation of a glutinous lump of potato balanced on the tines of a fork. But the halftone was at least appropriate; Allenstein colored Prippet neutral.

That morning he had trouble seeing him. A section of the Monument was visible from the office, a gray and unrelated column which might have been an airshaft awaiting delivery to substandard housing, and Prippet sat with his back to the windows. Through a trick of the morning light he seemed to be growing out of the stone, his features sometimes so indistinct that only the stiff smile remained. The Cheshire-like illusion was complemented by the three men who sat facing his desk: Howard MacFarlane playing with his pipe, John Stirby tugging at an ear, Allenstein with a hand to his brow to keep the glare off his glasses. It was a full staff meeting. MacFarlane was Prippet's administrative assistant and Stirby the deputy bureau chief.

Prippet kept them waiting while he leafed through a set of papers. From time to time he looked up to grin or frown and the others would come to attention, but then he'd shake his head as though they couldn't be expected to understand what he'd been reading. Allenstein was familiar with the performance and had nearly fallen into a semi-stupor by the time Prippet seemed satisfied that he'd prepared the way. He carefully evened the sheaf and placed it center forward on the desk, leaving just enough room for him to fold his hands and lean toward his audience.

"Flipover's on," he said. "Case positive."

Allenstein came alert while Howard MacFarlane scratched

his jowls and John Stirby sat even more erect.

"And it's our ball game entirely," Prippet added.

"But with that Scanlyn in it, I suppose," Stirby said. "There didn't happen to be a last-minute change for the better."

"I think we might look at that differently, John. The printout gave us exactly six names, and Eliot Scanlyn was available and willing. He seems to have an adequate background."

"Civil rights," MacFarlane said.

"*Whose* civil rights?"

"That's not the real question at this point." Prippet's voice went down and his jaw set sincerely. "If he fits the overall pattern established by the computer, we'll just have to assume he's the best man for the job."

"I take it there was some consultation with actual human beings," Stirby said.

Prippet glanced at MacFarlane and then placed his fingers together near the end of his nose in a pious, vulgar gesture. "I'm sure there was," he said. "But more important—and this is for our ears only—we've had word that He has a definite interest in the project."

Color crept up Stirby's neck. "That's news to me," he said. "I would have thought that my position was of secondary importance here and that such information would have been made available."

"Somewhat privileged," MacFarlane said.

"From who?"

"There isn't any question of your position, John. I think Mac meant we wouldn't have counted all the way down to launch if our checkout sheet hadn't been cleared all the way up."

"If He's for it, then of course I don't have any further questions about the thing itself . . . but I still can't see this Scanlyn in it. Damn well I know that background everybody seems to be so high on. And so do you, Frank. It wasn't so long ago you were investigating him and others of that like ilk."

Allenstein watched Prippet recede until his voice seemed to come from among the granite chips of the Monument. "I was simply a part of the senator's staff," he said. "And those were very different times. The point is, I don't think our personal opinions should be allowed to interfere with what we've been given to accomplish."

"Scanlyn wrote that book . . . what's its name, Lew?"

"Masses."

"And did it or did it not say that everybody ought to go on public relief?"

"Not exactly," Allenstein said.

"And as if he wasn't busy enough meddling with states' rights, he was also very active in pushing for an even worse gun-control law. To the point he attacked some very respectable organizations only trying to uphold their constitutional rights."

"Not very constitutionally," MacFarlane said.

"That sounds like a pretty personal opinion."

"We're all entitled to that, John, and since we were never invited to participate in that particular program, I don't see an application."

"I judge a man more by what he does than by what he claims not to be."

"And you're certainly entitled to your judgments as well," Prippet said. "We all are, although it would be an entirely different matter for us to make them publicly if we haven't been asked to."

"You mean about *this* particular program we're so-called participating in, this sending a pinko liberal on some kind of joke luxury excursion to sweet talk—if bribe isn't a better word—a runaway *Negro* into . . ."

"We'll be supervising a liaison." Prippet's mouth hardened in a downward swoop and his eyes rolled up under the shelf of his brows. "A very important one. And I don't think we need another go-round on the responsibility of doing exactly what we've been asked to do. We're all here because this administration has confidence in us, and the least we can do is return it. That's obvious to everyone, isn't it?"

No one answered.

"I mean to make myself clear. Discussion is always welcome, but we close ranks on the other side of that door."

Stirby sat as though he were frozen, knees together and feet planted firmly on the floor, so stiff that his jacket didn't touch the back of his chair. "I don't leak," he said.

"None of us do . . . unless we're asked to. That's understood, Lew?"

"Perfectly."

"Check," MacFarlane said.

"We're pulling together, then. We'll have a good deal more to discuss shortly, but in the meantime we keep it just where it is, between the four of us."

The light had softened, but Stirby's eyes were narrowed as he stared out the window.

John Stirby had come to the Bureau literally out of the blue, a former municipal police commissioner whose ideas of law and order had grown increasingly rigid and controversial. When the administration supporting him was voted out of office he raged so loud and long about jellyfish politicians that no other city would risk hiring him. As a professed party regular, Stirby was an embarrassment noisy and unemployed, and a state committeeman made the necessary connections to have him absorbed by the new administration.

Lewis Allenstein was shocked to find himself appointed Stirby's assistant. As soon as he could, he began a cautious probe to see if a change in assignment was possible, and one of the first people he encountered was an equally unhappy Stirby circling just as cautiously as he tried to get Allenstein transferred or fired. Prippet let both of them know that he himself hadn't had any say in the Bureau's composition beyond being allowed to bring along Howard MacFarlane, his law partner, and he gave them a harangue on teamwork which ended with a reminder that someone inevitably went over the side when boat-rocking began.

Allenstein had to contend with more than Stirby; he had to face up to the nature of the Bureau itself. In the early days he

The Best of Our Time

was patient, waiting for those meaningful projects and studies he had come to Washington to undertake. But the Bureau never got any real work of its own, only scraps, beginnings or middles or ends from programs under way not only at HEW but at other departments, and Allenstein finally had to accept the fact that he'd been recruited into limbo. He thought about going back to teaching, but couldn't see how returning to the campus smirched with an ultra-short record of government service would help his career. More important, he wanted to stay where he was.

He might not belong in the Bureau, but he was sure that he belonged in Washington, and if the Bureau was his only base, he would simply have to discount science and apply himself to politics as one of the many arts of the possible. Both the director and deputy director were expected to address minor gatherings as part of their official duties. While Prippet was an experienced bland catechist of government handouts, Stirby's approach was pure blunderbuss. The administration didn't object to him because they scheduled his appearances before audiences matched to his style, but Allenstein was appalled at the thought of being identified with Stirby's "folks." Yet, as a junior striver, he had no other identity except as Stirby's man. He had to find a way to be able to work for Stirby, as well as a way for Stirby to work for him, and the only possible escape from his situation lay in his trying to change the deputy director's image.

Allenstein's early attempts to modify the speeches were disastrous, and the only thing which kept him and Stirby from openly attacking each other was their joint fear of toppling into the briny. He might have given up if he hadn't had such vivid memories of his recent obscurity, and if he hadn't felt an occasional real pulse in the apparatus and longed to become a factor in that enormous power field. He took a grim pull on his belt and moved closer to accommodation.

Stirby was deeply suspicious of Allenstein's initial approaches, but he gradually became convinced that his assistant wasn't trying to change what he said, only his manner of saying it, and little by little he allowed his semi-articulate ranting to be transformed into the homilies of a rough champion righteously wroth over lost values. As a result, he not only held his old audiences but attracted so many new fans that he began to gain some notoriety as a speaker.

Frank Prippet wasn't pleased by his deputy's success. At first he tried to be offhand about it, but he became waspish when Stirby's popularity continued to grow, and even went so far as to recommend that he devote less time and energy to his activities outside the office. Prippet was checked, however, by the administration's approval of Stirby's increasing influence with a segment of the electorate, and he was forced to rearrange his public smile to reflect the small glory being gathered by the Bureau as a whole.

As Stirby became better known, so did Allenstein. He was gratified that insiders were aware of the source of the words coming from the horse's mouth, but there were times when he was afraid that it was actually the other end speaking, and he was often unhappy with what he had to write. In his worst moments he had visions of a shouting sweaty-faced mob brandishing torches, and had to console himself with the idea that he was actually a temporizing influence, bringing Stirby's people around to a less emotional viewpoint. He never allowed himself to think that he might be moving toward them.

At the end of three years Allenstein and Stirby were grudging collaborators still miles apart. They never argued over Bureau policies because the few it was given to implement were almost completely inconsequential—but Flipover was something altogether different. An earlier Allenstein would have been enthusiastic over the project, and even now he was for it in principle; Stirby called it abject surrender in his calmer moments, pure treason in his wilder ones.

The deputy was furious now as he stood behind his own desk, a big man with carefully brushed silver hair, his person bandbox-neat even after the long meeting. His office was on a lower floor than Prippet's, and the Monument filled the windows like the oncoming edge of a gigantic plow, the lagoon beyond invisible except for a small corner where litter bobbed in a greenish scum.

"At least I reflected my opinion," Stirby said.

Allenstein paced back and forth, his hands clasped behind him beneath his jacket. "That was a little like shooting off a flashbulb in a whorehouse."

"You mean I said what they really think."

"You ought to get off Scanlyn, John. He doesn't have any weight or importance any more, and he isn't even actually working for us . . . he's only a factor in what we're supposed to be coordinating."

"I hope he coordinates himself straight to hell," Stirby said.

"He just might pull this thing off."

"Not with my help, he won't."

"I don't see that our help has been particularly asked for."

"What we want to do is make our position known right away."

"I had the impression Prippet was telling us we should avoid doing just that," Allenstein said. "But let's play The Game for a minute. Question: is this administration especially known for its sympathy to what is loosely called the civil rights movement?"

"A sight too much for my taste."

"Answer: no. Question: why then is an administration which is not particularly known for its sympathy to what is loosely called the civil rights movement extending this sort of an invitation to a black radical? Answer, part one: it needs some sort of spectacular move to prove it isn't dead on its duff domestically. Government by the tube hasn't turned out to be all that was expected of it, and the only enduring image He's developed is of a man who sweats a lot. That and the double peace sign— two fingers up yours if you happen to be on the other side."

"Let's leave out the smart-ass," Stirby added.

"But a black radical who also happens to be wanted on some fancy warrant no one has bothered to explain to me yet?"

"They ought to pick him up."

"Until a month ago they didn't even know where he was.

Answer, part two: they don't want to pick him up. That was the old plan, when what we seemed to be running was a sort of inquisition specializing in baby doctors, poets and people who looked like Jesus getting gagged and shackled while judges broke their gavels left and right. And then there were the nuns and priests. I think I know what He's been doing since He stepped back for a good look at that whole balls-up. He's been praying for rain."

"There's a lot of your talk I could do without, Lew."

"They don't want to pick Buffre up because they can't afford another circus built around a black man. But what to do? When Buffre was out of sight they could write him off as a fugitive and forget him, but when some dunce found him they couldn't just leave him out there to maybe be discovered by the press who'd add a few heart-wrenching interviews to their problems. If they move toward due process now, they'll wind up with another political prisoner on their hands. What's the alternative?"

"There doesn't need to be one," Stirby said. "Laws are meant to be kept."

"Unless they're unenforceable and turn out to be an embarrassment to the makers. It really isn't a bad dodge they've thought up, John. Buffre doesn't wear a beret and carry a water pistol on his hip. As far as I know he doesn't even talk dirty in public. And he's young and has a following. I think a few of those dim bulbs at the top might have finally gotten the message that they're going to have to do a lot more than stitch samplers to bring it all together. Since they're not doing such a good job collecting rednecks, they might as well give blacks a whirl."

"That's a favorite tactic, making out someone's harmless while all the time they're boring from within."

"Whose favorite tactic?"

"Damn well you know who I mean."

"Me?"

Stirby looked stubborn.

"I know it's difficult to get the image of the liberal sheeny out of some of these red-white-and-blue-dyed skulls, John, but I thought you and I had worked that out pretty well. I've been sweating too hard on your account to—" Allenstein began.

"And hoisting your own end up in the air at the same time, ready to take off for the first rainbow you see."

"Don't think I haven't had a tickle from here and there."

"Hah, but that Mr. Somebody in Housing isn't about to go anyplace, except maybe back to the farm."

"That's better than being shoved back on a beat."

"I'll start to worry about my prospects when I see *you* jumping ship."

"Neither one of us is going to keep afloat simply by hanging onto that nightstick of yours."

They glared at each other for a moment, and then Stirby looked down and began to pick at his blotter. Allenstein cleaned his glasses.

"I never begrudged you your help," Stirby said.

"You're not the only one I'm trying to help, John."

Allenstein resumed his pacing, stopped, looked at the ceiling, then settled in an armchair. "Okay, I'm for it more or less and you're not, but I don't think our respective attitudes are going to matter. This is the first time anyone's tried something as strong as a Buffre. If it works, the press is absolutely going to have to give them an *A* for effort, and they might even indulge in a little soul-scratching and find that their past attitudes have been too harsh. That would be welcome, Commissioner, most welcome. And if it works, the Bureau's bound to come in for some of the credit and Prippet's going to be right up there with his front feet in the trough."

"Whatever I say about Frank, I say to his face."

"Which one?"

"That smart-ass is going to do you in, Lew."

"I've heard you call him a shyster, but never while we were in there."

"I call all lawyers shysters."

"This one is going to be so busy gobbling up glory he won't leave much for anyone else."

"Damn little I want."

"Myself either, as a matter of fact, but with Prippet making as much noise as he can to call attention to himself he's going to call attention to the Bureau as well, and we're part of it. What you call your 'folks' aren't going to like it at all."

"We'll make our position known right away, like I said."

"I don't think so. I don't think there's a chance that we can get away with trying to sell the overwhelming pressure of those scruples of yours this time."

"You act like you invented them."

"There are people who believe I invented *you*, John."

"And there's those that say you'd be back to wiping kids' noses if you didn't have somebody to hide behind."

"We'll both be doing something else if you open your mouth and He decides to put His foot in it."

"I'm going to hear from those folks of mine."

"Probably."

"Then you'd better put that fancy education of yours to work and find something for us to say."

Stirby turned his back and looked out the window. Allenstein opened his mouth, closed it, then got up and resumed his pacing.

THREE

When Scanlyn awoke the next morning he thought he was in a surrealistic light box. He'd drawn only the inside curtains the night before, and now the entire curved wall was filled with the glare of the nine o'clock sun while he lay washed by a slightly tainted flow from the air conditioner and remembered where he was. It wasn't a typical ambience for an urbanologist or demographer or sociologist, whatever it was he'd become over the years, but perhaps he was turning into something new: rebirth through a freshly sterilized and banded toilet seat, through the water glasses wrapped in plastic, the antiseptic landscape.

He took his briefcase downstairs and had it put in the hotel safe. The lobby was almost deserted. There were four tables still operating in the mushroom glow of the casino but no customers other than himself in the coffee shop. Breakfast was served until three. Scanlyn had the Chuckwagon Special of eggs and steak and potatoes and found it threatening to run away with his stomach. Only one taxi was parked in the driveway. He decided to walk off the meal.

There was a heavy flow of commercial traffic along the boulevard, but the sidewalks were deserted. Sand ground audibly beneath his feet. The brilliant light flattened and nearly eliminated perspective so that mountains miles away seemed just down the street. The lush hotel gardens were curiously bleak, and the wonderland of the night before was stacked in tiers of dead bulbs. Story-high names on the cold glass seemed slightly forlorn, as though the acts had already closed.

Scanlyn began to sweat, a fine lubricating film which made his movements easier. His eyes went slightly out of focus in the hammocks of shadow behind his sunglasses and he had to fight off a sense of remoteness, the distinct feeling that he'd wandered onto a deserted movie set. The fluted palaces he continued to pass were only a screen, an exotic foreground backed by a skimpy border of apartment houses and trailer camps, and then by nothing but brush and sand. The hotels diminished in size and style as he approached the city, and a gaudy filling of strip joints, horse parlors and marriage studios offering especially lucky wedding rings appeared between them, but still there was no activity anywhere.

If it wasn't an ambience for Scanlyn, it didn't look as though it would be suitable for George Toussaint Buffre, either. There was nothing for a black to blend into, nothing of the angled shadows of cities or the heavy shade of southern towns. Scanlyn caught himself trapped in thought patterns colored by his own skin, working with the hackneyed image of eyeballs rolling in the dark. He gritted his teeth and tried again, as he'd tried before. There were attitudes he'd never been able to overcome, and yet he still had hopes that he could make some small change in the circumstances which had bred those attitudes. They were tattered hopes, but he clung to them as the only support of one of his last beliefs; no matter how roughly, society could be made to function.

All of which was difficult to find relevant in a land probably named by a conquistador in a blazing steel corset, then decreed to be Xanadu, a pleasure dome, by some Kubla in a business suit and Stetson hat. But now Scanlyn was encountering supermarkets and service stations and people as he worked his way downtown. He passed ordinary stores, seemed to be in an unexceptional small western city—as long as he didn't look up, didn't take notice of the massive buildings hung with bold glass sails which dominated the hub of the downtown area. It was a simpler version of dreamland, the big daddy of all the fancy casinos strung out along the boulevard, and perhaps even more bizarre because the buildings rested on open arcades where townspeople on everyday errands cut through aisles lined with hundreds of slot machines whose cherries and bells and silver and gold bars could be combined to bring instant wealth.

He found the High Heel and wandered through glittering hedgerows where players jerked and bowed as they grappled with levers, some so adept they used both hands to milk and feed simultaneously. Within the crook of the machines was a large room filled with tables, most covered with dustcloths but three open to gamblers who didn't seem to find anything unusual in cards and dice at eleven o'clock in the morning. Scanlyn went to the bar and had a bottle of beer, which was cold and peppery on his tongue. There was a restaurant beyond, and to one side of it a glassed-in area which he at first took to be the waiting room of a bus terminal but which turned out to be a Keno pit filled with women surrounded by grocery bags and shopping carts.

Scanlyn sipped his beer. Seen from the coolness of the bar, the street blazed like a bone. He checked the time, drank up, and went through the restaurant. At the swinging doors leading to the kitchen he nearly collided with a waitress who gave him an angry look. The kitchen was hot and filled with unpleasant smells. A young man shifted baskets of potatoes bubbling in dirty oil. Scanlyn identified him as Chicano, thinking wryly that he would have called him Mexican years ago, Mexican-American until recently. He sighed. "Hi," he said, "I'm looking for Joe Jones."

A drop of sweat from the other's chin fell into the oil and sizzled. "Watch?"

"Jones," Scanlyn said. "I think he works the dishes."

"Leffy!" The Chicano shook one of the fry baskets, the backs of his hands dotted with tiny silver scars, then gestured with an elbow.

Scanlyn turned to see a man in a white hat and stained T-shirt watching. He went over to him. "Leffy?"

"Lef*ty* . . . yah." There was a tattoo of a woman with astonishing blue breasts on his upper arm.

"I'm looking for Joe Jones."

"You hadn't oughta be in here, mister."

"Only for a minute. I'm trying to get in touch with . . . "

"Yah, I heard. I bet you want to pay him back some money you owe him."

"I wouldn't give you that old dodge. It's a personal matter."

The man scratched idly at an armpit and inspected his fingernails. "You probably mean one of the nigger dishwashers," he said.

"Probably."

"You going to pinch him?"

"Nothing like that."

"It wouldn't bother me none if you did. He's one of them mouth niggers, you know?"

Scanlyn nodded.

"Yah, he's on the second shift, comes in at one." Lefty took Scanlyn's arm and turned him toward a door. "He's got to come in through there because it's a rule they ain't allowed in the dining room."

"Thanks," Scanlyn said.

"You wait out in the alley and you can get him."

"At one."

"He won't show up more'n a minute before."

Scanlyn thanked the cook and went back to the bar and had a second bottle of beer, then strolled between the rows of machines. They were more magical than any childhood toy he could remember, filled with whirrs and oiled clicks and gold which perhaps only his touch could coax out. He went over to the Keno pit and stood with his forehead pressed against the glass. A gaunt man in a string tie was monitoring the game. Runners distributed cards to the women on the tiered benches.

The caller's words were muffled. Scanlyn slipped through a door and sat at the rear. When a runner came by and offered a card, Scanlyn paid for it. He read the instructions, sat forward attentively and began checking off the numbers as they were called out.

At one o'clock the instrument of governmental policy still sat as a sort of outrider for Keno-fixated granddaughters and great-granddaughters of pioneers, their corded necks and intense faces exactly those Scanlyn had seen in old photographs.

He'd changed the plan as he sat idly losing four dollars. Confronting Buffre on his way to work could be a serious tactical error. If Buffre insisted on the Joe Jones identity and kept going into the kitchen, there would be no way for Scanlyn to follow him and continue the discussion there, and that would leave Buffre free to respond to whatever voices he heard within the clanking dishwasher mechanism, a side door and those wide-open spaces only a few yards away. If Buffre tried to run he was certain to be leashed, and there was no way for Scanlyn to make his pitch to a man in handcuffs. He thought it best to wait until the end of the day when Buffre might be tired enough to listen, when Scanlyn could try to keep up with any move he made.

The downtown area evidently had a more regular meal schedule. They not only served lunch but even opened up three additional blackjack tables, a desert version of the noontime quickie. After Scanlyn ate he went to a movie, a motorcycle film; he slept through the defilement scene featured on the posters but caught the finale where the two male leads roared off into the sunset on a single hog, leathered crotch snug against leathered bottom.

Once outside he found a sky too grand to be anything but artificial, a pure blue scrubbed in one corner by a clutch of small clouds. He was amazed to see that the lights had already been turned on. The huge outslung signs and the panels with crests of jerky spume and the ovals where hare-and-hound colors chased each other were still pale and ineffectual, but they waited ready to blot up the first faint shadows of twilight.

He walked through the streets, passing casino after casino where the action at the tables was still light. But more people seemed to be staggering between the machines, having a fast one on the way home. Scanlyn wondered what happened then, as they sat after dinner watching television life blander than the action in their hometown, conscious of the thin fold in the hip pocket and aware there was more to be had just down the street, more than more, a choice between staying even with mediocrity or risking everything in hopes of breaking out and breaking clear.

With a little bit of luck . . . Everyone needed it, Scanlyn particularly, if his work was to come to anything. And he would have settled for less than luck in his life, for any indication that grace still existed. He found a cocktail lounge with a minimum of local color, the twanging music muted, as many men wearing regular ties as the shoelace variety clipped with steerheads and miniature revolvers. While he sipped beer and ate stale peanuts he wished someone warm and uncomplicated would find him so interesting she'd ask his name. When no one appeared he drifted into memory, half expecting Judith but finding his ex-wife Catherine instead. It was understandable; Judith was much more the bar person, but she would have found this one unendurable. She liked places with broken light and blurred music where the men were usually vain and slightly haggard and the women no longer looked sure they could afford to wait.

Good old Kat, or young Kat—though she wasn't quite so young now. Scanlyn never took a student to bed but he took one for a wife. He had met her during an intensive graduate seminar at Cornell, and he often felt he'd resigned his way into marriage. Quitting government meant getting away from grappling secretaries looking for a leg up as much as for a leg over, from hostesses and hostesses' friends whose yes or no depended on his status and prospects at the moment. Kat was uncomplicated, a beacon of unrestrained adulation which he danced in at first.

He'd been concerned about her being too young, but it actually would have been better if he'd been older, beyond his thirties and somewhere near his present age. If he'd been more venerable, growing fat and stiff, he mightn't have had to try so hard to live up to her opinion of him. But the early days had been exciting, Scanlyn with a grant and a purpose, doing the interviews and research for *Masses* while Kat did the collating and typing. They lived in New York, and she built him up into a small figure among people who were contemptuous of politics and offered brilliant impractical alternatives that Scanlyn dozed through. He traveled to Boston and Chicago, so driven by her energy and absolute faith he nearly came to believe he was engaged in heroic work.

But he lost the sense of his own high purpose halfway through the book. Sifting through the lives he'd taken down in notes and on tape, Scanlyn realized he was merely accumulating particles of personal history, documenting an awful sickness he had no remedy for. He continued with his work only because he hoped the exposures might contribute toward change; but Kat saw it as pure revelation which would bring down all the old rotten walls. Scanlyn knew differently, and although he was grateful for the reception given the book, he was sure those walls would continue to stand, his efforts more graffiti than anything else. But his wife insisted that society should recognize the existence of a manual of salvation. She mimeographed excerpts and distributed them like religious tracts until Scanlyn, touched and embarrassed, made her stop. She was hurt by his attitude, he was exasperated by hers, and they began to bicker over politics and conditions which neither one could affect in the least.

There was a freshening between them when Scanlyn went back into government service. Kat opposed the move at first, then saw it as an opportunity to get to work from the inside. She was so eager to help that he had to restrain her from charging up the Hill and inflicting her visions on boggy legislators. It was only for the sake of his position that she set her jaw and adopted a low profile. Nevertheless, their home became a sort of tatty salon for malcontents addicted to permanently lost causes. Scanlyn sat with them and wearily acknowledged the goodness and correctness of their views, said yes nearly always; there was nothing else he could do. Between the aristocratic towers of the administration and their famous Frontier was a wood where roads became tangled, all things practical rather than possible. And when that shining city came tumbling down and the streamers of myth evaporated, Scanlyn was able to see himself more clearly, only one among the many clutching the king's shilling and hoping for a raise.

Then came the first voter-registration drives in the South. Kat's urging and his own guilt set old fires sputtering again, and Scanlyn had himself appointed an official observer, gradually losing his objectivity and edging into participation until he grew active enough to have his front teeth knocked out by an enthusiastic deputy. Kat was filled with pride and tenderness while his gums shrank enough for the plate to be fitted, but he'd had it. He was getting too old for combat, was better off slightly out of range, teaching what had happened and suggesting what might be done. Kat said she understood, but afterward he often caught her looking at him with a failed light in her eyes.

In what Scanlyn found a gesture of reproach and deliberate irritation, she increased her own activities. She annotated book margins and clipped newspaper articles and worked through the fat looseleaf which was the ad hoc of a half-dozen committees—not without some effect, since the politicians who dismissed him as a paid hand sometimes turned a tinny ear to her for the sake of whatever influence she might have. Scanlyn didn't care what she did as long as she let him have some kind of peace, a homonym for what arrived in the form of Judith. He would come home with nothing but a shrunken sac to show for his evening's work, and find his wife weary with concern, her hair not so much defiantly pulled back in a schoolgirl's ribbon as lacking any arrangement at all, so fair that the strands losing their color didn't seem to have turned gray but to have undergone further refinement. She'd say hello and immediately tell him of some catastrophe in the great world. It was far too much with them.

The marriage lasted nine years. Later, while they picked

through the ruins and played sourly at being adult, they wondered if it would have gone better if they'd had children. But people they knew wondered if their own marriages would have succeeded if they *hadn't* had children, or if they'd had more or fewer. Scanlyn had been inclined toward a family; it had been Kat who hadn't wanted to bring anyone into the world until she'd scoured it a little cleaner. And although they weren't really careful, chancing conception as though they controlled it through the brightness of their intellects, Scanlyn wasn't surprised that there was never as much as a near-miss. Sex with Kat was calculated exercise. There was too much talk about what did or didn't suit, too many mutual adjustments, and he often felt like the harassed commander of a miniature dirigible trying to insure a perfect mooring before discharging all passengers. He had release without satisfaction, her heat so arid he thought it must have withered each tadpole of seed.

Then he met Judith and was afflicted with typical fortyish intimations of mortality, off on his last romance. He let his cup run over, but he did understand that the hot flashes were partially due to his time of life, and he didn't think in terms of Kat against Judith, of making such a complicated exchange. In that ninth year he'd actually come to see himself as growing more mellow, content with a life where both he and Kat could go on with their work and he with his play. Things were going so well he never even bothered to rehearse a defense, and so he was unprepared when he came in grayly one particular night, his parts reduced to something like a shriveled walnut. His wife's face was cold and cunning as she proceeded to act out a highly improbable lust, using crude words and gestures to describe how she'd been pulsating all night long and wanted him, it, immediately, Scanlyn still clutching his hat if necessary. He was shocked. And then she shrugged up her skirt and the slip with a frayed border to show him that she was so far gone in heat she'd even forsaken her Lollipops.

Scanlyn flinched. He might have found the revelation of only mild interest at any time, but he had seen so much in kind during that afternoon and evening he couldn't have cared to whom it belonged, particularly when it was exposed like some sort of magic curative. And then he understood that was exactly her intention. She knew, and was offering a solution of sorts, giving him a chance to prove she was wrong that one time at least. She was willing to suspend her disbelief if he could manage even a mechanical response she'd be able to accept as proof that he'd been even titularly working—or if he had been with whoever she was he hadn't coupled so exhaustively he couldn't, through an act of will, give her enough dignity to be able to lie to herself in the future. Scanlyn was too empty in mind and body to answer with anything except an ardent evasion of her chill pursuit.

In those few minutes of her coldness and his heat their marriage was stripped of future conditions. But it continued to function. There were undercurrents, digs and small cruelties, yet each found something to admire in the other. And since sexuality had lost its importance because it was no longer shared, there was a milder, damper climate which might have nested a child they could raise with kindness and concern, only gradually allowing it to learn how little love there was in the world, even between father and mother. Time might have worked to their advantage; events didn't.

Scanlyn drank his beer and sighed and wished he wasn't a failed husband and failed lover and such a featherweight influence in corridors of power. But the clock turned no matter what he was or wasn't. He glanced at it and took a final swallow and went out to meet Buffre.

FOUR

Gloria MacFarlane sat at her dressing table, a towel draped over a ribbed undergarment which not only supported her breasts but collected stray whorls of muscle and flesh in a stockade of plastic stays. Her hair was piled in a lacquered rick.

"And you're really going to work with that Totty Scanlyn?" she said. "Well I never."

"You have, once or twice I know of for sure." MacFarlane was in the adjoining bathroom, bent toward a mirror as he tried to inspect the liver spots freckling his skull.

"You devil." His wife made a scandalized face at herself. "But Howie? You don't know as much about him as some of us have been here just a little bit longer than you all."

"There's a complete enough file."

"That won't say how a person really is, though." She edged a brow to look like a blade. "He was just awful to Mizzie Towbaugh's husband, the one in Agriculture, when Mizzie was married to that gentleman owned the chain of specialty markets."

"Grocery stores," MacFarlane said.

"Brought in a pretty penny, whatever they were. That Totty made him out to be some kind of Hitler."

"I remember reading he was trying to organize a private army."

"And people still say those Reds aren't trying to take over by violent force."

"The grocer, Gloria."

"But he was so sweet and mannerly. I remember it was just after I divorced Ernest." She bit her lip and looked toward the bathroom. "Howie? *Excuse* me, Howie, but it was only mentioned to establish the time. Before we met, darlin'. You weren't here, so you couldn't imagine what a nasty fuss was made."

"Private armies aren't legal."

"That Totty's for sure too smart to be caught out . . . but all poor Mr. Towbaugh was trying to do was protect himself from that raving trash wanted to ruin his stores. Times I think you're too liberal, expecting the law to protect everybody."

"It has to be obeyed."

"You wouldn't know that these days. All these people making ructions in the street don't seem to care much."

"We'll take care of them." MacFarlane came out of the bathroom, his head still bent, and stooped toward his wife. "Are there more, or is it my imagination?"

"Oh Howie, 'course there aren't." She peered at the smooth skin. "What's this? I swear, it's the cutest thing, looks just like a teensy pussycat, ears and all—just the head, I mean."

"A what?"

"Well I wouldn't call it exactly a pussycat."

"It feels tight."

"Poor baby. A good rub's what you need."

MacFarlane knelt before his wife, placed his arms around her waist and hooked his nose into the bridge spanning her breasts. She took a jar from her table and, humming, applied a white cream to his pate. His shoulders began to shake. "A pussycat?" he said.

"Just a teensy one." A small bubble of laughter escaped from her. "I lawn."

They quaked together while she went on rubbing.

• • •

The Best of Our Time

The Prippets and MacFarlanes lived in Acquarelle, a new apartment complex in a green belt outside the capital. Many of the residents had come in with the change of administration, and they were stacked so that the cream rose to the top. Howard MacFarlane's apartment was on an upper floor because of his personal wealth. Frank Prippet lived below, his rooms so shadowed by the staggered overhang of terraces, they were frequently gloomy. Prippet hadn't either the money or the position of most of the people in Acquarelle but he was tolerated there as a retread from days of earlier glory. He understood the basis of his acceptance and put on an agreeable face while he rankled at the theoreticians and glib critics who'd become prominent only after the party was out of power, who'd had all the benefits of the opposition's mistakes and had coasted in on business and academic credentials. They'd been condescending to men like Prippet, old hands who knew what it was like to have to perform under pressure.

But there had been a change over the past three years. The administration wallowed in troughs more often than it hit modest peaks in the polls, and the whiz kids were no longer confident. That evening at an upper-floor party Prippet had to hide his satisfaction at seeing those superior faces lined and sometimes twitching. He made polite inquiries and often got worried replies. On a few occasions he even had his advice asked for by men who made it clear they were desperate enough to listen to anything. He enjoyed their unhappiness all the more because they had no idea of the existence of Flipover and couldn't know of his involvement with it.

At eleven o'clock he slipped out to the deserted terrace. The night was unpleasantly damp. Prippet turned up the collar of his dinner jacket and practiced his new walk. There had always been an odd stiffness in his upper torso which gave him a sliding nearly effeminate gait, and when he'd tried to compensate by exaggerating his shoulder movement, he'd swayed suspiciously. It was only recently that he'd developed a brisk step which was an improvement but made his calves ache, and now he had to stop to rest, shifting his weight from one foot to another while he shivered in the still air carrying the elusive smell of something like rot.

Prippet loved the city. He'd never gotten over the thrill he'd felt when he first arrived in his early thirties. During his period of exile he'd sought work with MacFarlane because the firm was located in Philadelphia and he was able to visit Washington often, a tourist when he had no real or political business there. There had been some talk of his running for elected office, but he hadn't been interested in subjecting himself to voters' whims, particularly not for a minor position. He thought of himself as having the more durable stuff of a warder, a keeper of stamps and seals, keys to the city's doors. At fifty-five there was still time for things to come his way.

He swung his arms to keep warm as he practiced his walk again. Eric Krug was late. Krug was one of the new people, and Prippet couldn't help but resent him. If it hadn't been for a failure of party leadership, Prippet wouldn't have been so dependent on Flipover as a factor in his comeback. He would have had twenty-three years of service and success, and someone would have been on the terrace waiting for *him*. He stopped to ease the cramps in his calves. From that height a few of the capital's illuminated buildings were visible, the view like a Byzantine dream of grace and power.

He drifted toward the sound of phantom trumpets, but then his attenuated ear picked up a subtle change from inside. There was a cold spot of near-silence close to the vestibule, an indication that a personage had arrived. It moved across the room as each separate group of guests became aware of the presence. Prippet was sure it was Krug. Voices in the area of the foyer brightened. Evidently Krug had taken off his coat and was now greeting people, perhaps accepting a drink. The current of chatter moved toward Prippet, and he rolled down his coat collar and positioned himself before the French doors, then realized he'd be seen as soon as they were opened. The voices veered away. He went to a corner of the terrace and pressed against the concrete wall. The ripple ran parallel to him, rose slightly, then died to a hum. When Prippet shifted position he saw that one of his sleeves had become powdered. He was awkwardly stroking his arm when he heard a click and saw the glint of glasses outside a small door at the far end of the terrace.

"Psst, Eric."

The glasses turned. Prippet hissed again, his arm still extended as though he were exhibiting a wound. Krug moved through the rectangles of light from the French doors.

"I was trying to keep out of sight," Prippet said. Krug looked at the outstretched arm, and Prippet doubled it behind him. "I meant so I wouldn't be seen from inside."

"From a lighted room you cannot see out through the windows into the dark."

"I know you don't want the conference made public . . . yet."

"It should be at least quick if we have to stand out here." Krug rubbed his hands together. "But perhaps it is time for this business to suffer a slight exposure. Not officially, you understand."

"A leak?"

"A hint . . . discreet, and involving yourself directly. The credit should come to you."

"That's very generous."

"And to the Bureau. It has been unprominent, too soft. Some call it a rubber stamp for rubber checks—ours. Rubber checks are no good, you know."

"That's right . . . Not that I'd agree that the administration has been passing . . . I mean to say, we've done exactly what we've been asked to. And done it well, I think."

"Yes, yes. He is aware. There will be the guidelines, of course, but in this case, *your* inspiration. You will see it like falling down over a ditch . . . *Zugsbrücke.*"

"I'm sorry, Eric."

"Yes, the ditch around a castle, with water in it."

"A drawbridge," Prippet said.

"Exactly. We will let you down. The first one very narrow, but after a while bigger and bigger drawbritches so that the people can come to us and we can go to them. You will be the first to succeed."

Prippet grasped the railing and gazed toward the softly lit government buildings. "It sounds very exciting," he said huskily.

Krug hooked his thumbs in his vest and looked pleased. The vest was brocade and the jacket had an Old World cut, yet both looked new.

Suddenly Prippet wanted a tuxedo exactly like Krug's. "I'd like to assure you that the team is up for this one," he said.

"Everyone agrees."

"Perfectly—no matter what you may have heard."

"I have heard nothing."

"Only intradepartmental discussion, Eric—chalk talks so we can be ready for anything the other side may try to pull."

"Like running up the flagpole to see who salutes? But not with visibility, not so argument shows. We would like you to reflect new enthusiasm as well as new ideas."

"There is no question of . . . "

"You understand, I am certain." Krug raised three fingers. "An attempt to escape—preferably with shooting but not actually dying—will mean an arrest. In this no one will be able to discover any blame. If the subject disappears, the difficulty is eliminated. And if the last choice is made . . ." Krug shrugged and folded his fingers. "This is not a business of all or nothing. There can be gain in the negotiation even if there is no result."

"I do understand." Prippet bit his lip. "The only question raised has been over the suitability of the man carrying the ball."

"You raise it?"

"Of course not, Eric. I would never have anything but absolute confidence in any choice of yours. But we do try to keep a certain balance of opinion within the Bureau. I'm sure John Stirby only meant to arrive at the broadest possible picture."

"The Hungarian?"

"Well, John isn't . . . "

"Born Janos Stirbea. We have a joke, that if you go into a Hungarian restaurant and order pork, the first thing the cook will do is go out and steal a pig. With holes in their boots they wear fur hats."

"John's views may be too rigid at times, but they're very helpful."

"It would be better for him to be useful, to keep his mouth shut unless someone tells him what to say."

"Well, I don't think John should be included in the final briefing. There may be a certain amount of antagonism."

"Agreed."

"Then everything appears to be set and ready to go as soon as the final details are ironed out."

Krug took a figured silk handkerchief from his inside pocket and wiped at his glasses. "You were wise to think of avoiding the difficulties which can be brought about by meeting too many people. Mr. Scanlyn has all the information he needs to begin. He has been instructed to report to you, directly and only."

"I'm gratified by the extent of your confidence, Eric, but I do feel a personal meeting would be helpful. After all, I've never seen him except . . . " Prippet pressed his lips together. "In an operation as delicate as this—"

"There are various ways to be in touch," Krug interrupted, "and the moment will come to be acquainted, but it is not possible at this time. He is already gone."

"Gone?"

"Yes." Krug waved his glasses at the overcast sky. "He is there."

FIVE

The file on George Toussaint Buffre wasn't a simple folder. It was more like a safe-deposit box which contained not only written information but film clips and fingerprints and photographs, even scratchy recordings. Between those artifacts and his own suppositions Scanlyn had developed an image of the man the administration felt it needed rather than wanted: a twenty-eight-year-old with a Louisiana boyhood and a Northern education, an honors graduate who'd turned to bitter, reasoned public debate which sometimes sent people into the streets.

Buffre in person was impressive, literally black, burly in a denim jacket over a T-shirt. Scanlyn didn't think they'd be able to mold that blocky body into a three-button image, to bleach him enough to conform, and he felt a growing excitement at the prospect of bringing back much more than a report they could file away. This time it would be substantial meat on the hoof. If the move was to have any value, they'd have to make a show of giving Buffre some sort of authority whether or not they liked or trusted him, and no matter where he came to stand, white or black or gray, he'd be at the very least official and very visible. It was also possible that Scanlyn's own visibility might improve; he wasn't beyond distrusting his motives even though he told himself that the only important thing was to get the job done, that he didn't really care if it turned out to be his swan

song or comeback. He wanted to coax Buffre into a situation
where he'd be incessantly hammered not for his own good but
in order to give society one more feeble chance.

As they maneuvered among the wilted leaves and splintered bones in the alley behind the High Heel, the slot of sky
overhead burning in multiple colors, Buffre was balanced so
warily he seemed about to disappear into the few folds of brick
which escaped the glare.

Scanlyn had brushed past the slackjawed *Suh?* Buffre
affected as Joe Jones, and he'd shown him he wasn't carrying
either a gun or a warrant—but he hadn't suggested there wasn't
someone beyond the shadows at the mouth of the alley with
both. He had Buffre in a state of poised alarm and was trying
to turn him toward accepting an invitation to dinner in his
room. Scanlyn had already resisted the inspiration to take out
his front plate and exhibit it as part of his credentials because
he'd pictured himself waving the fragment of artificial gum
while he lisped an explanation. He thought he'd at least convinced Buffre he wasn't an aging fag, and now as the other
shifted position Scanlyn tried to keep his voice calm even as he
reasoned against running, asking what could possibly be lost
through a good meal and an hour or two of talk when Buffre had
already lost his disguise and would have to assume his real
identity for at least as long as it took to develop another one.

Buffre did not so much agree as allow himself to be led
away from the spoiled vegetables and congealing fats and into
a cab, where they sat apart in the rotating barrel of light along
the boulevard, each colored blue and orange and gold while the
cabby's eyes cut back and forth in the rear-view mirror. The
doorman's smile stiffened when he saw Buffre, and the desk
clerk was chilly when he brought Scanlyn's briefcase from the
safe. As they threaded through mists of different perfumes,
patches of fancy cloth, the sounds of chips and money and what
sounded like a hundred brass pieces playing the supper show,
Scanlyn caught several dead white looks. He tried to act natural
in the face of the elevator operator's smirk, but he had begun
to sweat slightly, and he nearly sighed with relief when he was

at last able to close the door of the room against all those people he was trying to get Buffre to join.

Scanlyn pulled the drapes and let in a wedge of sky, where the lowest stars were smoked over by the electric fire but the higher ones were as clear and bright as new glass. While Buffre looked out the window, he tried to arrange a smile.

"I still can't believe it's real myself."

The other turned so that only a corner of his eye showed, and Scanlyn gestured at a chair. Buffre perched gingerly on it.

"Would you like a drink?"

"You're supposed to tell me my rights and give me a chance at that phone if this is a bust."

"I told you it wasn't. I'm not with any enforcement agency." There was nothing in Buffre's face to show whether or not he believed that. "I'm a messenger boy at worst," Scanlyn said, "and a minister without portfolio at best. It's been a while . . . Do the street gangs still have ministers? Are there still action groups and cadres?"

Buffre's smile was small and slightly amused.

Scanlyn went on. "As I said, it's been a while and I really don't know where it's at these days, but I'm not sure you do, either." Buffre blinked slowly while Scanlyn sat cold and gray and running to fat, chill drops sliding down his ribs. "I told you my name was Eliot Scanlyn," he said. "I've been a teacher and written a book about the urban poor called *Masses* and had my front teeth knocked out during the early SNCC action."

Buffre's lips twitched.

"I mentioned that for whatever it was worth . . . and shouldn't have. But it was worth something at that time, no matter how things may have changed since. I do believe that."

Buffre raised his eyebrows and put his hands on his knees. "Go right ahead."

"Whoever I am and whatever I've done, the only important thing is what I'm doing at this moment. It could be called liaison work. There's an official connection with the federal government, but I might have to deny that under certain circumstances. At present I'm a simple link to The Man."

"Between the cuff and the ball."

"I'm trying to make it clear that I had nothing to do with your present situation, with the warrant. It was a mistake, and they recognize it, but that won't keep them from serving it if they're forced to."

"Who's doing the forcing?"

"Let me finish," Scanlyn said. "Or rather, let's begin, with you. This doesn't seem to be such a good place to hide in but it evidently has been. They've been looking for you in the cities for a long time. If you hadn't kept in touch with so many people I don't think they ever would have found you."

"They always find a scab to pick."

"Whoever it was, it wasn't Mrs. Hattie Jensen in Detroit. She's your aunt and she's been taking care of your two children. She receives money orders from Joe Jones regularly. The handwriting varies and they're usually sent from San Francisco. Joe Jones gets no mail at all here and there's no phone listing for him, so whatever contacts you have with the outside are direct, personal. They've let the money orders go through, incidentally, and there's no reason you shouldn't continue to send them."

"I really appreciate that," Buffre said.

"Until recently I hadn't heard your name except in passing. Any information I have comes from the briefing I was given. I'm not and never have been with any enforcement or investigative agency. They told me you have a code name, Jade. They were concerned about that; they thought there might be a background of Maoist ideology, but there isn't any evidence of it, or of any Marxist tendencies at all except for some general tubthumping when the occasion suits. You don't appear to be part of any particular group. You've worked with different organizations from time to time, but from all the available information it doesn't appear that you're actually affiliated with any."

"Whatever you say."

"It's what *they* say, what they told me. I haven't found anything to the contrary in my own review. You don't appear to be getting financial help from the outside. At least there's no

'Save Buffre' committee, and there haven't been any concerts or cocktail parties to raise money . . . and to give the promoters a chance at a great rip-off. I knew of one where you could get to shake hands with a real snorting Panther for fifty dollars. They weren't quoting a price to get laid."

"Now that's the way to come on, Cap'n," Buffre said softly.

"In summary, the only reason you're out here is because you're hiding, and you've had to wash dishes and your wife has had to work as a chambermaid to support yourselves and your children." Scanlyn looked at Buffre a long moment while the other blinked steadily, as though each frame might bring a change in image. "Did you plan to go on this way indefinitely?"

"Only until I got caught."

"That's happened in a way."

"Then I'd better make that call."

"If you want to . . . but it isn't necessary."

Buffre's eyelids slid up and down. "I know you're not charging for the tape," he said, "but I had a long day at that sink, and if this isn't a bust I'd just as soon go home."

"No one's taping us. It's the truth." Scanlyn wished he'd stop sweating. "Check out the room if you want to."

"They could be next door or upstairs, or even out in the desert with one of those giant ears." Buffre teetered on the back legs of his chair. "I've been around a couple of corners with that whole scene. There's the creep who stands around with a newspaper with holes in it, and the one they might just as well put shoe polish on and give him a banjo and a sequin suit, the *infiltrator*. What's your specialty?"

"I asked you before if you'd like a drink."

"No, I would not."

"I suppose it's safe enough up here to light a joint if you want to."

"Do you really think I'd be holding?"

"No, I'm only trying to impress you that I'm semi-current. How about dinner, then? They've got a special steak . . . "

"No chicken 'n' ribs?"

"Is that what you want?"

"They feed me down at that greasepit. Get yourself some dinner if you want."

Scanlyn considered a moment. "I'd like to," he said, "but I'm afraid I'd have the feeling of stuffing myself in the dining room while you were out on the kitchen steps waiting for your bread and molasses. Or am I supposed to feel that way?"

"You've got a problem, haven't you?"

"But mine isn't legal. They never quite told me what the warrant was for. You'd know better than I what they can tag you with—conspiracy, incitement to riot, crossing state lines to avoid prosecution? That's none of my business."

"I can believe that," Buffre said. "You'll leave the getting busted part to me." He brought the front legs of his chair down. "But what I don't understand is why you're bothering to unload all this bullshit on me when you've got enough muscle to give me one tap and Gracie another and put us in some hole nobody could find for a million years."

"I don't think that could happen."

"Don't you now?"

Scanlyn rubbed his forehead. "I'm not sure. It might if things don't start to get better."

"They're going to catch *you* on that tape, too."

"There's no tape." Scanlyn thought for a moment. "But is that why you've kept in touch with the outside, to let people know you're still around? A sort of insurance policy?"

"Like I don't need one."

"Maybe . . . maybe. I wouldn't know because I've never been in your circumstances. I don't mean this current situation. I've had more contacts than most with blacks but I haven't ever deluded myself into thinking I knew what it was like to *be* black. All right? Can we proceed along those lines of acknowledged ignorance? And can we get back to what I asked earlier, if you and your wife intend to go on this way indefinitely? Did you take all those chances so you could end up as classic menials?"

"Oh Cap'n suh, it don't make no mind."

"That way of talking just might become natural again if you

spend the rest of your life in a kitchen." Scanlyn paused. "There's a way out, though. I'm here to give you—and us, too —a chance. And if you're convinced this is being recorded, don't say anything, just nod or shake your head. But please listen.

"They're aware now that the warrant was a mistake, as I've already said, and you and I know why. Last year's countermeasures are this year's bad news. But it *does* exist, and something's going to have to be done about it. One solution is to have the source of the problem disappear."

Scanlyn picked up the briefcase, feeling melodramatic as he worked the combination lock and took out a heavy envelope. Buffre was frowning slightly.

"There's a cashier's check for ten thousand dollars and three passports in here," Scanlyn said. He placed a small table between them and put the envelope on it. "There are separate passports each for you and Mrs. Buffre and one for Mrs. Buffre together with the three children. We had pictures of you and your wife, but the one of her and the children is a composite fake. It's a good job."

Buffre looked at the envelope.

"You can touch it," Scanlyn said. "We have your fingerprints already—in fact, we even have your voice print."

Buffre opened the envelope. He pushed the check aside and looked through each of the passports, longest at the last one. "Georgie lost another front tooth," he said.

"They're the latest school pictures. Mrs. Jensen probably hasn't gotten around to sending them to you yet." Scanlyn leaned closer. "According to our records you've never had a passport." He pointed. "That's a visa. If you want to enter that country from the United States you need a visa, and that's it. We want you to go there first. In fact, you'll *have* to if you go through with this. From there you can go anywhere you want to, and for most countries you won't need a visa, but this has to be your first stop. We want you officially logged in. Tickets will be provided; they won't have to come out of the money."

Buffre put everything back in the envelope.

"There are three choices open to you," Scanlyn said. "You can go by yourself, you can go with your wife, or you can take everyone. There are other blacks already there; you may even have been in touch with them. And you'll probably be able to get housing and a subsidy from the local government. The money should last you a long time. If you don't think it's enough I'll see what I can do, but I don't think they'll come up with much more."

"That looks like enough," Buffre said.

"Think about it. I don't want an answer tonight." Scanlyn put the envelope back. "It's an important decision and I'm sure you'll want to talk it over with your wife. Or perhaps you'd rather not let her know. Her part in this isn't at all important to us. You could begin an entirely new life by yourself if you wanted to—leave everything behind. It wouldn't be possible to come back until this whole business has cooled off, but I'm sure you'd find things better there than they are here right now. There's a variety of junk easy to come by."

Buffre looked at him a long moment. "That's ugly work you do," he said.

"This phase isn't very pretty." Scanlyn locked the case. "I'll keep all this until I hear from you. You pick the time and the place for the next meeting."

"Suppose I don't pick anything?"

"I don't want an answer right now. In fact, I couldn't accept one. If you make an attempt to disappear "—Scanlyn shrugged —"then I'll be out of this. Another plan would take over and so would another person. It's a big apparatus."

"It's a mother, friend."

"It's what we've got at the present. I'd like you to call me whenever you're ready to meet again. There's a certain amount of pressure . . . they won't give us much time."

"I'll think about it."

"Tomorrow?"

"To make sure I'm still here? I could be calling from Alaska."

"And I wouldn't do anything to stop you from going.

You've got to accept the idea that my only role is what I'm doing right now. I'm not responsible for apprehension or detention or any other enforcement function."

"I've *got* to accept that idea."

"It's true whether you do or not. How about tomorrow?"

Buffre stood and went to the window. "I could tell you I was buying and then take the bundle and go off on my own."

"You could. I'm sure they've thought of that."

"That *they* is you, isn't it?"

"No, but that's not important . . . any way you want it. Tomorrow?"

"Well we'll see."

"That's good enough. Do you want me to go down with you to get a cab?"

"You think I'll need somebody to talk me past that general at the door."

"I don't think he'll . . . "

"Call me a cab. That's big news."

Scanlyn gave him a card. "I've written down the number and extension."

Buffre looked at the card. "It doesn't say where you're from."

"No."

Buffre made a noise in his throat.

Scanlyn had a thought and reached into his pocket. "Cab-fare back is probably . . . " He held out a ten-dollar bill until it seemed to wilt under Buffre's stare. "I'm sorry," he said.

"Yeah, that's the way it is." He shook his head and went out of the room.

Scanlyn took a step after him, hesitated, then stretched out on the bed. He reviewed the conversation carefully, and when he got to a part that had gone wrong he changed what he'd said and got a more satisfactory answer from Buffre. In the improved version Buffre shook his hand before he left, gave him a warm and grateful smile. Cap'n knew best. Scanlyn groaned aloud.

The phone rang. "He went directly home," a man said.

"Who is this?"

"Cyrus. They gave you a name and a number, didn't they?"

"For an emergency. There hasn't been one. Don't get in his way . . . it might spoil everything if you do."

"I have instructions, Mr. Scanlyn."

"I don't think I'd like to know what they are."

Scanlyn hung up. They could print that too, if Buffre was right and tapes were spinning in every corner, recording all Scanlyn's groans and murmurs. He couldn't bring himself to see a real plot, but there were implications he didn't want to think about, and he was still hungry and getting a headache. He had to get out of the room.

He and Buffre were head to head in a scooped-out place between mountains, a natural arena. Scanlyn was finding pictographs better than words. Buffre was a shadow and the mountains might turn out to be false and Scanlyn crossing the lobby might be his own hallucination. Las Vegas *was* Xanadu, a dream which might be interrupted at any moment.

In the meantime it was the beginning of the evening and everyone was on the move—or the beginning of the peak of the evening, and then the peak of the peak. If there was ever a decline it would have to come somewhere near sunrise, but he supposed the engine would continue to idle smoothly, ready to use or be used. He was becoming adjusted, beginning to see straight images in the distorted glass. The people were not really all alike. There were sports and flashy couples and fading ones, habitués and vacationers and one-nighters—all with different accents and in different clothes, all American in that severely offset mid-America which advertised itself as the place everyone had to visit at least once in order to do all those things either law or custom prohibited back home, things which were natural in a place where time had no meaning and no one grew old or looked foolish while they ran as far and as fast as they wanted to and never had to worry about a closing hour shutting down either love or luck.

Of course it was the perfect meeting place for two contenders as weightless as though they were on the moon. They'd slug it out right in the middle of the slithering American dream while nobody watched and nobody cared. He had come out there to fight against someone whose side he'd always thought he was on. It wasn't an arena after all; it was a pit.

He took his first real tour of the casino. There were forty or fifty tables and hundreds of machines. The room gave the impression of being full without being crowded. There were empty places on the high stools at the lips of blackjack tables and at the long low boxes where craps was being shot and at the corners where ladies were parked to play low-pressure roulette while their escorts followed the heavier action. Real money was hardly involved, the bills snatched up and stuffed into slots. Mere chips were changing hands, all losses plastic, a high-roller's version of Monopoly. Cash was used only in an area roped off by velvet, the dealer there in a tuxedo, wielding his paddle like a foil while twenties and fifties and hundreds fell in neat sheafs.

And there was more than gambling—something for everyone. Girls in short skirts and net stockings served free drinks to the players. A huge line waited for the last show at the theatre restaurant where star and superstar and famous orchestra waited to peal as soon as the dinners had been gobbled down. The revue lounge was just opening. And for those who weren't satisfied to look without touching, there were ladies of the evening or the morning or whatever time going round and round the cluster of tables, singly and never too close together but in perpetual promenade, all pretty and nearly all young. They weren't allowed to distract the gamblers by twittering around the tables. They had to wait on the move for other moves, pausing every now and then to drop a small coin in one of the machines.

Xanadu was real after all. It was too perfect a sink to be artificial, a gathering of all the corrupt dreams from the cardboard towns and cities beyond the crumpled-paper mountains. But Buffre's concern with surveillance had made Scanlyn conscious of being watched, and in the casino everyone was watching. The dealers kept cold eyes on the gamblers, burly men in dark suits watched the dealers, and uniformed guards with pump guns across their knees stood in corners or sat on platforms. Scanlyn had to get away from all those eyes. He went to the bar and ordered a double bourbon which trickled warmly into his empty stomach. He sighed, turned and found himself being watched by a gallery of birds with long and short legs, round and pert bosoms, all more or less exposed. He looked away, finished his drink, and decided to have something to eat in his room.

But the whiskey had been so relaxing he found himself flowing into the charged atmosphere, caught in the currents around the tables. He circled among the nightingales, their rears insinuatingly atilt while on one side people sweated and howled at craps and on the other pulled feverishly on the handles of slot machines. At each turn he passed beneath the eyes of a man with a gun, and he finally grew so dizzy he forced himself to struggle crosscurrent and through the doors of the revue lounge.

It was only half full for the first show. He found a table down front and was surprised to hear himself order another double. The lady on stage was also belting down a long drink as she stood at the piano between numbers. Scanlyn recognized her, a soulmate who'd become prominent but never famous and was now ever so slightly in decline, a remembered name more than an existing talent. She stepped to the microphone and began a song which had been one of her biggest records, one she'd sung well countless times. Now she struggled to keep her breath and phrasing from going ghostly. Scanlyn nodded sadly; he knew how it was. He drank and listened and when she finished he applauded until his palms stung.

The piano was hauled off before the singer had taken her last bow, and the pit band struck up the moment she left the stage. Four girls skittered out of the wings and were instantly in total motion, four heads of lilac-tinted curls bobbing over gaping satin vests and hip-hugger bell bottoms tight at the thigh and cut out at the rear to reveal eight solid halves marbled by the stage lights. They were all young and lean; they had to be to keep up with the frantic dirty rock the band was beating out. The bodies went into turn after synchronized turn, hams taut and navels popping, demonstrating all the stretched-out maneuvers youth was capable of in that new age which most of the people watching were too old to participate in. But Scanlyn would have liked to try—to have painted himself blue, perhaps, and gone up on the stage to rub and be rubbed, a sort of stamen among the domino petals of soft cloth and hard flesh.

There was a break in the music. The girls hurried to the rear and struck a pose just in time to form a background for an identical set who danced the same way. He studied the first group, sweat beading their compressed lips, delicate rib cages heaving, then did a double take because a particular set of eyes seemed to be peeping out at him. It could have been a trick of either the light or the bourbon, but when he looked more intently he saw a definite movement among the glittering lids and tarred lashes, and he was about to gesture toward them with his glass when there was a new musical cue and all eight became galvanized. Scanlyn tried to follow his lady but could catch only one shoulder, part of a face, a line of indistinguishable rumps. Then the chorus ran off, to be replaced by a couple banded with sequins who began a dramatic pas de deux.

Scanlyn wondered if he should buy flowers and go to the stage door. When the couple went through a glittering and overextended mime of copulation he smirked because the real thing was probably waiting in the wings, a warm dark place he could disappear into—while someone called Cyrus photographed him at the supreme moment. He was going to order another drink and wait for the next nubile spectacular, but then he saw himself as the nation's stable paunchy pride playing the part of a fully absurd visiting fireman panting for a child who might light him up. He paid his check and left.

It was unsteady going, too far to the room and the telephone and the waiter who'd arrive too late to save him from collapse into a sour-bellied nightmare. He went to the coffee shop, not caring what name they put on the meal they were serving as long as they fed him. Only two tables were occupied and the waitresses were collecting salt and pepper shakers. Evidently people didn't want to eat with Scanlyn; he began to feel like a known carrier. Then he saw a face at one of the tables set at a certain angle, and looked for a topping of lilac curls. But of course that would have been a wig. The rest was there, her gummed lashes and lids even more outrageous in ordinary light. She wore a duster over the costume, or perhaps over nothing at all, and there were strokes of color in her cheeks. He could barely distinguish the real outlines of the face shaped like a slender heart, her chin narrow and mouth wide and full, and as he went unsteadily toward her he wondered just what among all the things he really needed a freaked-out dancing hooker might provide.

She looked up from a bun oozing yellow filling, gulped slightly, and then waved her napkin. "Hi," she said, "I thought it was you I saw."

Scanlyn wondered which *you* she could possibly be referring to, but he asked if he could sit down.

"Sure, but I have to get back soon." She gestured with the dripping bun. "I eat this for energy. It's nearly pure sugar." She gave him an odd close look and then her mouth turned down and she sat back.

"This may seem strange," Scanlyn began, "but I don't—"

"—know who I am." She laughed, a dull coughing sound. "That just came to me, Prof. You thought I was giving you the come-on to do a little business, right?"

"But you seem to know who *I* am."

"You're a fast zipper. How about for a quick fifty? I get a twenty-minute break after the next set."

"How?"

"Any way you want it."

"How do you know me?"

The waitress arrived, quintessentially Western in a calico dress with puffed sleeves. "Is there anything I can get you, sir?" she asked in a strident New York accent.

"More coffee?" Scanlyn said to the girl. She shook her head.

"Well, I'd like a rare steak and some broiled tomatoes. Plain green salad, and if you could—"

"We got coffee and buns. Like huzz." The waitress pointed.

"A couple of hamburgers?"

"We're closing, sir. The regular restaurant serves dinner until three."

Breakfast at three in the afternoon and dinner at three in the morning; it was a proper balance. Scanlyn ordered coffee. The waitress left and the girl licked her fingers.

"Sure," she said, "everybody in town got the news about you. The big tool from the East was on his way."

"That's a dubious description," Scanlyn said, "but you *do* know me."

"Five years ago. No, four."

"I'm sorry."

"At Berkeley."

"A seminar?"

"Right. Neighborhood self-help. You read my preliminary paper to the group. The only one."

Scanlyn could feel tufts of gray hair beginning to sprout from his ears, Mr. Chips incarnate. He remembered the seminar because of the fee. He tried to remember the girl. "That's a lot of students ago," he said.

"Body stack, you mean. They don't even have to be breathing, just as long as they're slightly warm." She gave the odd laugh again. "I never got involved in throwing bags of shit around, but I wish I had."

"It's hard to see your face clearly. The make-up, I mean."

"It used to belong to Laura Nunenburger. 'The Desirability of Community Sharing As an Antecedent to Social Programming.'"

"Why yes, I believe . . . " He made himself half believe.

"I doubt it . . . but the full paper got me my master's."

"The prelim alone was very impressive."

"Couldn't get it out of your mind. And it really took me places, like to this body shop. I have to get back now."

"I wish you didn't have to go. Couldn't I see you later?"

"For the fifty?"

"We could go to dinner."

"I get through at four-thirty."

"I'm sure we could find a place for at least a snack. Laura Nooneyburger, imagine . . ."

"Nun*en*burger, or Lorry Noon now. There's more snow on the roof, but the old potbellied stove is still roaring, right? The Lit Two instructor claimed you screwed her."

"I'm afraid I'm not in a position to either confirm or deny that, and I don't think it matters. Seriously, *Laura*," stroking neatly, he thought, "couldn't we get together to talk? I've been away from teaching recently and I'm curious about today's students . . . even more so about my old ones."

"This one is shaking her box four shows nightly."

"Why?"

"Because I listened to people like Dr. Eliot Scanlyn." She pushed her chair back.

"Couldn't we . . .?"

"I doubt it."

She was gone before Scanlyn could say anything more. The waitress brought the coffee, cold, a sodden check in the saucer. Scanlyn paid it, pushed the cup aside, and went to look for the restaurant.

SIX

Sitting in bed with a lapboard propped against his knees, Lewis Allenstein opened a folder and clucked. "Fifty years from now they're going to be using these charts as classic examples of the logistics of futility," he said. "It's incredible that it all started with soup kitchens. Imagine a simple expedient like soup and bread to keep people from starving growing into this mess. We're supporting whole infrastructures—and I mean family *life*. They're humping us into bankruptcy."

His wife grunted without looking up from her book.

"Bea?"

"You intellectuals blew it," she said.

"*We* blew it?"

"Academics particularly."

"What are you reading now?"

"Hoffer."

"You're kidding. One of the favorite fans of our late great President? You're regressing to the world that never was and never will be."

"He's got this Scanlyn of yours in a couple of footnotes."

"Hoffer's one of the few people in the world who would even think of lifting something from *Masses*."

"Wrong. It was some kind of report Scanlyn did for Kennedy."

Allenstein snorted and went back to his papers. His wife marked her place with a bobby pin and closed the book. She put out her light, stretched and rubbed her eyes.

"Be with you in a minute."

"Don't rush," she said. Allenstein looked at her. "I don't know if I can go on giving my all to a reactionary," she said.

"I might question just how much all you've got left to give, babe, but since when have I become a reactionary?"

"That's a dumb tag, isn't it? God, you get so used to all the pigeonholes here. But aren't we sort of accepting it all a little more than we did when we first started? I mean it wasn't such an absolutely solid front of nothing then."

"You have to consolidate before you can move, Bea."

"*Move?* Oh boy, and you're talking regression to me."

"Do you think things were any better before, with all those old wheezes and half-assed programs? What worked?"

"At least they had some style. This bunch of farmers . . ."

"They had some sell, you mean, and now this so-called bunch of farmers has to clean up what they sold. Where are all those golden boys now, after they expressed their polite regrets and disappeared? If they were so full of principles and concern, where are they now?"

"Maybe they're a little more particular about the company they keep."

"They prefer aristocratic types like booze distributors and beef peddlers? Come off it, Bea. You were willing enough to accept our present company when we were back in Montclair."

"It looked better from there than it does from here."

"You mean it looked better to you than gobbling a half-bottle of pills a day to get through the routine of being a No-where U kitscher, better to me than teaching nothing to nobody. It still does. And it's getting Dana's teeth straightened and keeping Ruthie in tutus."

"Oh no you don't, Lewie—not on us."

"Exactly the point, that I don't have to put it on you. I'm just where I want to be, and there's meat on the table too."

"Hustling for the Cardiff Giant."

"Who happens to be in the final stages of petrification. Stirby's going to go sooner than he thinks. In the end . . . "

"In the *meantime*." She punched her pillow and turned her back to him.

He gathered his papers. "Bea, nowever little is happening, it's happening right here. Would you rather be back pouring tea and trying to make points with my department head?"

"The kitsch in this town can make Nowhere look like the East Village."

"I'll buy you a red armband and you can jiggle around without a bra. All right, the packaging is a little lousy right now. Who else is doing anything, anything at all . . . who?"

"But what are *we* doing, Lew?"

"What we should be—trying." He put the papers and lapboard on the floor and turned to her.

"What you're trying right now?" she said.

"You're the one who brought up ends."

"Don't think you're going to change my mind."

"That's only a means."

"Not that I'm knocking it . . . you're randier since we got here."

"Access to all that power."

"Oh hey . . .!"

"Revolutionary fervor?"

"If it was I wouldn't be here. Is this going to make *us* go broke, too?"

"Anybody not on welfare is entitled. Oh Bea, it's going to work."

"Why don't you . . .?"

"It will, it will, Bea. It will work. It will."

"Why don't you shut oooooop *up?*

The next morning Frank Prippet faced the mirror in the entryway of his apartment, his hands raised to the level of his face and his wrists bent at acute angles, a gull-wing effect heightened as he flapped his stiffened fingers against the undersides of his chin where the flesh tended to be slack and sometimes gave the appearance of a small store of nuts having slipped to the bottom of either cheek. He'd read about the exercise in one of his wife's magazines.

"Frank?"

"Um." It came out in a phlegmy vibrato. Prippet cleared his throat and adjusted his shirt sleeves. "Yes, Betty?"

"Breakfast."

At that hour of the morning the dining room was completely shadowed by the overhang of the terrace on the next floor. The tops of a few of the city's buildings could just be seen above the trees. Since the floodlights had been turned off and the sun wasn't fully out, the stone had the dull smudged appearance of a putty replica. Prippet gazed at it fondly. "Well," he said, "I guess it's more than time."

His wife looked at a wall clock. "No, only seven-thirty."

"Out there, I mean. For the contact."

"Oh, yes. Do you think it went well?"

"Considering that we have to work with what they gave us . . . I suppose he's as good a man as any for this job, no matter what we might feel along the lines of personal preference."

"Gloria hasn't anything good to say about him."

"Has she been talking?" Prippet asked sharply. "I mean to anyone besides you."

"You know how Gloria is, Frank."

"This is too important for her goddamned back-chatting, goddamn her."

"Frank, I—"

"Goddamn her to hell."

"Frank."

"This is one time she absolutely cannot be indulged. I'll speak to Mac. For all the good that ever does. Couldn't *you* say something?"

"I don't think she'd take that very well."

"I'm serious about it being important."

"I'm sure it is."

"Not only for me, Betty, for you and the girls, too."

As Prippet's voice rose there was a slight tightening at the corners of his wife's eyes and mouth, a touch of apprehension.

He looked away. "I don't mean to imply that you don't
. . ." he mumbled, and then recovered and gave her a rigid
smile. "Eric hasn't said anything definite, but of course he never
does." She didn't react to the diminishing chuckle. "And after
all these years we both know better than to count on anything
that floats over the transom, but I do know they're planning to
split responsibility in the full Department . . . *two* associate
directors instead of one."

"Oh, Frank, those things—"

"I know, Betty, I know, and you're absolutely right. It's only
that this time . . . well, everyone knows how bad their internal
organization is, and there isn't anyone special . . . I certainly
think the Bureau has proved what it can do, and if Flipover
turns out right . . . ."

"Nobody deserves recognition more than you do." She said
it so firmly her voice nearly splintered.

"Thank you." Prippet looked away again.

"Of course I'll talk to Gloria." His wife seemed to gather
herself. "And I'm sure you've talked to John."

"He'll stay in line."

"He's speaking tonight, you know, at a meeting of that
police chiefs' association."

"Tonight? I saw that memorandum, but I thought he'd
already . . . I don't know what he could say about this. What he
could use to his own advantage, I mean."

"Isn't that man a fugitive?"

"That's very complicated. John hasn't been brought in on
all the fine points. It would serve him right if he made a big
thing out of it and then had to wind up making a public retrac-
tion—the stupid bastard."

"Frank, you simply have to—"

"I know . . . forgive me."

"I only mentioned it because I thought Eric didn't want
any publicity at all."

"Certainly not that kind, though he did say he wanted me
to open this thing up on my own. I was only waiting until we

had a little positive news. Perhaps we'll hear today. I can't say anything even semi-officially until I know which way it's going. Though I suppose we could prepare the ground a little. That Jaycee dinner tomorrow night . . . I wouldn't bring out the entire thing, you understand."

"If you think that's the proper place."

"It could be tied to, um, tied to being willing to work with the younger generation even when they . . . I'm really very pleased to be working this dinner. I haven't had enough contact with young people. The Jaycees are a very important part of the future, more important than police chiefs. Much more."

"It sounds good, dear."

"And then if Stirby was dumb enough to get himself going in the wrong direction right at the beginning . . . But then I suppose he'd be running around beating his chest if the project flopped."

"But if you took the position expected of you, Frank, and made the first move . . ."

"It's what I've been asked to do, after all. I'll work over the speech at the office and we can polish it up when I get home. We'll play down that section on tariffs, or take it out altogether, and . . ."

His wife listened attentively, a look of determination brightening her eyes until they almost glittered.

SEVEN

Though the guests around the pool were from a younger group, the men were edging toward flab and some of the women showed the effects of baby-stretching. Scanlyn lay gingerly in the sun, his body white and veined, slathered with something which guaranteed a mahogany finish within a few hours.

Those bodies he'd seen the night before . . . Laura Lorry Noon Nunenwhat? He could stand a little of that, though he didn't know how much. She was too young. It was the reprises that were difficult. But when were they ever too old? Judith had been a do-it-again type and she'd been turning forty. He'd done it the best he could, his nose twisted aside by the high bone of her pelvis, chin nested in the moss, eating candy, Ju's Ju-Jube, until she sat erect with a cry and flattened her belly against his head and hiccupped.

Scanlyn had raged with enthusiasm in those days. He wondered if he would have sustained it on a long-term basis. If it hadn't been for Ju's boy—but then, it was the boy who got him started thinking seriously of remarriage in the first place. Little Paul, age ten, went down the stairs and came back up again. He was supposed to have been at the movies while they played their own Saturday matinee, Scanlyn going home to dinner later and shining as spouse of the week.

Paul claimed he had come back because the line at the

theatre was too long, but Scanlyn wondered if it hadn't been to see what was up with his mother. And it was, as far as possible, Scanlyn inspired that afternoon, Ju kneading his ribs with her knees. All the winking and blinking apertures in that overprime flesh must have been a spectacular sight from the eye level of an undersized ten year-old. Ju had seen him in the doorway and gasped, and Scanlyn, misinterpreting the signal, had let himself go in a final surge which took Judith's eyes off her son and rolled them back into her head. It seemed minutes before she croaked over Scanlyn's shoulder. He turned and saw the blurred face for an instant before the door shut, and then lay hoping it was a dream while Ju went on and on in a dull voice about there now being three of them who knew mother was a whore. Scanlyn rocked her until tears were trickling through the chilled sweat on his chest.

The affair had been going on two years and showed no signs of cooling. Kat knew; their life together was static and empty. Scanlyn brooded. There wasn't any real reason he shouldn't make a move. But not out of pity, Ju insisted, not simply because she was alone and getting old and hopelessly compromised in her son's eyes. Scanlyn was touched, enough to feel that he should give in kind; a superfluous wife was a fair exchange for that much devotion.

Kat stormed at him and he stormed back, and it wasn't until they'd exhausted themselves fighting that they became bleak and adult. She was willing to have him in the house until final arrangements were made, but Ju thought Kat would find some way to hold him if he stayed, and the lawyer recommended separate residences. Judith wanted him to move in right away, but he was against smirching family-life-to-be any further. He took a hotel room and put a decidedly more avuncular cast on his relationship with little Paul—the meanwhile continuing to grab his mother whenever it was convenient. Ju told him he didn't have to marry her ever, she'd be happy having him live with her without bonds; if love wasn't enough, law wouldn't help. Scanlyn was so moved he planned to set up house as soon as the preliminary decree came through.

The Best of Our Time

They usually spent Saturday together. There was dinner at her apartment and afterward television until Paul was asleep, then the show of shows in the big bedroom mirror. Since Scanlyn always left at first light, the boy never knew he slept over. He worked hard at knitting something between the two of them, but he still found it difficult to think of him as a son-to-be.

One Saturday afternoon Ju was out shopping and Scanlyn was struggling not to yawn over a game of casino, when Paul looked up from his cards and told him Uncle Bruce had a bigger dongie. Uncle Bruce was the lawyer who'd represented Judith during her divorce, and Scanlyn wondered what on earth he kept a donkey for and whose it was bigger than. Than Scanlyn's, Paul said. There were a few seconds when Scanlyn thought the boy was being silly, but then he understood and tried to keep his voice even, tried to ignore the distinct impression of something slipping away, while he asked Paul how he knew. He had seen Uncle Bruce doing wee-wee, the boy said. Scanlyn told him that Uncle Bruce should close the bathroom door, and played another card. Sometimes he didn't, Paul said, and sometimes he took off all his clothes before he did wee-wee.

The child matched his card and picked both up. Scanlyn looked at him sharply. The bud mouth said baby words but there was something very like malice in the eyes. He suspected Paul of making it up, and then suspected he had no choice except to think that. There was another slight lurch. Scanlyn suggested that the boy hadn't seen Uncle Bruce that way in a long time. No, Paul agreed, not for a long, *long* time. Scanlyn reminded himself that he had to be both practical and fair-minded. He couldn't have really believed Judith lived a solitary, emotion-starved life while she waited for him to come along; but they'd certainly get a new family lawyer. Then the boy said Mommy had told him Uncle El was going to come live with them. Uncle El said yes, very soon. Then where would Uncle Bruce stay when he slept over? Scanlyn put down his cards; he wouldn't encourage the child's storytelling by asking any more questions. Paul reminded him that it was his turn. In a minute, Scanlyn said. He had difficulty lighting a cigarette, looked at the tip, then suggested it must have been a very very, long *long* time since Uncle Bruce stayed over. Yes, Paul said, it was. Not since Halloween. It was then a week to Christmas.

Scanlyn went out to the nearest bar and watched the college Game of the Year. Later he remembered nearly every key play in spite of the bourbons the bartender kept bringing, and he was able to discuss the finer points with the man on the next stool even while *lying little bastard* were the only words in his head which made any sense. When he came back to the apartment later Judith was pacing back and forth with a cigarette. He glared and told her she smoked too much. Her hand was trembling slightly as she ground the cigarette out, then faced him and said Paul had told her about his talk with Uncle El. Scanlyn pasted a superior look on his face and sat down to listen.

She would have gone to pieces without Bruce. He'd been the only man in years who'd been good to her—before Scanlyn came along, she added. Scanlyn could understand how good Uncle Bruce must have been if he was bigger hanging down taking a leak than Scanlyn was at his erect best, and he asked what the hell he was doing getting out of bed at four o'clock in the morning if the goddamned kid was so used to boarders. Paul had never known what they were actually *doing,* Judith said. That famous Saturday when he'd caught her and Scanlyn had been the first time he'd actually *seen* anything. And what had she and Bruce been doing Halloween night—riding Bruce's broomstick?

She began to cry. Scanlyn sneered. Though by then he wasn't slipping or lurching but absolutely careening, he sat with his mouth twisted in a pose while he waited for the next wrench. She told him it had been sex, simply sex—nothing like what *they* shared. And Halloween had been the last time. Scanlyn told her she had it wrong; it had only been the last *day* of that particular month. No, the last time, and she'd told Bruce so. She was going to be faithful to Scanlyn because she finally believed he wasn't just using her, and really cared, and—And he'd damned well cared during the whole of those two years, Scanlyn said, during all the time she'd been weeping and bleeding all over him. She asked him to be honest, to admit she'd never made any demands and he'd never made any promises. To be *what?* She composed herself slightly and asked Scanlyn if he hadn't been doing the same thing Bruce had—And at exactly the same time, Scanlyn raged. With all that bullshit about heavenly bliss, what she'd actually been doing was riding those celestial elevators in tandem. She had—hell, she'd been getting more than *he* had. Not all that often, Judith said, and what was she supposed to do those times he couldn't get away? A woman alone—And that she could stay, Scanlyn said as he walked out.

In a more reasonable moment Scanlyn was able to see her side of things, but reason didn't help to keep him from feeling like an overaged horse's ass. It was over between them in nearly the same way it had been over between him and Kat—immediately, probably in the instant when that rotten kid had picked up Scanlyn's jack with one of his own. But it dragged on, he inflating himself with the idea she might do something desperate, calling sullenly to find out how she was and edging closer and closer until they met for a drink and ended up co-starring in the big mirror, making nothing like love, Scanlyn rooting and plunging in anguish and near-hatred, she grabbing it all with even more enthusiasm than when he'd whispered all the words people were supposed to say to each other. And coming grayly shrunken out the door, Scanlyn had decided firmly that it *had* been the last time.

There was a half-chance to pick up with Catherine again, but he had simply drifted, and the documentation unfolded steadily until he had a decree to go with his degrees, a free man for as long as he sent the check every month. He never saw Kat again, and Judith only once as they passed each other crossing a street. Even in that flickering instant Scanlyn felt the old pool beginning to open at his feet and hurried on, afraid to look back. There had been pickups and putdowns since, but not much of either in his recent past, and now, lying in the billion-dollar sun, he found that memories of the affair had distended his trunks slightly. He thought about the dancer. She probably hadn't been serious about the fifty dollars, but if she had . . .

It wasn't until he heard the announcement for the third time that Scanlyn realized he was being paged. Before he could say he wanted to take the call in his room the pool attendant had seated him at a table with a fringed umbrella and was plugging in an extension. He hoped it was Buffre, wished that it would be the girl.

"Mr. Eliot Scanlyn?"

When he said yes a secretarial voice picked up from the operator; Mr. Prippet was calling. Scanlyn didn't know what he should call Mr. Prippet. He hadn't seen him for twenty years, not since Prippet had sat on the other side of a table and floated memos from somewhere beneath the senator's scaly wings. Scanlyn had called him a scrimy weasel bastard during that period.

There was a short delay. Scanlyn shivered in the shade, chilled from having been out in the sun too long.

"Hello?"

"Yes."

"This is Frank Prippet."

"Yes," Scanlyn said.

"At the Bureau."

"Yes, I understand. How are you?"

"Very well . . . thank you. And you?"

"I'm fine."

"Well I was wondering how things are going."

"I met Buffre last night. I offered him the first alternative and didn't press him for a decision. He's supposed to call me back to set up another meeting."

"What do you think?"

"I don't know. These first encounters are difficult."

"When will you see him again?"

"It's up to him. Tonight, possibly."

"You don't think he'll take off, do you?"

"I had the impression he couldn't. Who's Cyrus?"

"Cyrus?"

"Whoever he is, he's watching Buffre."

There was a pause.

"That's probably correct," Prippet said.

"I wasn't told anything about a tail."

There was a loud splash as someone went off the high board.

"I couldn't hear you. What was that noise?"

"I'm at the pool."

"The *swimming* pool . . . Well. This late."

"It's afternoon out here."

"That's right, it would be. But there's nothing definite you can report, no indication?"

"None."

"Will you call me the minute there is?"

"Those are my instructions."

"That's fine. Listen, there may be some sort of news on this by morning. A mutual friend thinks it would be best to go public."

"As long as it doesn't spoil anything out here."

"More spadework than anything else," Prippet said.

"Don't let Buffre hear you call it that."

"What?"

"That's interesting," Scanlyn said.

"I mean a sort of overture to the larger coverage we'll probably develop. It shouldn't have any effect on what you're doing."

"I hope not."

"Well, good luck. And call me."

"I will."

"Maybe you'll have something by morning."

"I doubt it."

"They'll put you through at any hour. To my home if necessary."

"Good."

"Yes. Goodbye now."

EIGHT

I n the capital the sooty afternoon had begun to take on the additional speckling of twilight. Prippet pushed a button to shut off incoming calls, placed a yellow pad before him, and took up a pencil.

"Is Cyrus the name of the surveillance?" he asked.

"Code," MacFarlane said. "There are three of them rotating."

"He knows about it."

"No reason he shouldn't. Keep him from doing anything foolish."

Prippet smiled dimly. "Sounds as though you think *he's* the one we should watch."

"If it was up to me there'd be a man on him too."

"We'd need another set, Mac. We've gone over this. If we requisition any more we'll start to call attention to what we're doing."

"Now that we know the room he's in . . . "

"We can't risk that, either."

"Get it done without a court order."

"I agree that anyone with nothing to hide shouldn't have any objection, but people can get very touchy."

The dottle in MacFarlane's pipe bubbled.

"No matter what we may think of Scanlyn, we'll simply have to trust Eric's judgment," Prippet said. "And what if he found out and told Eric? Let's get off that tack. I guess you heard enough to know the meeting didn't produce anything definite."

"Didn't think it would."

MacFarlane's magisterial croaks sometimes sent Prippet drifting toward the image of himself as a beplumed prince squatting in conversation with a great toad. "Well, you were right," he said a little sharply. "And none of us expected more at this point."

"John's acting as though he knows something."

"He doesn't."

"Camel's got his head under the tent."

"For Christ sake, Mac." Prippet drew a circle on the pad, then filled it in as a pumpkin with a pipe in its mouth. "I know what he was hinting at last night. It's more like he has his head *outside* the tent, braying to anyone who'll listen. I haven't quite worked out what we should do about it."

"You'll be getting in a couple of licks of your own tonight."

Prippet's face brightened. "Yes, that came out well, didn't it? I'm sure it will at least establish our direction. If John wants to take off in a different one he'll be entirely on his own."

"You could come out more openly against him."

Prippet drew a series of tiny swastikas. "I don't think it would be wise at this point, not when things are going so well. We'll let the situation ripen a little before we make a definitive move."

"As long as we have the chance to do it first."

"You put things very baldly, Mac." Prippet looked up. "I didn't mean—"

"That's the way I think."

"I know, and I'm deeply appreciative. Your alternatives are very practical."

MacFarland disappeared momentarily in a cloud of smoke. "Not sure John will be entirely on his own," he said. "Clark Lumney isn't going to be very happy about the way this is being handled."

Prippet drew a police club that looked very suggestive, and hurriedly added a thong and a serrated grip. "Lumney hasn't been happy for twenty-five years," he said. "Not that I intend any offense, but I do think he sometimes over . . . Anyway, we're only following instructions."

"But not strict routine."

"If it was a routine assignment they wouldn't have asked us to handle it. This is a very imaginative move, Mac, and I wouldn't like to see anyone else get credit for it. We could use a little boost."

"As long as it isn't in the tail."

"Anything that goes wrong will be Scanlyn's fault."

"He's operating under our authority."

"*Direction*, not authority. Whatever authority he has doesn't come from this Bureau. We certainly aren't going to give him permission to do something dangerous if he asks us for it, and whatever he does on his own is none of our concern. All we want is a form of control over the situation."

"Not sure we have that."

"Over what's happening out there right now? No. We're not supposed to be policemen. Cyruses . . . Couldn't they think up separate names?"

MacFarlane smoked for a few minutes. Prippet drew a club smashing a pumpkin.

"All right," MacFarlane said.

"What's all right?"

"We're covered."

"Yes, I think so." He drew a skull crunching a club between its teeth. "Do you?"

"No reason not to."

"No reason not to *what?*"

"Think so."

"Are you sure?" Prippet broke the pencil point.

"Looks good."

"I wish you sounded more certain."

"It ought to be all right."

"There isn't anything more you can suggest?"

"Put an ear in his room."

"*Jesus,*" Prippet said.

Seen from below, the Monument was a deep gray, conducting the dark from sky to earth. The lights had already been turned on in Stirby's office, and he stood dignified and neat behind his desk as he read out phrases from the pages in his hand.

Allenstein folded his shirt-sleeved arms and nodded from time to time. "It's a medium goody," he said.

"Maybe for the Boy Scouts."

"Don't you think you had enough to say last night? That stuff you put in yourself?"

"Damned if I can depend on you if you're going to be running scared."

"I've been slightly terrified ever since I stepped into this office, Commissioner. Come on, hold off on that other barrel for a while."

"You can't stand heat."

"What I can't stand is the prospect of being out of work. That speech is all right. There's enough of this and that in it to give them a few chuckles."

"Is that what you think?" Stirby let the papers drop to his desk. "Well I think it's a bowl of mush when what my folks are looking for is something to get their teeth into."

"Like human flesh."

"You will, won't you? When you don't like the right answer you turn it into smart-ass."

"It takes my mind off what I'm really saying."

"What you ought to be saying is why this country's falling to pieces because nobody has enough guts to stand up for what's right. And why that coon's out there living the high life while law-abiding people have to work for a living."

"I presume you mean Buffre."

"We've only got one on our hands that I know of."

"I don't remember anything about high living in that report."

"That report was written before our special representative went out there with a million government dollars to throw around."

Allenstein inspected his arms. "Exaggeration's a good thing in the right place, John."

"Why there's nobody begun to tell the truth yet, let alone exaggerate. You get so taken up with being clever you don't even realize it when you're not telling the truth, Lew. I believe you. I believe you get so wrapped up in your own words you don't know what you're saying. Now I'm telling you, I want something a little closer to the bone for that property owners' dinner."

"We could distribute pickax handles."

"Damn well I know a few places where they could be put to good use, but all I want from you is something a little nearer the relevant facts. And if you can't bring yourself to doing that I'll just have to find someone who can."

"It's going to be difficult to find anyone as anxious to get kicked out on his ass as you are."

"There's likely to be a hell of a lot more kicking than getting kicked."

Allenstein smiled and nodded. He cleaned his glasses, replaced them, settled back in his chair and looked at Stirby.

"I don't believe you've really gone out of your mind," he said, "so I'll ask you to assume that I recognize the problem we're facing. Don't you think I *know* this could roll back over both of us? We've got to hang loose until we find a way to handle it."

"That way just may be available."

"Bigger and better speeches?"

"That wouldn't hurt neither." Stirby jammed one hand into his jacket pocket, stood looking at the wall for a moment, then took out his hand and smoothed the pocket flap. "Right now it seems to me there would be no real problem if the law was simply allowed to take its course. We can advise F. Clark Lumney of this Buffre's whereabouts and he will bring him in."

Allenstein rubbed his forehead. "You don't think Lumney would already have brought him in if he hadn't been told to keep his hands off."

"Such does not happen to be the case." Stirby looked a little smug. "I have availability to certain information which you may not. It wasn't the Agency who located this crook, and as far as I'm aware they still haven't been informed just where he is. I'm sure the director would be very grateful for that advice."

"Lumney would be grateful for any kind of credit at all these days."

"The proper credit can be made part of the arrangement."

"If the administration had wanted to arrange anything, they'd have let Lumney out of his cage themselves."

"They should."

"But they *haven't.*"

"Then let the fault be theirs."

"Only let it not be *ours,* John." Allenstein got up and began to pace. "You have got to understand that this balloon may be just going up, but it has to come down eventually, and what we have to do is try to be in the vicinity when it does. You want to let all the air out before it's two feet off the ground—*His* balloon, if what we've been told is correct. They'd bring the firing squad right into this office."

"We'll give Lumney anonymous information."

"In this town there is absolutely no such thing. Besides, where would the profit be for us in doing that?"

"The right thing would get done."

"You go right ahead and do it, Commissioner, and I'll go back to my desk and write a memo in triplicate advising you against it. You're not taking me with you when you go."

Stirby's lip curled. "The boat's leaking."

"The boat will *sink* if you leak that information. You've got to get it straight. This is His project and we're not to pull any switches at all unless we're asked to. Isn't that clear?"

"Which doesn't make it right."

"God is never wrong."

"I don't like that talk, Lew."

"John, if it came to likes and dislikes . . . But all right. I was trying to work this out a little more clearly, but if you've absolutely got to have something to make you feel better, there *is* another angle. There might be an overwhelming reaction to

Buffre if they do get him to come over. I'm talking about the prospect of those November Valentines being blown away. If it goes bad they'll nail Prippet with the responsibility, and if Prippet has grabbed as much credit as I think he will, he'll be left very visibly straining his poop in the cold wind."

"That's his lookout."

"Nothing would make me happier," Allenstein said. "But *then* what? If Prippet looks lousy, so will the entire Bureau—unless we can arrange to have it look as though He's made at least one brilliant appointment. But who would that be, who might salvage a reputation out of the mess? Old aw-shucks, aw-shit John Stirby, that's who. The man who told us so all along, who held that white-starred, true-blue fundamental line, risking his job in defense of his principles. But we've got to be the loyal opposition, for God's sake. We've got to rig it as though it's against Prippet, not against *Him.*"

"Old aw-shucks, aw-shit."

"Or Sir Launcelot, or whatever you have to be when the right time comes."

"And meanwhile?"

"We'll hang on. And we can if you'll just listen."

"Frank's not the only one could get killed," Stirby said.

"You and me together, baby."

"I don't know but what it wouldn't be worth it if I was sure I'd take you along."

"Neither one of us has to go, John. Keep the volume down and we might even have a chance to come out of this better than when we went into it."

Stirby fingered the pages of the speech, put on his glasses and began to look through it. "It's still mush," he said.

"But nourishing."

"And I still think you ought to be able to do better."

"I will, I will. Endure my mediocrity for a little while, until I can see daylight."

"As long as that's not too long, Lew."

Allenstein shrugged and held up both hands in an ancient helpless gesture.

NINE

The cabby was dubious, but Scanlyn had taken down Buffre's instructions carefully and was sure he had the right address. They went beyond the city and through an area which had a surprising number of suburban homes. Evidently not everyone worked at stuffing money into slots or providing slots for stuffing or carrying suitcases or guns. People who sold shoes and butter and chickens lived a more normal life than those who fed off the blazing straightaway.

The houses were arranged in clusters rather than in blocks, and quickly petered out into single homes set at the edge of the desert. The driver looked smug when the cab stopped at a remote intersection where there was nothing except a phone booth, but Scanlyn checked the street signs against what he'd written down, and got out. The cabby shook his head as he streaked away.

On the other side of the city a cone of fire reached into the night sky. Scanlyn waited beneath a web of stars, his sunburn chilling him, while cars passed flat out in either direction. He planned to tell Buffre about Cyrus. It was the fair thing to do, and it would save having to make tortuous arrangements to meet at remote places. He shivered. The brush rustled under a faint wind carrying the last of the day's dry scents. Coyotes barked not far away. He felt like a key figure in one of those flat unsparing paintings of American midnights. And then an unlikely clanking came from nearby. He looked cautiously behind the booth and saw a form topped by metallic horns and black feelers edging out of a culvert. Buffre's head and shoulders came into view, then the bulk of the motor scooter he was pushing. He walked it to the highway's edge.

"Hop on," he said.

"I don't know if I can." Scanlyn looked at the machine.

"You'd better can if you're coming."

Scanlyn got on the rear seat and put his hands around Buffre's middle.

Buffre looked down the highway, toward the mountains. "Your mother's parked just down the road," he said.

"What mother?"

"Shit." He kicked the starter until it caught. He wore the same denim jacket and half-boots, and a pair of old-fashioned goggles pushed up on his forehead. He cocked his head as he twisted the throttle. The headlamp came on, a yellow furrow across the road. Buffre revved the engine and slipped the glasses down. "Let's see you eat this, mother," he called.

Scanlyn was nearly thrown backward as the machine bucked, crossed the highway and went down the shoulder on the other side. There was a shower of grit while Buffre's legs kicked out for balance, and then they were on a track which wobbled in the pale beam of the lamp. Buffre's stomach was sucked in beneath Scanlyn's hands, his muscles tense with the strain of steering. The machine sputtered and slowed to a stop at an embankment which cut off the track.

"Come on," Buffre said, "come on," and began to push the scooter up the rise.

"I didn't . . ." Scanlyn panted.

"No you didn't. Come on and *push.*"

The road at the top of the embankment was unlit. Scanlyn looked back toward the telephone booth and saw a car slewed across the highway at the point where they'd entered the desert, its beams falling away into darkness. "That wasn't . . . my idea," he whistled.

"It wasn't any idea. They'll be waiting in a half-track next time. How does that taste, you mother?" he shouted. "Get on."

Buffre turned off the headlamp, pointed the scooter toward the mountains and gave it full throttle. Scanlyn hoped Buffre's vision was better than his own double blur of tears and windscreen. The night rushed by as though it had been torn into streamers, and when they hung aslant on curves he felt as though the road itself had been tilted. Buffre grunted and stiffened. Scanlyn squinted over his shoulder and saw two buttons of light far ahead. Buffre moved to the furthest edge of the road but didn't turn the lamp on. The oncoming lights straddled the white dividing line and they brightened until the scooter was supended motionless in the glare while the line pulled the car toward them; then there was a screech of tires, the lamps swerving, and a horn blast which fell behind like a long tail.

The wind whipped under Scanlyn's jacket and through his shirt, icing his sunburned back and the sweat running down his side. His fingers were locked so tight that the joints ached. The demon ride went on in a pocket of noise, his head tucked into Buffre's neck. At last they slowed again and dipped down another shoulder, then more sharply, Scanlyn's legs kicking out in tandem with Buffre's. The scooter's headlight was on again, and they jolted along the hard bed of a watercourse. He thought of all the fanged night things watching, waiting for them to falter. They stopped under a small bridge and pushed the scooter up a bank, Scanlyn clutching it so he wouldn't fall across a poisoned burrow.

The bridge supported a narrow road. He remounted and hung on, nearly stupefied as they moved along the uneven surface. He swayed with Buffre as they went down a gentle incline and onto a track where gravel sprayed up into his shoes. Finally they came to a gentle stop, and when Buffre closed the throttle Scanlyn sat in a roaring stillness, his legs still tucked up and his face in the other's neck until he was elbowed away.

Scanlyn's hair was gritty and sand grated between his teeth. His back was stiff and his shins quivered from the stones' pinking, and each of his joints seemed slightly out of line. He was too shaken to be surprised at finding himself before what was certainly a set trucked in whole from Hollywood Hills, a tile-roofed stucco bungalow framed by a hedge of cypress, behind it a gleaming rectangle which could only have been a swimming pool. They were far from any house or lighted road and only a dim fan of color showed on the other side of the city. Buffre's teeth gleamed in the dark. "Got your bearings now, pops?" he said.

"I thought it was mother."

"All you mothers. Know where you're at? Nowhere is where."

Scanlyn followed him into the yard. The house was dark except at two corner windows. Buffre opened a door and they went into a kitchen where two candles burned on a table. One of the shadows moved.

"There's one of them still out there tearing up the road and probably halfway to L.A. by now," Buffre said.

She moved closer to the table and Scanlyn was suddenly functioning again, thinking of how he must look, disheveled and disjointed, the gray tufts sticking out like a fright wig, while she was slender and round and had skin of an unimaginable color —but then the passport picture hadn't been taken by candlelight.

"How do you do, Mrs. Buffre? I'm Eliot Scanlyn."

His throat was too dry for the practiced musicality he used on students. She didn't answer, only stood with one hand wrapped around her waist, the other at her throat. Like dark honey, Scanlyn thought, and probably like silk to the touch.

"Here's Mr. Man," Buffre said. "Did you bring your package? Gracie wants to see all that stuff."

"I don't need to see it."

"I have it," Scanlyn said.

"He'll be disappointed if you don't let him show you the great fake they did on the picture of you and the kids. He's real proud of that one."

She and Buffre took chairs at opposite sides of the kitchen table and left Scanlyn to find one at its head. He tried to smile at each one of them but their faces danced away into the shadows.

"Talk about conspiracy," he said, "this atmosphere alone ought to be enough to get us all busted."

"You don't have to worry about any tapes."

"You may be right." Scanlyn pulled his aching parts together. "I mean you may have been right about my room. I didn't think they would, you see, but then I don't really know them. And that other car . . . I didn't know anyone was following you until last night after you'd gone. I was going to tell you about it."

"Were you now."

"Yes, even though it would have been a waste of time—you know more than I do. But who did he follow tonight, then, you or me?"

"Whichever one, he didn't have much luck."

"To where we met, I mean. At the phone booth."

Their eyelids drooped slightly.

"You're wrong," Scanlyn said. "I didn't . . . unless they *are* on my phone . . . They must have followed *you.*"

"They didn't follow anybody across those flats."

"No, they didn't. It must make you feel more comfortable being on your own turf—if they still call it that."

"Didn't I tell you, Gracie?"

"I brought the check, too." Scanlyn took out the envelope. A few grains of sand fell to the table. "Your turn for that business of the tap on the head and the shallow hole among the deer and the antelope." He smiled.

"Since somebody knows approximately where we are and since they saw me hauling you away, trying to take off with this doesn't look like too smart a move."

"Of course." They looked as though they hadn't expected him to be any brighter. "There's still tape . . . not that it would bother me. You could have one running in the next room."

"We're not using candles because they're romantic," Buffre said. "There's no power."

"Battery-operated," Scanlyn said nearly triumphantly. "If

there's anything incriminating you want me to say for the record, I'll be happy to oblige."

"Make me that deal again."

"I don't want to hear it," she said.

"Not even the part where he wants me to leave you and the kids?"

"It was one of the alternatives," Scanlyn said.

"I keep thinking I've seen the entire bottom," she said, "but you people always turn up something new."

"My name is Eliot Scanlyn and I am officially authorized to offer George T. Buffre and his wife forged passports and ten thousand dollars to leave the country. Will that do?" He thought for a moment. "You can't be renting this house."

They looked at him as though he were an idiot.

"Not even if you could afford it," Scanlyn went on, "not out here. But it doesn't matter. If you don't want to see the passports and the check, does that mean you aren't interested?"

"Do I have a choice?" Buffre asked. "Leave the country or make the pigsty, isn't that it?"

Scanlyn didn't answer.

"Can't you get yourself to put a name on that stick you're holding? The fat part's for me, but what do you think that is oozing around the end you've got hold of?"

"Tussy means the shit end," she said.

"I know what he means, but that isn't an answer."

"I'm still waiting for you to tell me what choice I'm supposed to have." Buffre looked more as though he was waiting to pounce.

"The alternatives—"

"I'll tell *you,* and it's that we're staying here just one more week to get a few things straightened out and give you a chance to serve that warrant any way you want to. After that we're moving on. I'll try to make bail if I get busted, but if I can't she'll just have to get by on her own. At least she'll be with Georgie and Edna."

"Then you aren't interested in leaving the country."

"My own time and my own way."

"Do you feel the same, Mrs. Buffre?"

"She was ready to go if that was what I wanted."

"Why don't you want to?"

"I told you, didn't I Gracie?" Buffre shook his head. "Because we don't push any more, that's why."

"I'm very pleased you're not going," Scanlyn said.

He didn't expect to be believed but he was grateful for the slight shift of expression on Buffre's face. His wife didn't seem to have heard him.

"To my mind, going abroad would have been as great a mistake as continuing to slave away here," Scanlyn said. "And I use the word in its full context. What could you possibly have done from over there? More empty manifestos from another revolutionary in exile? I'm sure you'd have been a showpiece on the diplomatic circuit, but what would you have had in common with an Arab society? They're the ones who originally sold your people, you know. Could you adopt their history, their dress, and really believe it was your own? I think not."

"Yours is better," she said.

"*Yours* is better, but only when it isn't distorted by make-believe. And would you be satisfied to be Jade to the crazies dropping in for the latest word? Would you be content with a soul slap from the junkies looking for a connection to the hot line? You'd be of no use at all to the movement, to any movement. All you've worked for and all you've risked is going to be wiped out unless you can continue to be effective."

"Cap'n got real trouble with all that bad stuff's backed up on him. But don't count on this nigger to be your enema bag. Whatever reasons we're not going for are personal, and none of them would make you feel any better."

"But isn't it true that you couldn't help from there any more than you could hiding here?"

"Tussy already figured that out," his wife said.

"I was sure he would. Fine then, we don't have to discuss that any more. You've made one choice. I'm going to give you another, one I'm fervently hoping you'll take." Scanlyn put the envelope back in his pocket, then settled himself and tried to look directly at both of them. "We want you to work with us."

"With *you?*"

"A better job than that." Scanlyn looked at the rings of light on the ceiling and felt used and useless and uncertain. "If I'm the best they could find to send out here, things are pretty bad."

"They're going to get worse."

"Very likely, unless there are changes. Wouldn't you like to be part of them?"

"Doing what?"

The woman didn't move her head but Scanlyn saw her eyes gleam as they shifted toward Buffre.

"Being the man between," Scanlyn said, "another link, if you still want to call it that. And a chain, too, with you as the other kind of prisoner this time—the keeper. Become the link between them and the pluralistic you."

"You've got that problem that you can't say it."

"A visible prop?"

"An *ornament.*"

"You already had those," his wife said. "You always did have. Tussy, has he got your nose open?"

"Do you think so?" Buffre said.

"I don't know."

"Which one of those Toms has got to the point he can't stand it any more?" Buffre asked Scanlyn.

"No one."

"Then they're giving somebody the shaft again."

"This is a brand-new position."

"Created just for me." Buffre was amused.

"To fill a vacuum."

"But for *me* to fill."

"Someone like you," Scanlyn said, not believing it. He was sure the administration wouldn't make another effort like this one. "A person who can accept being hired as an ornament and who'd try to turn the job into something worthwhile."

"What job?" Buffre turned to his wife. "My nose is all right, Gracie, I just want to hear this."

Scanlyn felt a quick flush of anger and as quickly felt it ebb.

Condescension was as much as he had any right to expect. "We'll arrange a satisfactory title," he said. "The position would pay between eighteen and twenty thousand dollars a year, with certain expenses. You'll have a guaranteed year's contract, so even if they fire you or you quit you'll still receive full payment for the year."

"Does that other ten go with it?"

"It may seem to you that I'm merchandising sellout, but this arrangement will be absolutely legitimate; no, that other ten doesn't go with it. And you *can* be effective if you get that nose a little harder and sharper. There's a good chance this time because there's a motive of absolutely cold politics behind it."

Buffre's wife snuffled. "Some news."

"I didn't think it would be. But this time the politics aren't merely ceremonial. They're willing to work with someone they'd never have identified with before, someone they've opposed. It's window dressing to them, a radical move that can be made to look like a whole program . . . But you can use *them.*"

"They'll do the using," she said. "They'll use Tussy to keep themselves where they are."

"Not if he won't let them. He's going to be very visible. He can have a real audience instead of a parkful of trashers and heads, and he won't have to share the platform with rock bands and splinter groups. He'll be center ring and full spot."

"They'd have a bandanna knotted four ways on my skull in no time at all," Buffre said.

"You ought to be able to avoid that. You've got the advantage of having seen how they did it to the others. Sure, they'll try the same tactics with you, the same pressures and slights, but you can beat them if you stay absolutely straight, if you don't try to make black beautiful every single time, if you dress more or less the way they do, if—"

"All those chances have already been had," Buffre's wife said, "by all those people right on to do something. What did *you* ever do?"

"I did what I could," Scanlyn said. "It doesn't look like much now."

"I told Gracie about the teeth," Buffre said.

"And I've already said I shouldn't have mentioned it. All right, our day is past. Is yours?"

"It's coming."

"Not unless you force it. You've got to do something more than congratulate yourself on your own virtues."

"You'll do it for us."

"I don't think so," Scanlyn said. "If this system breaks down, the new one won't be built up exclusively by blacks. You'd better find a place—"

"Know our place," she said.

"All of us had better find a place." He paused to let that sink in and found they were not quite there, their faces fading in and out of the background. "But we're into aspects beyond those I originally had in mind. I only wanted to present the official position and to give you an idea of the use I think you can make out of it. If you want to go on to graduate school, say, you'd have to take turns putting each other through unless you got something very special in the way of scholarships. And with two children? Would you feel any better as ornaments on a campus? Take the job and then take the money and run if you want to. It could be like turning a trick; do it and you'll have enough to put both of you through school."

"Is my wife supposed to know something about truning tricks?"

"Never mind. If—" she began.

"That's not close to being fair," Scanlyn said.

"Never *mind*. If there's anything left of him to *put* through."

Beyond the outline of the candle flames her face was hard. Scanlyn had a vivid recollection of Nefertiti in dark stone. "I think we've said as much as we should for now," he said. "You've got enough things to think about and to talk over between you."

"Do we, Tussy?"

Buffre turned to Scanlyn. "I thought there wasn't time to talk about anything."

"You said you were going to be here a week more in any case."

"And suppose I want to bring in a little outside advice?"

Scanlyn hesitated. "Publicity would ruin things at this stage. Later they'll certainly give it all the notoriety they can as an act of solemn faith, but I'm sure they'd deny the whole business if you tried to turn it into propaganda at this point. And they'd get away with it. At this stage I'd have to support them myself—I owe that much."

"Then all the jazz about willing to be taped . . ."

"Does it really matter? We both know what they can do, and if publicity comes into it now, they'll find some way to work the disclosure to their advantage."

Buffre's wife sat back with her arms folded, her face turned in planes of bitter amusement.

"I said advice, not publicity," Buffre said.

"If you can obtain it quietly, you should have all the advice you can get."

"He's worried you're going to embarrass him," she said to Buffre.

"Can't we leave this just where it is? I recognize my guilt, Mrs. Buffre. Won't that do for the time being?"

"Depends on what you do with it."

"Let's come down for a minute, Gracie."

"And let the tapeworm start to eat us up again."

"I'm tired," Scanlyn said, "and I don't think we're going to get any further tonight. Will you call me, or can I call you?"

"You already told me I don't have a phone."

"Then you'll have to call to arrange the next meeting."

Buffre looked at his wife. She looked down at the table. "I'll see," he said.

"And next time can we do without the elaborate precautions? I'm too old for all that cross-country travel."

"I said I'd see."

"Could you take me back a more direct way tonight?"

Scanlyn saw her eyebrows shift a fraction.

"You won't know any better how to get here," Buffre said.

"Then I can honestly say I don't know if I'm asked."

"The way you've been honestly talking to us," she said.

"As honestly as I can, Mrs. Buffre, and no matter how much you do or do not believe that, I think we've done enough talking for one night."

"Suppose I get you to one of the main roads?" Buffre asked. "You can thumb from there."

Scanlyn pictured himself as a grubby midnight image moving at ninety miles an hour past every car. "That's fine," he said. "I'll say goodnight to you then, Mrs. Buffre. I hope to see you again."

She didn't even bother to nod.

His sunburn crawled in the chill air as they mounted the scooter. He turned up his coat collar, Buffre kicked the machine into action, and they went off into the land of the rat and the snake and the lizard.

TEN

In Lewis Allenstein's opinion the press had grown as ponderously as the government it covered, sharing the same shadowy and formless succession until it was itself as warren-ridden and institutionalized and secretive. He didn't see it in terms of loyal or disloyal opposition, but as much a victim of self-image as the various departments and agencies and bureaus—and yet he thoroughly respected its power.

Stirby spoke so often for himself Allenstein was rarely called on to act as his outlet, and so he was surprised when Edmond Carruthers phoned him directly. He knew the names of most of the Washington regulars, even a few personally—or rather was identified and categorized by that few as an adjunct of Stirby—but he'd never heard of Carruthers. For whatever reason the reporter was calling on him, it wasn't important enough to warrant dinner or lunch or even drinks; the appointment was at Allenstein's office, during working hours.

His office was situated along an inside wall and had a view of the windows of others very much like it. The indirect lighting meant to create an illusion of daylight gave an industrial tinge instead. Carruthers inspected the surroundings openly while Allenstein inspected Carruthers. He didn't like "black" as a generic term because it so often did not literally apply; Carruthers was a case in point. His skin was tan, even touched with freckles, and he had a bristling mustache that swooped away from either side of his mouth.

There was nothing in Carruthers' accent which gave any hint of his roots. "I suppose you know I originally asked to see your boss," he said.

Allenstein hadn't known, and made a note to rap Stirby on the knuckles for not telling him. "John's got a wild schedule these days," he said, meaning that no schedule of Stirby's was likely to include speaking officially with a Negro. "But I'll be happy to try to fill in, and I'm sure Frank Prippet or Howard MacFarlane—"

"They sent me over to catch this half of the act." Carruthers smiled.

"One way of putting it."

"My editor has the idea there may be something going on."

"I hope so." Allenstein tried a smile of his own. "We get paid to look busy."

"I don't know exactly what my editor has in mind, but I'm on the honkie circuit. That's why I asked to see your boss."

"I don't think you can call John . . ."

It was more Allenstein petering out than Carruthers breaking in. "At least I *try* to see them," he said. "Usually I wind up with a safe delegate who also happens to be unquotable. I'm only trying to save us time, Mr. Allenstein."

"I don't think I'm going to turn out to be very attributable."

"We could disguise you as a highly placed source, but that would imply your boss was even more highly placed. He's just noisy, though, isn't he?"

Allenstein suddenly wished he'd been able to afford the luxury of being unavailable. "I hope we can find something we'll be able to talk about, Mr. Carruthers."

"We could try a little question-and-answer."

"Sure."

"My boss wonders if he's correct in feeling there may be a shift coming in the administration's present racial policies." Carruthers raised an eyebrow. "We can leave the race unspecified if you like."

"I'm afraid I'm far, far away from the source of administration policies," Allenstein said.

"Right. And that sort of thing wouldn't normally be in the line of this Bureau's activities, would it?"

"Our work can be very diverse."

"Enough to include a swing toward the liberal side—and to include Stirby in it?"

"Very diverse." Allenstein could feel his face going stiff.

"Obscure, anyway. We had some trouble actually locating you physically. Sort of an *eminence gris* without any *eminence*, isn't it?"

"We're simple bureaucrats."

"Stirby seems to be simple enough, a law-and-order type with a touch of the old-fashioned seg. Racist would probably be a little strong."

"I don't think you expect me to agree to that definition. I'd certainly call him a man of rigid principles."

"So was Hitler. That line's pretty old even by bureaucratic standards, Mr. Allenstein."

Allenstein tried to look impassive and swivel away smoothly, but his chair needed oiling and it screeched.

"In fact," Carruthers went on, "I've seen your form sheet, and if I read it right I don't see you as a type to be working for a honkie."

"I'm not . . . and I'm wondering if you were planning to call him that if he had been able to see you."

"That's what I get paid for—my shock value. Journalistic confrontation. No matter what I may call your boss I'm sure you know we wouldn't print it, and the truth is he's not very much by way of being news except that word has it that the administration is finally creaking in one direction while he seems to be taking off violently in another."

"John Stirby is hardly a violent man."

"I'd say that depends on your viewpoint. From some of his stuff that I've read—or should I say your stuff?—he's definitely opposed to violence . . . from the people. He doesn't seem to mind it from anyone in uniform." Carruthers paused. "I'm getting drawn off a little. You just might have a better technique than I do."

"I think we ought to get back to questions and answers."

"You don't provoke, as they say."

"I can't afford to, Mr. Carruthers. I'm bottom man here."

"Okay, what do you see from down there, then?"

"I don't understand."

"Right. Have you any indication, do you make any inferences, are there any implications, to the effect that the administration or some part of the administration is adopting a more conciliatory attitude to a certain unnamed minority group?"

"I think the administration has always taken an interest in the welfare of so-called minorities."

"Right. And has this Bureau—so-called—been assigned a particular role in this *volte-face?* You can see how carefully I read your form sheet, Mr. Allenstein. I know about the French."

"I'd recommend Frank Prippet as your best source of the Bureau's specific activities."

"What's he doing that's got Stirby so bothered?"

"I hadn't noticed he was."

"I'd still like to see him. Can you arrange it for me?"

"I'm not his secretary."

"Would you care to tell me just what you are, Mr. Allenstein?"

Allenstein turned so abruptly, there was a sound like tearing metal. "I'm the administrative assistant for the deputy chief of a minor bureau," he said. "My civil grade and salary are on file."

"And are you planning to stay in that civil grade?"

"All of us have hopes for some sort of future, Mr. Carruthers."

"As hacks for a throwback to the Stone Age?"

Allenstein sighed. "I think we're wasting each other's time."

"While you're working toward that future, you're probably going to need some cooperation from the press."

Allenstein hesitated, and Carruthers waited with a per-

fectly neutral expression on his face. "I think I'll need cooperation from many areas."

"Yes, but from the press."

"I may even need a letter of recommendation from what
may turn out to be my ex-boss." Allenstein was surprised at
what he'd said.

There was a flicker of interest from Carruthers. "I could
easily misread that into a hint that moving day might be near."

Allenstein shrugged and spread his hands.

"Right," Carruthers said.

"It's the very best I can give you. You should be talking to
John, even though we both know he couldn't expect anything
close to sympathetic treatment from your paper." Allenstein
held up his hand. "I don't suggest you shouldn't take that position, only that we both recognize it. Anyway, John will do what
he thinks he has to, no matter how it's received."

"Then maybe you can tell me just what it is he thinks he
has to do."

"I literally can't," Allenstein said.

"You could try."

"Mr. Carruthers, for three years I've been trying to keep
things in this office as level as possible. Definitely *not* for attri-
bution, I can tell you that rather than hyping up public state-
ments, I've been struggling to keep them toned down."

"I see." Carruthers drummed the arms of his chair. "Well
aren't we all."

"I beg your pardon?"

"Victims of circumstance. I would think there are probably
some very good-hearted people grinding out stuff in support of
preventive detention and bus-burning and anything else that'll
bring us back to the good old days. It's a shame they can't get
credit for their intentions."

"I'm not trying to cop a plea," Allenstein said too quickly.

"Oh no."

Allenstein waited, but Carruthers appeared to be waiting too. "I'm not, and I am sorry I don't have more to give
you."

"Me too." The reporter put away his notebook. "I'd still like to see Stirby."

"I'm sorry, I can't help you."

Carruthers got up. "If you ever feel you'd like to try a little harder, give me a buzz. I think I'd be interested in hearing what you've got to say."

Allenstein came from behind his desk. "If I can—and I mean that—I will."

There was a moment of clarity between them, and Allenstein felt his eyes going out in what might have been beseeching. The other's expression of indifference became touched with contempt. "Right," he said. "If you can."

Allenstein fumbled with his glasses, recovered, and then saw Carruthers to the door.

ELEVEN

Buffre's outside advice was more expert than had been anticipated, and Scanlyn felt at a distinct disadvantage caught loafing at poolside, wrapped in a patchwork of towels which covered the red skin and exposed the white. Julian De Berg wore enormous sunglasses and his thin hair flowed over his ears and collar. His tie was wide, his shirt striped, his trousers belled.

De Berg had made an early reputation as an inveterate defender, and he'd prospered, but his commitment to civil liberties had grown until he'd gone off what some of his colleagues clucked at as the deep end. His clothing was not nearly as outrageous as some of the costumes his clients appeared in, and he'd become a prominent figure in chaotic courtrooms where precedents were often set. But Buffre had never been one of his clients, there was no record of a Buffre defense fund and no known connection between him and De Berg.

Scanlyn fussed with his towels while they talked about the hour and the weather, decided on limeade, and acknowledged that they had a mutual interest in George Toussaint Buffre.

"Isn't he remarkable?" De Berg said. "Some of the others . . . I know they have every reason to rage, but that unremitting hostility . . . I have to bite my tongue to keep from saying it isn't *me,* not now it isn't." He reached over to touch Scanlyn. "But George isn't like that. I think he still has the capacity to love."

"He doesn't flaunt it."

"You mean you don't think he shows enough gratitude. I might ask for what. It's our last chance, you know, our only hope —love."

Scanlyn made a face and sipped at his drink. "When that last chance slips by we'll find another one."

De Berg smiled. "Haven't I heard you called Totty?"

"Probably."

"Most people call me Jerry even though my name is Julian." The lawyer's eyes drifted for a moment, then brightened behind the blue glass. "It isn't that you haven't tried to do good things, Totty, only that it's been from the wrong side of the street. Nothing can be done properly if it's done *their* way. They know that; it's part of their technique. They eventually wear you flat. It was happening to me before I began to see my work in the proper perspective. I wasn't helping enough people and couldn't ever have as long as I played by their rules."

"I don't like this business of 'they' very much. Let's say I'm doing what I think is best."

"But that's just where it's all gone wrong. We start out with our hearts full, and then . . . I can see shreds of sincerity, I can see that you feel your attitude has some value." De Berg sat forward. "But that's not going to do George any good. Whether you'll admit it or not, you're still looking at things the way you wished they were rather than as they actually are. The dreams you're trying to sell him were exhausted a long time ago, before they ever began to work. He knows that, and it would be terrible if he began to believe in those fantasies again. He'd never survive a second disillusionment because he doesn't have our advantages or resources—we've already been through so much, after all. The greatest favor you can do him is to let him come to trial and learn what it's really all about."

"You think he'd be likely to survive that better."

"There's no chance of a conviction. These cases are nearly impossible to prosecute, and judicial error is the easiest thing in the world to force. They sit there in their bought robes and feel themselves threatened and bang, down it comes—unwarranted contempt findings, erroneous jury charges, all the rest."

Scanlyn shielded his eyes and looked toward the mountains. "I know you've been mixed up in some gutty cases," he said, "but I haven't always had a clear picture of the virtuous public defender."

"Of course you haven't. The rapacious lawyer . . . in my case, revolution for profit. That's what everyone thinks. And expenses *are* met, because they have to be. But there's far more to be made in any corporate tower. Why don't you ask Howard MacFarlane what he's worth?"

"I don't happen to know MacFarlane personally. And I don't care what you or anyone else make on Buffre, only what you're trying to make out of him."

"You can't think I need to enhance my reputation. Everyone already knows I'm a flamboyant self-serving charlatan currently reliving my late adolescence. I take smaller fees in some cases so I can get at the little girls. Or at the little boys, if you want a really dirty story. I can find grander causes than George Buffre. Where's my gain in being linked with him?" De Berg sat back. His forehead was dry, and a breeze stirred tendrils of his hair.

Scanlyn was sweating inside the little tent made by the towel draped on his head, but he was afraid to expose the back of his neck. "Or his in being linked with you," he said.

"Indecent exposure." De Berg smiled. "I'm interested in the trial as a public exhibition. The apparatus itself is enough to disgust anyone. Let it be seen functioning as arrogantly as it can —and then let it fail miserably. That's my profit. As for George, he'd gain prominence and stature, he'd be listened to by more people."

"Until the day after the verdict," Scanlyn said, "when the newspapers dropped him and some lecture bureau picked him up and squeezed out as much as they could before he was completely forgotten. He'd be prominent in front of audiences principally *not* black, kids looking for any excuse to raise the fist. Your boy would have all the stature of a minstrel show."

"Which is exactly the use you plan to make of him."

"One of the reasons I find the picture of the public defender muddy is that this concern of yours is fairly new. What happened to the days when your biggest involvement was getting the widow off so you could collect half the insurance?"

"That was a long time ago. I've gotten away from all that."

"I see." Scanlyn tried to correct the downward pull of his mouth. "Well, I haven't been that fortunate. I happen to be doing what I've always been doing, and if I don't believe in last chances any more, at least I've got a few hopes left."

"Hopes, even though you must be aware of the kind of company you're keeping these days? Come on, Totty, you know George is nothing but meat to them. You've hired out to entice him to a slave auction, to see him sold into bondage to . . . Why, I'll even give you that much credit, I'll call it an ideal. But it's your ideal, not his, and it hasn't ever worked."

One of the younger unstretched wives went by. "Marvelous," De Berg said, looking after her. "The really young don't know how to draw a man out. They're sexually shallow." He looked at Scanlyn. "Are you married?"

"No."

"Divorced?"

"Correct."

"You have that look. I've been through it myself. I'm remarried and I've got two children now. It's a pity George has a family, because the less he has to lose . . . I'm afraid he's swayed by what he feels to be an obligation toward them."

"He damned well should be."

"Just as you were—the divorce, I mean. Were there any children?"

"No. And you?"

"That's fair, but I think we're getting small. You'll catch him any way you can, won't you?"

"By the toe if I have to."

"That's a curious echo."

"It was meant to be. What's going to happen when you move on to the next cause and leave him with nowhere to go?"

"We would have moved a fraction of an inch forward in the

meantime. George sees that point and even agrees with it in principle—but alas, he can't bring himself to participate. It doesn't look as though there's going to be a trial."

"He's made up his mind?"

"Your offer, you mean? Oh no. That's a vicious piece of maneuvering, but George isn't frightened by it. I've told him he shouldn't be, that you'll have the warrant canceled. He won't talk to you until you do."

"I don't even know what it's for," Scanlyn said. "I don't know anything about it. How can I have it canceled?"

"Get them to return it. It's very simple, and it was a filthy warrant anyway. But you didn't know? I can believe you didn't." De Berg touched Scanlyn again. "You're not a *bad* man. Well, it's what they call a John Doe warrant. It doesn't even carry George's name. They can arrest anyone who can be proven to have been at the scene of the agitation and who reasonably—and that means very roughly—can be identified through a general description. The warrant could apply to a number of people."

"And if they promise not to serve it?"

"Not to have it executed. But you don't know the extent of the dirty business they were set up to do. After the arrest they could have charged him additionally with having crossed state lines. He doesn't become the criminal until he's apprehended, you see. Would you expect us to accept a promise after that? No, there's no one to trust any more, and I include you. We won't even begin to believe anything until we see the warrant returned and canceled."

"I'll try." Scanlyn felt that things were beginning to slip out of his grasp.

"They could get another, of course, but it would be extremely irregular. They'd have to gather and present new just-cause information. We might be able to make something embarrassing of that."

"I said I'd try."

"I'm really helping you even though I don't want to. George might be a little more inclined to listen if you do this.

He may take it as an act of faith, even though you and I know it would only be expediency. And I'm sure they'll go along. It makes sense to smooth the whole business over as though it never existed. A very angry young man would be one thing, and a fugitive from justice quite another. Since there was never a warrant issued in the name of George Buffre, they can deny everything. You see?"

"Can't we do without all the damned intrigue?"

"I don't see why not. You'll want to remove those watchers in the shadows, of course."

"That wasn't my idea."

De Berg paused to watch a lady who'd been lying on her stomach with the bra of her suit undone sit up and clutch the cups as she tried to fasten the straps. There was a slip and a white pink-eyed breast showed. The lawyer sighed. "Totty, I don't think you understand—and if you do, I don't understand *you*. There's no way of separating yourself from their reasons for doing what they're doing. You're their representative, acting on their behalf. I have the same problem; someone I represent and sympathize with may make an outrageous and perhaps even illegal move, but I have to protect him, to remain mute, and in so doing, I share the responsibility. We're all becoming blurred by general identification. None of us is really all of one piece or another, but we have to join a group, to take visible positions. You and I are antagonists through identification." He tapped Scanlyn's forearm. "If George takes your offer he'll be changing sides."

"Not if I can help it."

De Berg gave him a bemused look, then turned toward the pool. "I do think you're deceiving yourself rather than trying to deceive anyone else, but I'll have to stay in this until I'm sure George is on absolutely firm ground legally."

A drop of perspiration dangled from the end of Scanlyn's nose. He removed the towel and hid his face in it and wished that the ground he himself was on wasn't quite so shifty.

TWELVE

F rank Prippet sat on a bench along the Mall and dreamed of the days when the fruit trees had seemed perpetually in blossom, when he and his wife had been in the last bloom of their youth and all things had been possible.

He glared at the tourists who drifted past, their voices high, cameras pointing. Some day it might be *his* photograph they'd be after. Things *were* still possible. He wasn't making the errors he'd made during his first stay, committing himself to causes which turned out to be only temporarily popular. A career had to be built like a picket fence, one carefully aligned slat at a time, each supporting the whole. A neat solid background, and perhaps a screen of ramblers to soften the line, perhaps a house —but he only permitted himself an oblique glimpse of the house.

It wouldn't be likely that they'd have the chance to photograph him on a public bench, of course. More probably on a balcony, his hand raised, smiling, while the tour groups below gaped and their tilted cameras strained to catch his shadow. And then with a slightly melancholy wave he'd return to the great work of caring for them all. They didn't realize how much guidance they needed. In their ignorance they were constantly electing untried new people when it would have been far better to let men of experience do what they thought was best.

Prippet believed that correct intentions must bring correct re-
sults. The people had to be guided toward what they needed.

He looked at the huge clouds boiling up behind the arches
and columns, heightening the somber inscriptions. It was
grander than anything in all antiquity, and if it was simply
allowed to function as it had been designed to, it would be a
beacon of perpetual glory. But there was always some new
panic, some unbalanced temporary surge. They forgot that no
matter how rapidly situations changed, the old foundations
were still there. Corrective machinery existed. And the lack of
belief and respect. The President spoke to doubtful audiences;
Secretaries' pronouncements were treated with contempt.
Government had lost definition and direction. If it would only
assert itself, the nation's dormant pride would rise again and
everyone would work together.

Direction: the need to be given something better than bent
nails to use in his construction of neat pickets. Prippet was
overwhelmed by cross-pressures. Flipover lacked proper control because no one had laid out a definite line, and now it had
taken a preposterous turn. Buffre could legally be considered a
fugitive; he had no position at all. Yet now he was dictating the
terms under which he might consider—merely *consider*—joining the administration. The fugitive aspect would have had to
be pruned away at some point, of course—but what were the
prospects for successful assimilation if Buffre was calling signals
from the very beginning? Prippet's own answer was no, a definite checkoff; it was time for the situation to be brought firmly
under control. But there might be considerations he wasn't
aware of. It wasn't fair to expect him to exercise total responsibility when Flipover hadn't been his idea in the first place. It
was up to *them* to decide on an answer. But Krug had been
completely noncommittal on the phone, and now he was a
half-hour late.

Pigeons picked through the litter along the Mall. Prippet
couldn't understand how men like Krug had become so important. It was impossible to tell where he stood, what position he

advocated. Krug was like most of the new men, specialists who had no roots and cast no shadows. They seemed to be nothing more than transmitters for the synthesis of all the information sucked into the computers. And he lacked style, as well. He didn't behave the way an official should. Rather than receiving people in an office where one could get a sense of texture, of moment, he arranged conferences in strange places, almost as though there was something dirty about legitimate business.

Prippet spied Krug walking along with his head down, wearing a strange suit with a belted jacket. No one paid any attention to him. Prippet found that undemocratic; people should recognize advisors. If he'd been in Krug's position he'd have made himself visible, so that everyone would know just who was working so hard. He would have set certain hours for them to stop in and chat. People wanted their officials to be accessible and sincere and dignified. Krug looked like a nobody. He stopped before a cluster of bobbing pigeons, searched through his pockets, then held out his empty hands. He might have been some kind of eccentric bird lover. As he approached, Prippet scrubbed his thoughts and tried to muster a proper expression, but he felt his facial muscles going in contrary directions and could only gather them with a smile.

"Do you have peanuts?" Krug asked.

"I?"

"They will get sick from eating garbage, the birds."

"Actually, they're supposed to be discouraged, Eric. I think they carry some sort of disease."

"So."

Krug sat down and took off his glasses. His pupils flared and the skin around his eyes seemed to sag inward so that he looked half-witted and distant. Prippet felt uncomfortable.

"Do you think someone is listening to your telephone?" Krug asked.

"I'd never . . . Do you think they would, Eric? But why?"

"To hear what you say." Krug peered at him. "If it is important."

"It certainly wouldn't be anything I'd be ashamed to have overheard."

"For me, yes. When you began to mention this legal business I thought it would be better for us to meet like this."

"I see . . . of course. Well, you already know Buffre isn't interested in leaving the country. I would say that was the preferred development, and I think we handled it very well." Krug smiled encouragingly. "Scanlyn is at the next stage right at this moment. I presume the presentation he's making is adequate, but it's certainly had a strange response, one we'd never anticipated. I wonder if he provoked it. Not deliberately, you understand. And De Berg—where did he come from? There was no suggestion of a connection in the file. Did you know of one?"

"I have heard of him," Krug said.

"He claims to be speaking for Buffre. Which may or may not be so . . . though Scanlyn believes him. And it seems that De Berg has insisted there will be no further discussion until the warrant is canceled."

"Whoever insists, the result is the same."

"I suppose so. Buffre is also threatening to make his whereabouts public, even at the risk of being arrested. He says he doesn't care any more."

When Krug nodded he looked like a foolish old mouse.

"So we appear to be at an impasse created by this ridiculous demand," Prippet said.

"The matter is closed unless you do what he asks." Krug nodded again, and smiled. "And?"

"I'm not a policeman, Eric. It looks to me like something for the enforcement agencies to decide."

"A matter of law, certainly." Krug pinched the sleeve of Prippet's jacket. "And you are the lawyer, my friend."

"I didn't have anything to do with the warrant. *I* couldn't have it canceled."

"Directly, no. But if that is what you think would be best . . ."

"I? This surely isn't a matter for me to decide on my own.

Buffre might be bluffing, mightn't he? I'm sure we have options other than agreeing to his demands. Don't they strike you as arrogant?"

"Yes or no appears to be the option."

"Eric, I don't think I can be expected to do anything but give an opinion. We'll certainly follow whatever course of action you think best."

"Yes, you are handling it very well, and that is correct, for the Bureau to be prominent. After all, a simple business of arrest could have been arranged without you." Krug put on his glasses and immediately looked brilliant and cunning. "But to do it now might make it necessary to use the Bureau, and I think that would look more like the law and order of the Hungarian." Krug shrugged. "And of course He will be disappointed."

"It's Scanlyn who's brought Buffre to the point of not being willing to discuss anything."

"As long as there is the warrant."

"*You* can have it canceled, Eric."

"We can arrange whatever you wish. If there is not to be a drawbritch, then He will have to look for another way . . . though this appeared to be a good one. You think otherwise."

"Of course I don't. You know how much I want this to succeed. I'll follow any suggestion you make."

"We talked of the gain in negotiation even when there is no result. But now a condition is made, and if you refuse it, there is not even a negotiation."

"I can't believe you're serious, Eric."

"You are amused."

"Not in the least. The project wasn't our idea, the agent wasn't chosen by us, and yet what might be the most crucial decision is suddenly entirely ours. It isn't fair."

Krug folded his arms and looked at the sky.

"Is it?" Prippet said.

"Fairness?" Krug shrugged. "How can you gain without risk?"

"But according to Scanlyn, Buffre isn't even promising anything. What if we have the warrant canceled and he still refuses to negotiate?"

"What if?"

"Then we'd have given away something for nothing."

"If we have nothing now, I do not see what we would lose."

Prippet looked more bitterly at the people going by; they had no idea of the anguish which went into the decision-making process, of just how much was done for them. "I'll have to talk to Mac about it," he said.

"Your assistant?"

"He's a colleague."

Krug brushed an invisible something from his trousers. "But not like us. He is what they call a sunshiner, here for only one season. If it is our intention to stay, there are so many little things, like this present nuisance, that decide whether we will or not."

"I'm aware of that, Eric." Prippet's jaw set. "I've been here for more seasons than you have."

"But to stay? The things we must do." Krug continued his brushing, and when he had brushed his way to both knees he stood up. "It is time for me to proceed."

"But we haven't decided anything."

"I would like it if you would call me when you do." Krug bit his lip. "There are certain pressures for the arrest. Mr. Lumney, the policeman, also knows now. He may want to talk with you."

"Lumney? But what in the world could I *tell* him, Eric?"

"It is difficult to know. Perhaps it would be better to avoid him until this is settled. Mr. Lumney's way is safe for him, and we win nothing and lose nothing. Certainly there will be no gain for you, and I think there may even be some risk if you do not tell your decision by five o'clock today."

"And the surveillance?" Prippet cried. "They insist that we lift that too. We may lose him entirely."

"I would see that possibility."

"Then don't you think we should discuss this more?"

Krug patted Prippet on the shoulder. "On the telephone, please only yes or no." He bobbed his head. "Thank you."

As Krug walked away the people paid no attention to him —or to Prippet, either, sitting on the bench and chewing a knuckle.

THIRTEEN

There was no word from De Berg or Buffre or Prippet. Scanlyn stood at the window of his room and watched the light bleed out of the sky and onto the boulevard until there were a dozen separate colored suns.

He stood so long in one position that his knees grew stiff. He was getting too old to play Mercury. If it weren't for the project . . . But he needed more than the project. No matter how brilliant his week's work and no matter how much personal success he extracted from it, it wouldn't combine those fragments of broken worlds ringing him, wouldn't begin to fuse that trashy cluster into something he could use as even a tentative base for the future. And yet he had nothing except the project to support him, and so he shut his mind to anything beyond it and squeezed those unthinkable thoughts, those insupportable probabilities, into a concentrated whole-effort application of will which would levitate Flipover clean and shining from the rubble of his career.

Though Buffre had youth and conviction and right on his side, Scanlyn had wit and guile and a conviction which might be even stronger because it was born of necessity. He had every reason to need to succeed, and enough confidence to feel sure he could shift Buffre if only logic was required. But he suspected there would have to be emotional appeals as well, and probably nudges toward visions of personal glory. Scanlyn was prepared to do what he had to. He arranged his thoughts to match all contingencies, trimmed his approaches to meet every counter, and couldn't see how he could fail to bring the operation off. What he was not able to do was make his phone ring.

He had been afflicted with increasingly dumb telephones over the past few years, and often sat for hours waiting for a trick of memory to cause someone to discover that the gap in the structure of a newly formed committee had exactly his shape. He waited to be asked to dinners where the talk was serious, to drinks which would pave the way to an invitation to join forces with other good men and true. His palm was often sweaty with expectation, and his disappointment was intense when the phone did ring and it was only his secretary asking if it was all right to go to lunch—to go anywhere, he supposed, away from the tedium of guarding a door so few people wanted to pass through.

He looked at the telephone tinted pale blue to match a prominent motif in the wallpaper. There were perhaps a dozen people he could have found an excuse to call, and each one would have become dry and cautious when he announced he was in Las Vegas for no reason he could openly admit, probably losing his money and his mind and contracting a filthy disease. He had no wife to lie to, no mistress to scheme with, no interest in the girls here and there who had always hesitated a fraction too long before saying yes or no. He was damp with the effort of willing the phone to ring. He went to the window again and watched the city burning with a hundred intolerable delights, then took up the hotel directory and ran a slightly humid finger down the listings.

She'd remember his name, though in the course of the evening she'd probably forget it and end up calling him Sport. The captain at the revue lounge told him he couldn't speak to her. There was a hotel rule about personal calls, another about giving out the addresses or home phone numbers of performers. Scanlyn hung up, fumed, then wrote a note which he took downstairs, he and the captain pretending they hadn't just spoken, Cupid's bow in the other's tie and a look of total indifference on his face as he took the envelope and the five-dollar bill.

Would she be touched? More important, would he be? He could have avoided the suspense, had satin meat sent up in a variety of wrappings—in a cake, a basket of fruit, dressed as Little Orphan Annie if that was his taste. The sniggers were probably spreading through the hotel that very moment. He called room service and ordered a salad and something called a Bullburger, unable to resist the implication of magic ground horn. The waiter would probably arrive sly-eyed, and under the covered dish there'd be a discreet card from an agency specializing in joys for randy elders. Scanlyn qualified in terms of years but he wasn't actually possessed by that insensible urge, only hoping for temporary rebirth in the form of Snorting Totty. Acronym Snotty, Snelly? Cyrus could send off a coded Telex: AGING BUFFALO BILLHOOKERED.

He could see himself as an infra-red figure in a sniperscope. Would they tape him, strangling their laughter while they listened? He didn't care, and by two o'clock when nothing but the position of the moon had changed he was on the verge of going out to dig up any bone he could find just so they'd have something to chew. He'd try another casino, another lounge—try them all until he ran into one more of his thousands of ex-students, lettered but untaught, shaking what could be made into his heart's desire.

When the phone actually rang he missed a beat or two, and then nearly let it slip through his hands. She was cool and slightly mocking and he didn't find much promise in her calling him Prof, but he offered to take her to the best dinner in Las Vegas, and he saw himself attentive to her least need, sincerely interested in any story she had to tell while all the time looking for a break in attitude which would allow a glimpse of soft parts, a peek at his prospects. Her "no thanks" held no hint of thanks and he pictured her impatiently rubbing a spangled sweaty thigh. He hurried on to all the improbabilities which had to be available in the after-hours. She seemed to grow more distant, then actually left the phone, came back scratchy and indistinct to tell him he could take her to a party.

Scanlyn said he'd be delighted, and after she hung up he sat wondering what sort of doubtful figure he'd cut in a hip and totally permissive atmosphere, if he'd be able to go anywhere near the distance in a slippery group roll-around. It wasn't an ideal prospect but it was better than being dominated by a mute telephone, better than trudging through streets filled with hysterical strangers as he tried to find someone to break silence with. He bathed and shaved again, read and dozed, and at four-thirty he went down to the bar.

There was a curious dimness in the air, a slatted effect he could not at first identify, then recognized as darkness. Just at the point of near fading, it had finally seeped in to fog the lights and shadow the eyes and creases of the players. Many tables had been shut down, and most of the action was concentrated in craps, the shooters hoarse in their last intense runs, the previously cool faces of the stickmen and moneyhandlers edged with greed. There was a fine prickly air of concentration, as though the next hour would tote up the whole night's make or break.

The ladies with gaudy wings were no longer circling. A few sat in the bar lounge, evidently hoping for their own final score in the form of an all-day sleeper they could bring home. They were all attractive and looked capable, and Scanlyn wondered why he didn't simply fall backward into a set of anonymous arms, admitting failure in all things while the dregs of hope seeped out through an orchestrated gland. *Hello, Beautiful . . . Hello, Sport.* But he had a half-chance at something better, someone who'd known him when he was almost a personage.

The drink warmed and loosened him slightly. He went to the lobby and found the deferred midnight chiming there too, people arriving with pumped-out slightly dazed expressions and trailing shreds of their evenings as they went to their rooms. The musicians and revue girls began to drift through, a collection of tuxedos, worn instrument cases and bodies which looked intensely fragile away from the stage. Lubricity had been disassembled, the girls scrubbed clean of most of the theatrical make-up, only their eyes still colored and stiff-lashed. There was a willful edginess beneath their fatigue, a sense of alertness toward any new possibilities in that free time along the rim of day.

The warmth of the drink was receding under fresh doubts, but when Lorry Noon appeared with her hair gathered darkly and her heart face wounded red, Scanlyn's pulse quickened. He was effusive, she slightly thorny as she introduced a girl named Vikky, a pair of gray eyes bobbing under a cap of fine platinum hair. When Scanlyn was told Vikky was coming with them he cranked himself up to be twice as young, but they didn't seem to expect much from him, and after he was given an address and allowed to find a cab the girls talked across him as though he were an accidental passenger.

Although the huge signs still blazed, many of the in-between lights had been dimmed or extinguished and there were dead spaces all along the boulevard. The cab turned onto a short cross street and stopped at an apartment house built in a jumble of white rectangles, a haphazard fort at the edge of the desert. They went up an open stairway and there were chimes, a door swung open, and they entered a vestibule of bone walls and dark wood. A woman in beads and a silver lamé jumpsuit greeted the girls by name. She looked at Scanlyn and then more significantly at a bowl cupped by a wooden hand jutting from the wall. Scanlyn added a ten-dollar bill to the others. There was a shuffling of eyes and feet until he threw in another ten, wondering if the entrance fee was deductible from later costs, if they were planning two for the price of one, a triple joining which would leave him in an ashen stupor of all bolts shot.

The bone and umber continued into a long room vividly splashed with Navajo rugs. Scanlyn's whorehouse visions faded when he saw some thirty people arranged in the standard poses he might find at any party, moving against a background of muted rock music. The girls didn't want anything to drink, and he stood hovering while they indicated people with their chins and eyelashes, murmured names he wasn't expected to recognize. He excused himself and went to a table which held a variety of bottles, and there came under the direct gaze of a lady with glittering feral eyes. Scanlyn smiled, and when she did not smile back he realized that she was looking through and not at him. He fixed a straight bourbon, disregarding his own warning against spoiling opportunity, prowess.

The girls weren't where he'd left them. He looked around the room and found female faces which were slightly weary, as though from guarding knowledge no one any longer bothered to keep secret. Most of the men were older. On inspecting the group more closely, he saw that they lacked the attenuated poses of partygoers. There was a loss of outline, a blurred effect, and the talk had no peaks or vitality. It was like the fellowship of a dream nearing an end, an hour when metabolisms were at an ebb, time downsliding. They were the leftovers who'd somehow missed all Xanadu's promises, and this was the last chance at a connection before the new day came with another set of circumstances, a different puzzle to be arranged.

Scanlyn's glances were returned emptily as he edged around the room. He tried to grasp the nature of Western come-and-get-it, wondered where he was in the indistinct area between whoring and assignation. The clusters of words he heard gave no clue, and no one spoke to him until a hand touched his elbow, insisted that he take it in his own.

"Jesse Tomburn?"

Scanlyn was about to deny it, but then understood and gave his own name to the boots and whipcord suit and string tie, the rubbery face beneath hair streaked white and yellow.

"Real pleasure," the other said. "You look to be in as strange parts as I find myself, but I wonder if you might not have some idea of just what is the proper go-about here."

Scanlyn's shrug of hopelessness included both of them.

"Just two ole boys a long way from home. I can't quite remember how I got put onto this place." Tomburn scratched his chin and looked around the room. "There's a for-sure one, I know—fella gave me a card. But I don't care for that sort of arrangement unless it comes down to bein' absolutely necessary. Not that there isn't times it does; the goat can get to runnin' a little high."

Scanlyn wondered if flapping his arms might stimulate his dormant musk sacs.

"I will admit to havin' come to this whole crazy town with the thought of a little such recreation in mind," Tomburn said. "No point in a man even setting out on a little pleasure excursion if he doesn't plan on coming back with his belly full and his eggs empty. I been eatin' good and I haven't won or lost enough to matter, but that other department's comin' around to needing taking care of."

Scanlyn didn't think Tomburn would have any difficulty in finding relief.

"I don't believe there's much hope for anyone who does have," Tomburn said. "I can remember Galveston when it was, and there was some very unusual things done there, but what I would call the personnel wasn't much compared to what I've seen hereabouts. I understand there's one establishment specializes in nothin' but local high school ladies. You don't happen to know if that's a fact?"

Scanlyn shook his head, busy watching his fancy cross to him in no hurry, stopping for a word along the way. A hand belonging to someone he couldn't see stroked her rump during one pause. She didn't seem to mind.

"Yes sir, yes sir," Tomburn said, and swayed.

When Lorry Noon circled to Scanlyn's side he caught the bitter breath of gage, saw slightly weed-deadened eyelids. She wanted a drink now, ginger ale.

Tomburn declined. "I have had about as much as I can stand . . . and stand. It may not show but it is for sure there, and good whiskey's one thing can be gotten enough of back home. There's others can't."

"Like what, Waco?" Lorry Noon asked.

"Oh no, ma'am. Oklahoma. Jesse Tomburn?"

"Why not?"

Scanlyn went to get her ginger ale, thought about sneaking

something into it, then thought it would be much more sensible to sneak something into himself, his money's worth a drink while someone else got the feels.

She was still listening to Tomburn, her arms folded, and made no move to take the glass Scanlyn offered.

"Well now, Miss Lorry, this is a real pleasure?"

Scanlyn supposed it would end up that way, his government scrip no match for Oklahoma oil money. He half extended the glass again. She ignored it.

"But I was telling your gentleman friend here I am just not completely sure of my whereabouts," Tomburn went on. "And I certainly would not care to give anyone offense."

"Just drop a silver dollar on the floor," she said.

"Oh my."

"And the first one who does a split to pick it up, right?"

"Oh my, Galveston."

"I mean *flat.*"

"Indeed I understand, Miss Lorry."

"Do you, Prof?"

Scanlyn crinkled his eyes over his glass.

"Waco, did you know you were in the company of an honest-to-Jesus doctor of philosophy?"

Tomburn examined Scanlyn, the whites of his eyes bruised a tomato color at their edges. "I feel honored," he said.

"We all do. Give us an inspirational sample, Prof."

Scanlyn was inspired to utter a few unkind words but he sampled his drink instead.

"Prof's tongue has been got by the cat," she said. "And you're looking to be got by a tongue, Waco. I bet you are."

"I never bet against a lady."

She took Tomburn's arm and pointed to the shimmering bowl of Vikky's hair. "That's the one."

"That child."

"She stows it and blows it and sticks-up-her-nose it."

"You're not funning me, Miss Lorry?"

"Just mention my name."

"Not that I believe that child would . . . but doesn't she have an interestin' face. I would surely enjoy talkin' with her if you're sure it wouldn't give offense."

"No way."

"Then I do believe I will." Tomburn held out his hand. "I'm deeply obliged, ma'am." He bowed, turned the hand to Scanlyn, who could only wave one of his glasses. "Sir."

He walked across the room carefully, as though afraid of stepping on his own eggs.

Lorry Noon finally took the ginger ale. "Do you think she doesn't?"

Scanlyn had no opinion.

"Do you think she shouldn't?"

Scanlyn didn't think what he thought mattered to her at all, and he wondered why he'd been asked along.

"I thought you'd be hot to research the local zoo," she said. "You could write another book. You could call this one *Asses.*"

She laughed uh-uh-uh. He was distressed.

"After all you've done for us, right? And for me in particular. I've got to be alienated. I'm dysfunctional."

And how about a poor old punched-out ticket of admission with broken ends of his own?

"That's tough shit," she said.

Undoubtedly a line out of her master's thesis, The Desirability of Sharing something or other. Scanlyn had no doubt what was being shared and how freely, but he was beginning to wonder how really desirable it was.

Lorry Noon put out her hand as though reaching blindfolded into the room and touched a short man in a tuxedo, his tie undone, sweat beading his nearly bald head. "Matty, we need an ingratitude gag," she said.

Scanlyn remembered having seen him as a gray-white shadow on glass, sweating then too, wringing his handkerchief.

"*You* need a gag. I did two turns tonight at what I believe was the armless mutes' convention. Next time I furnish golf shoes so they can at least clatter. Ah, isn't that nice—he's smiling. How do you do, sir? Isn't this lovely—fading sunset and rosy dawn cheek to cheek."

"A full professor, Matty."

"He's from the home, he's come to take you back."

Scanlyn told the comedian how much he'd enjoyed his work.

"If you would only write and tell my mother, she'd be so happy. Strange-looking as he is, kiddo, I've got to admit he's kind. I wish I had a father like that."

"Father to the word, not the deed."

"You mean you have to talk it up a lot. Like the queer Indian who blew cobras to make his flute stand up. He didn't smile, kiddo."

"Matty, you should—"

But he saw someone on the other side of the room and scuttled away.

"You can tell the wife when you get back," she said. "You almost touched him."

Scanlyn said there wasn't a wife and noticed his glass was nearly empty.

"Are you a slosher, Prof?"

Rarely, and it certainly wasn't helping that night. But what about *her* addictions? If he was there to see and taste all, why hadn't she offered him a leaf from the incense-bearing tree?

"You mean you'd risk it? You aren't afraid of getting hooked, ending up on smack? A man for our times, right?" Uh-uh-uh. "You're folks."

He was willing to be. If she really wanted to stretch him out on that tour through the caves of ice, why wasn't she lining up pill and needle, why hadn't she put a cold price on her own bending?

A new face slid out from behind the other as though the moon were changing phase. He was surprised to see dust in the corners of her eyes and in the creases of her mouth, but it was powder, visible now because the lamps had grown dimmer. Scanlyn looked at a window. The dark was fading, gray seeping into the room and leaching away the last pretense that night and all its possibilities still existed. The changing light caught lines and furrows. It ringed eyes and turned faces vague and uncertain.

People were leaving. Scanlyn knew he should go, should have gone, should not even have come, but that admission looped him back to a dead telephone and all its implications of past and future. Beyond an open glass door was a terrace where he had seen people dancing, and when he picked up a thread of music he thought he could manage, he caught her hand. The tiles of the terrace were dewed and slippery. Her face was shadowless, and when his fingers curled around hers he saw his age spots black on a dead-silver hand. She deliberately brushed her padded middle bone against his thighs. His flesh engorged but didn't rise, a plumb bob tracing their erratic circles.

"What's it worth?" she whispered coarsely.

At that moment it was worth nothing. Perhaps if he'd caught her that first time fresh from the stage, damp and breathless, her make-up smearing them both in a sort of body painting, it would have been worth a shower of fifty-dollar bills. But now they were no longer total strangers and he could only see them dry-eyed and evasive as they coaxed the worm to spill its milk.

While the music swirled at their feet a moist breeze unraveled Scanlyn's hair and sent Lorry Noon's in a cloud across her face. He looked over her shoulder and saw the people in the room pasted against pale-yellow glass, a world watching without seeing. She ground her middle spitefully against him and for a moment he wished that for the sake of form, of continuity however pointless, it would pluck him upright.

She leaned against him for a few seconds, probing, then drew away. "One of us isn't making it."

He felt like a figure cut from the sponge of the sky, and he sensed time's edge in the morning and in his life and let it show in his voice when he wondered why they couldn't simply talk.

"That old salvation trail."

Another couple came out to dance, he unsteady, she smoking, the herbal smell wreathing them as they turned. The window of the room was now more gray than yellow, becoming overprinted with a transparent mountain tipped pale green. Scanlyn held himself away but reached toward her, asking for a telephone number, a chance to meet in a place slightly less unreal.

"Don't you know," she said, and stopped. For a moment Scanlyn thought she was going to laugh, but she turned her head away, the first real light tracing the fine bridge of her nose. "Don't you know it's always the preacher looking to save himself?"

He wasn't interested in pronouncements, only wanted a word or two to puncture the film he was wrapped in. She made a mouth and told him where he could call, then broke away and stood at the parapet of the roof. He followed, stood with her for a time watching shapes grow out of the desert, then asked if he could drop her off on the way back to his hotel. When he received no answer he asked again. She turned away with a sharp gesture, slid along the parapet and stood with her arms folded, excluding him. He said goodnight.

Tomburn and Vikky and the comedian were gone. There were no more than a dozen people left in the room. A couple slept decorously in each other's arms on the couch. In one corner a girl was doing a slow and provocative frug while one of the men watching waved money and begged her to take off the net briefs which showed each time she raised her arms over her head. Only a few girls were left now, and a man who was not as old as Scanlyn but fatter, his clothing off the rack of some prairie-locked emporium, looked toward the terrace where the dancers still turned like crippled dolls and Lorry Noon was standing alone. He patted his hair and went out to the roof.

Scanlyn saw himself to the door. The bowl was gone, the empty hand jutting from the wall as though looking for someone to grope. He went down the steps, into a pool of sage and sand and the elusive smell of some flower in its hundred-year blooming. The side street was empty. None of the signs on the boulevard had been extinguised, and all were dying.

FOURTEEN

The dining room of the Hotel McKinley had an
overused look, a reflection not so much of grandeur
gone downhill as of pretension to an elegance
which had never existed. Its shabbiness was beyond the remedy
of either paint or hammer, and yet all but a few of the tables
were reserved for lunch. In that city where both people and
buildings had such short histories, meeting at the McKinley had
become a tradition, and the elected and appointed who'd
managed to endure lined the walls and settled in the corners.

Howard MacFarlane's club in Philadelphia was older than
most parts of the capital. He wasn't impressed with the McKinley and never ate there unless he had to. That day he had no
choice. F. Clark Lumney had issued what had practically been
a summons to Prippet, and it was only through ingenious dip-
ping and slipping that he'd been able to beg off and have Mac-
Farlane accepted as a substitute.

Lumney's corner table was at the end of a windowed wall,
his own seat in shadow while the chair opposite was in full glare.
He didn't stand when MacFarlane arrived, and after they'd
shaken hands he rolled a napkin between his palms. MacFarlane sat, squinted a moment, then changed the position of his
chair. Lumney made a face. MacFarlane shook his jowls. He
considered Lumney's long career a reasonable success, but only
in bureaucratic terms, and he had no personal opinion of him.

People like F. Clark Lumney weren't taken into Howard Mac-
Farlane's club even as honorary members.

"Sorry Frank couldn't make it," MacFarlane said. "But I
should be able to fill you in on anything you don't know."

Lumney's small mouth parted to show a set of small regular
teeth. "That wouldn't be much. What's the matter with Prippet?"

"He couldn't get away."

"He must be a very important man."

"He runs the Bureau."

"Running that two-bit Bureau never made anybody important. I'd forgotten it existed until we moved to execute a warrant, and then Mr. Prippet's name suddenly came up. The action had to be cleared with him. Which was all right; we
cooperate. But before we could even get in touch, the warrant
was returned and canceled. Mr. Prippet owes me an explanation, but it appears he's afraid to see me. I wonder why."

"It's a delicate situation right now. Nothing to worry
about."

"I worry about people who're afraid to have lunch with
me."

"I'm not."

"But why is Mr. Prippet? According to the line I have on
him, he wouldn't have the nerve to turn me down. I wonder if
someone gave him orders to."

MacFarlane put a cold pipe in his mouth.

"And I wonder who that could be," Lumney said. "But
maybe I already have that information."

"That's a little complicated. But if you've got the information and want to act on it, there's nothing stopping you."

"I can handle complicated things. If your friend hadn't
made things so complicated he wouldn't have to worry about
the company he was seen in."

"I can speak for the Bureau."

"That warrant was canceled under Mr. Prippet's authority,
not yours."

"Not exactly under his, either."

The Best of Our Time

"I try to say things simply, so they won't be misunderstood. The cancellation wasn't made *by* Prippet, but he initiated the action. I'd like him to tell me why, but until he's able to break away from those important affairs of his I guess I'll have to settle for what you have to say."

"That warrant didn't have anything to do with Frank. He's not in enforcement."

"I'm aware of that. What I don't know is why he's meddling with people who are."

Lumney snapped his fingers at a Negro waiter who'd been hovering nearby. The waiter handed MacFarlane a menu.

"I never take a drink before six o'clock," Lumney said.

MacFarlane grunted and looked at the card. "Anything good?"

"Everything's good here."

"What are you having?"

"Peter knows."

The waiter made a buzzing sound and smiled condescendingly at MacFarlane. When MacFarlane finished ordering he handed the menu back negligently, letting it slip from his fingers just before the waiter touched it. The man had to stoop to pick it up.

"You were going to tell me why Prippet decided to interfere with our operations," Lumney said.

"His advice was asked."

"He didn't advise us. He knew where that bird was all the time and he didn't let us in on it. I could call that withholding information, aiding and abetting . . ."

"You can call it what you want, but that information was volunteered to us, not solicited. Why don't you try to find out who was holding out on you? Why don't you put the pressure where it belongs?"

"I don't need to try to find out, and I don't need anybody to tell me what pressure to use where."

The waiter served a clear soup to Lumney. MacFarlane nibbled on a plate of celery and olives.

"That can't be much of a job you have," Lumney said.

"It'll do."

"I *like* mine. I'm trying to get it done."

"I'm not aware of any business of ours which has anything to do with your Agency at this moment."

"At this moment. Your cute politics screwed us out of a kill. All right, Mr. At-This-Moment, we've been around long enough to know how to handle Johnnies who get in our way."

The waiter cleared their plates and immediately brought the main courses.

"I'd have thought you were busy enough with your own work that you wouldn't have time to concern yourself with ours," MacFarlane said.

Lumney's fork stopped moving. He chewed rapidly and was finally able to swallow. "I never have so much to do I can't keep an eye on the public's interest."

"These aren't bay scallops," MacFarlane said.

Lumney peered at the dish. "Sure they are."

"They're deep-sea," MacFarlane said. "Golfballs."

"If it says bay scallops on the menu, that's what they're serving."

"I know what I'm eating."

"I eat here every day."

MacFarlane looked around the room, sniffed, then bent to his food again.

"When your boss was around the last time he seemed to know what side of the fence was the right one," Lumney said. "What happened? How come you two went rotten?"

"I haven't been here long enough to go rotten," MacFarlane said. "And I'm not staying until I do."

Lumney's teeth showed again. MacFarlane noticed that the edges had been worn flat.

"Sammy Sunshine," Lumney said. "But Prippet's no whiz kid. He's a hack and he wants to keep on being one. He needs friends, and so will you when you get back on the outside."

MacFarlane looked at him coldly. "If you were serious about doing your job you'd get yourself a new warrant."

"I'd get *what?* The old one would still be good if you'd kept your fingers off it. What kind of games are you supposed to be playing?"

"If you think a new warrant's in order, you ought to apply for one. Unless you're worried about not cooperating. *You've* been here long enough to know all about that."

"I do my job."

"If I was an enforcement officer and had a defective warrant canceled under my nose and still believed someone should be picked up, I'd replace it with a corrected one."

"Maybe I will."

"I doubt it. But until you do, nothing the Bureau is currently active with is any concern of yours."

"The public's interest—"

MacFarlane faced him squarely. "That's bullshit, Lumney. Stick to your affairs and we'll stick to ours, and if that can't be worked out, Frank is going to have to ask someone to speak to you."

"Anyone I know?"

"Someone you know well enough to listen to."

Lumney pushed his plate away and wiped his mouth. He drummed the table for a moment, then broke out a frosty smile. "You act as though I'm harassing you. I'm only buying lunch."

MacFarlane signaled for coffee.

"The pineapple ice cream's good," Lumney said.

"No thanks."

"Real pineapple in it."

"Canned. I doubt they even have real cream for the coffee in this dump."

"Sure they do."

"Would you like to bet on it?"

Lumney looked dubious for a moment, then set his jaw and bellowed across the room. "Peter!"

FIFTEEN

For the third straight day Scanlyn came awake to a sky flooded with sunlight, and his first thought was of a Noon, probably high on pot while she did a languorous crawl with Chester Someone of Somewhere, Nebraska. He told himself he was not really concerned, and stood in the bathroom with his head twisted over one shoulder while he inspected the shreds of skin hanging from the broken blisters on his back. He was literally coming apart.

He picked up the hostile phone and called the front desk. No one had either wanted or needed him, and for several seconds after he was disconnected he held the instrument and listened to the unvarying buzz as though it were a code he might be able to break. When an operator came on with a bright offer of service he hung up. As he washed and shaved he found the face he'd put on his resolution slipping, the parts behind it gritty and askew. There was no frame of reference in Las Vegas; he had only his work to arrange himself in. He ordered a substantial breakfast and tried to set his mind in one of the old holding patterns he'd used when he believed that what he did mattered. An interim report was the next logical step, but that implied an assessment of what he was between, a position he could fall back on, and he was afraid that Lorry Noon had been right: he was slogging along the old salvation trail after a black Jesus more a stranger than any Nazarene.

When he let in the room-service cart he found a note beneath the door. Mr. De Berg would be in the lobby at four and would appreciate an hour or two of his time. The plain was ringed by Indians of every color. Mr. Scanlyn appreciated Mr. De Berg's thoughtfulness in not having awakened him by calling, then reflected that De Berg couldn't have known he'd gotten in so late unless there were spies working on his side too, a possibility he couldn't quite accept and couldn't quite discount. He sat in his robe and looked out at the burning day while he felt sorry for himself and ate too much.

Because he had nothing better to do, he dressed and went down to the lobby early, a stiff figure among the holiday straws and prints. Many of the faces were pouched with the night's wear but carried enough paint and sunburn to get them through until dark. Meanwhile the daytime rhythms flowed smoothly to the click of chips and dice and wheels in the casino.

When De Berg came through the front door he was a fading version of Now in fringed jacket, Apache scarf, bells and white moccasins. Scanlyn was touched by melancholy. They were all straining so hard in a race which was probably already lost. If he'd been able to see De Berg simply as a person rather than as an obstacle, he could have liked him. They might have been able to pass a few hours together in one of the foolish desperate pursuits Xanadu offered. But they only brushed against each other warily, nearly hostile, and when the lawyer suggested they pay a visit Scanlyn asked no questions.

De Berg had rented a convertible. As they rode along with the top down, the air whipped by in hot dry bands, a Western borealis. The eyes of the people downtown were hidden beneath wide brims or behind colored glasses, and they filed past each other on the shady side of the street in what seemed like either a civic drill or a mindless game. The suburbs in daylight were a collection of defenses, stone baked to iron and every patch of dirt beyond the reach of a water hose burned flat.

Scanlyn was sure he knew where they were going but he tried not to notice the route, fair to all parties in the game but most of all to himself. He wouldn't be able to tell if he was asked, not if they insisted, sweated him, threatened all sorts of . . . He really should have worn a hat in that sun. They turned off the road and onto the gravel track. The house was tiny and colorless against the bleached mountains and blue-white sky. When De Berg cut the engine there was such silence that the slam of his door was like an explosion, and the pebbles caught in the auto's joints dropped with a clatter.

Scanlyn shaded his eyes and looked back the way they'd come. "We don't appear to have been followed," he said.

"I know; I've been watching." De Berg touched Scanlyn's shoulder. "Such low skills we've had to develop."

A small Negro appeared at the corner of the house. He wore fatigues, a goatee and a beret, and hooked his thumbs in a web belt holstering a highly polished club.

"Hello, Reza," De Berg said.

The other nodded.

"Mr. Scanlyn's not one of us, but he's all right as long as he comes alone and there's someone in the house."

Reza looked at him as though he were a specimen to be grouped, and Scanlyn didn't offer his hand, put off balance by the paramilitary costume. De Berg held open the kitchen door and they stepped into a stream of cool air. An electrical generator popped softly somewhere outside the house. They entered a living room of plaid cushions and dark-stained western pine. An air conditioner hummed in the window.

"I was under the impression that Buffre didn't go in for that." Scanlyn gestured with his head.

"Reza Ahmed? Strictly a volunteer, Totty. He's been here all the time, you know, watching the watchers when he could. I think he might actually have tried to interfere if an arrest had been attempted."

"And probably would have gotten himself included."

"Probably. They can be fantastically loyal to someone they admire and respect."

"*They* can . . . and *Mr.* Scanlyn."

De Berg smiled. "I don't think we two should have to pretend that we are them or that they are us. I know you hadn't grasped that difference when you wrote *Masses*, but I thought you would have by now. I did read it, you know. Interesting, and a pity so little of it stands. Everything's a matter of blocs now, don't you think?"

"Within a system."

"A patchwork affair existing only through sufferance. Can you really not see that the central government is falling further and further behind actual conditions? Their new laws are mere cosmetics to disguise the fact that most existing ones are being totally ignored. All the scare talk about the country being on the verge of anarchy—it's not that at all. It's the government which is in chaos."

"Out of which you and all the hairy elect will salvage a new order."

"You see how we've all become reactionaries. You're better than citing hair and I'm better than calling the nation fascist, but each of us says those things. And I'm not one of the elect; simply a guide trying to find a path across the marsh. I'm only interested in seeing that George is on firm ground. That would seem to be the case now. You knew they'd canceled the warrant?"

Scanlyn stared into a corner of a room. "I didn't," he said.

"And the surveillance seems to have been called off. They're acting very sensibly. I'm beginning to believe they really mean to have George."

"What did he say?"

"I told him he was well out of it and should have absolutely nothing further to do with you."

"But what did *he* say?"

"Not very much—or rather, not very much that would interest you."

"I'd like the chance to make that judgment myself. Where is he?"

De Berg reached over to pat Scanlyn on the thigh. "You're all right, Totty." He raised his voice. "Grace? Can you come in?"

There was no answer, but Scanlyn heard steps, the movement of cloth, what might have been the rub of flesh. She stood in the doorway wearing a deep-blue terry robe, a matching band around her hair—walnut-colored silk wrapped in nubby ultramarine. De Berg went to her and took both arms and kissed her lightly near the mouth. Scanlyn thought she arched away but she could just as well have been swinging her hips closer.

"You've been in the pool," De Berg said. "I can smell the chlorine."

"All we had in that shack they allowed us to rent was a sometimes shower."

"Poor baby."

She took a cigarette from a box on the table, lit it and curled up in a chair, the robe parting briefly over a slender thigh. Scanlyn wondered what she was wearing underneath, not knowing whether he was trying to steal a normal eyeful or playing the part of the horny overseer. He wanted to cross the room and offer his hand, but she made some slight gesture to indicate her dislike and he simply said her name. There was a marked difference in her bearing, a changed atmosphere in the house. Scanlyn sniffed the air for traces of grass but found none. De Berg was relaxed, nearly amused. Scanlyn felt like an unexpected Sunday-afternoon visitor being tolerated until he had the sense to realize he wasn't welcome.

"Grace and George know they're under no obligation at all to see you," De Berg said. "They never were, of course, and now that those pressures have been lifted . . ."

"Then I'm all the more grateful for the time you're giving me, Mrs. Buffre." Scanlyn turned to De Berg. "Is this your house . . . Jerry?"

The lawyer raised his eyebrows.

"Then are you and your husband living here now, Mrs. Buffre?"

Her eyes rolled toward De Berg, then back again.

"Only curiosity," Scanlyn said. "I'm not trying to trick you into any damaging admissions. Is he coming this afternoon?"

"George is attending to some things," De Berg said.

"They're leaving in a few days, you know."

"I hope you'll be going in the right direction when you do, Mrs. Buffre. Do you think your viewpoint might be different now that things aren't so . . . restrictive?"

"Do I . . . ? Why, I don't know why we should feel different just because we're not expecting to get arrested every minute and the pig queers have stopped spying on us. We don't feel any different at all."

"Totty, do you really expect people to feel grateful when you stop beating them?"

"I never started," Scanlyn said. "And I've told you before I resent blanket identification."

"Whose bread you eat . . ." De Berg said.

"And whose song have *you* got them singing? How about it, Mrs. Buffre, are you programmed to the organ our friendly lawyer is grinding?"

He could see the twisted imagery even before the sound of the words died out. Eliot Scanlyn the clever advocate, the smooth maneuverer, was suggesting that the Buffres were monkeys performing to De Berg's sexual tunes. He needed a few hours to detoxify his libido, with Lorry Noon or anyone at all. And with Grace Buffre . . .

He pulled himself together. "That was badly put," he said. "I meant to ask if our friend has been as candid with you and your husband as he has been with me, if you understood that there are strings attached to any help he might be giving . . . strings like using you."

"They aren't stupid, Totty. They're aware I think in terms of the greatest general good."

"If I used that line you'd laugh."

"Jerry draws us pictures when the words get too big," she said.

"Then you know there isn't anything at all in his movement, or whatever it is, that can do you any good."

"Oh really, *really*," De Berg said. "That rubbishy shorthand is the worst part. The Buffres and I each may have special viewpoints, but we're both after the same ends."

"And so am I. We're one big family."

"Your views are as dated as your metaphors, and they've been made clear to the point of being stifling." De Berg's shrug set his fringes trembling. "I don't think there's anything more we can get from each other. I'll leave you to wear Grace down —or out—while I take a dip."

The lawyer left the room. Grace Buffre put out her cigarette and sat back. Scanlyn heard drawers being opened; De Berg evidently knew where things were kept. He went whistling past in a cap, bathing slippers and continental-style briefs. A door closed and the noise of the generator seemed to grow louder.

"I feel a little like an insurance salesman trying to convince a wife that her husband is underinsured."

When Scanlyn saw her face harden even more, he realized he'd made another slip. The Flipover file contained a profile of Grace Buffre's father. He was in insurance, a legitimate policy man who peddled dreams of security to the blacks of New Haven. He'd be a small bonus if Buffre could be coaxed into the administration: a prize exhibit in bootstrap elevation, squeezing out premiums until he'd crept to the most distant and pale spokes of his own neighborhood. They could point smugly to the magic wrought by a daily teaspoon of Dr. Snake's oil. Sis could even go to college—where she would find men like Scanlyn who'd blame the political process for her unhappiness between two worlds.

"But I've been lucky enough to be able to believe in my work most of the time," he said. "In its direction, I mean. I thought I might be helping."

"And all this"—she waved a hand at nothing, cutting lingering ribbons of smoke—"is helpful to just what particular person?"

"To your husband?"

"Not so's I can see."

Scanlyn had to make an effort to find a point outside the limits of his own itch where she could be touched—as a wife, a mother? They'd try to make use of *her* mother, too. He remembered all the manless enduring women he'd interviewed during his field work. Grace Buffre's mother had held her family together. Scanlyn could picture white gloves and a straw hat, elastic stockings ending just above the knee, grandchildren dandled—the straight and successful Negro family, a group study in exploitation and farce. He saw how wrong it was, how much there was working against it, and yet he had no choice but to try to convince Buffre's wife that his way was the only possible one.

"There are unpleasant statistics," he said, "patterns no one likes to talk about. Can you be sure your husband will stay with you?"

"What do you . . . ?"

"Please. I know it's a crude and distasteful approach, but I think you've got to give some thought to the future. You've shared enough time and experience to be able to realize that the kid-stuff phase is over now. These menial jobs may have been necessary while you were underground, but I'm sure you don't plan to go on with that sort of work. What if what each of you has to do pulls you apart? I'm assuming he's not going to hire out as a front for some splinter organization; he's too much his own man to do that. But when he tries to support you and the children, how far down the employment ladder will he have to go? Low enough so that after a time he might find himself becoming what he's working at? Do you want a real Joe Jones?"

"He can do what any of *you* do."

"No he can't. They won't let him."

"There's two of us."

"We've tried that, two parents working, and found it's bad news even under the best of conditions. Mrs. Buffre, there are many, many of us being smothered by what we do, and I don't have to tell you how much harder it is for blacks. Suppose he finds something adequate to support both of you, but only just adequate, with very little hope of improvement? Do you think he'll be satisfied to merely break even if he's going down the drain bit by bit every day? Will he allow himself to be strangled by a system he once risked everything to fight?"

"Tussy might just do a little strangling on his own."

"Playing games with someone like De Berg?"

"Jerry's been good to us," she said.

"For his own good." Scanlyn held up his hand. "All right, all right. He's been helpful. It was his idea to get the warrant canceled, and it was a good one. But now you're right back where you were. If your husband is still a concerned and dedicated man, won't he want to go on doing what he can? He certainly has something to give; we wouldn't want him if he didn't. But if he had to give up, instead, in order to support you, and if supporting you meant barely getting along, don't you think he'd feel he was a failure? He might come to the conclusion that he was wearing another kind of chain, that there was no chance of his being effective unless he was mobile. What could you say if he laid De Berg's line about the greater general good on you?"

She started to say something, made a move toward the cigarette box instead, then sat back again.

"You know your father and mother would probably take you and the children in. You wouldn't have any excuse for not letting him go," Scanlyn said.

He was talking himself into a vision of campsite fires, of urban halls and storefronts, Buffre the out-of-town thunder temporarily hoisting the crowd. And there was bound to be an admiring Sister afterward, very likely even some gray Jane waving her handkerchief from the wings while Buffre smiled grimly at the idea of scraping a little off Charlie by rooting in one of his whores. And then he saw that of course Grace Buffre might have accompanied her husband because she'd anticipated the very same thing. They'd left the children with his aunt because her own parents wouldn't have helped her follow a man whose chief talent seemed to be picking the wrong time and place to say everything they'd been careful all their lives not to say.

"I know it would be a terrible decision to make," Scanlyn said. "You two must care very much for each other to have stayed together through all that's happened."

There was a perceptible flutter to her eyelids. He took hold of the stick again, realizing she'd been right—it *was* the dirty end he grasped.

"You haven't stood in his way yet. Are you doing it now?"

The flutter stopped and her eyes went hot. "I was never in any way of his," she said. "He can go out and do anything he thinks he has to any time."

"Then you wouldn't have any objection to his taking this job."

"If that's only what it was," she cried. "Can't you say the right name for it, can't you find one?" She sat forward and the terry cloth bulged. "With all that talk of what he has to do for his family, what's he going to do *to* it?"

"I don't understand."

"You wouldn't. You would not consider for a moment what it would be like living down there. How long ago was it they had segregated transportation? And who's still in charge except those racist y'alls who've been getting elected for the last fifty years? And who is it that really lives there, has to, while all the good folks go home to Greensville every night? Slave city is what it is."

"You'd easily be able to afford something in the suburbs."

"And wouldn't that be like it, to get out the hair straightener and the flour and make believe we're just like *them?* The children—they could help dress up a model school. Maybe we could get in a magazine: How the Buffres Are Passing. Those suburbs you're talking about, that's the South, and anybody ever had a dream about changing that mess is out of his head."

Her heat had produced a flush like a ruby underglow, giving her skin the texture of warm stone. Let De Berg paddle until he'd equaled a Channel crossing, let the guard stand until he rusted; Grace Buffre and Eliot Scanlyn could find a world of stopped clocks. But there was no chance. He would have been unsure of how to bring them to the unicolor of man and woman in the best of circumstances, and now he'd lost her beyond the reach even of his sweaty dreams. Talking had given substance to those children who'd only been photographs. She was a mother now, a wife, a daughter. She was too many people, and he felt too much guilt and responsibility to all of them. He cared so much about her that he was extending an invitation to dinners carefully arranged to exclude anyone who might say the wrong thing; to committee meetings unattended by wives of the old cobs who had seniority and power; to be photographed with brisk legislators who needed the Negro vote or could afford to care because they were from states with negligible black populations.

"But what else can you do?" he said. "You're not foolish enough to want to go to Africa. Would it be better to preach revolution in Germany or Russia? The problem's *here*, Mrs. Buffre. I don't know what other role you want, what better chance a black woman could have . . . if she has *any*. I know it might be too late for you and him, but how about the children? He might be able to get something done. How about the children, yours and other people's?"

Which was the stone her father might have pushed an inch in his lifetime, leaving his children to find their way through a new landscape before they could push their inch, leaving their children . . . Dim prospects were all Scanlyn had to offer either her or himself.

"All right," she said, "them. But us first. Our own selves *first.*"

Not she and Scanlyn. "Is your husband coming today?" he asked.

"Maybe." She shrugged. "I don't think so."

"Did De Berg know that?"

"That's something you'd better ask him."

"Then can you tell me if your husband feels any differently? Under the new circumstances, I mean."

"He'll do that himself if he wants to."

"Only what he thinks or what you think he might think?"

"Tussy doesn't need me to talk for him."

"Can I call him here? Is there a phone?"

"I don't know anything about that."

"You mean I'll have to speak to the master of the house— or the ringmaster, whatever he is."

"You do that."

Scanlyn stood up. "I hope to see you again. If there are any questions . . ."

Once again she made a slight gesture just as he was on the point of offering his hand. He hadn't even a hat to twirl or look ruefully into, so he went outside.

The hot air filled his nose and ears, thickened his tongue. Reza was watering the shrubs. Scanlyn climbed the slight incline to the pool and found De Berg floating, capped like the head of a torpedo, his toes pink. He called, but the lawyer's ears were buried. Scanlyn splashed near him and he turned one startled eye over his shoulder, lost buoyancy, and went under. He came sputtering to the edge of the pool, a mat of ringlets leaking from the back of his cap.

"If Buffre's not coming I think I'll go along," Scanlyn said.

De Berg squinted at him. "Did Grace say he wasn't?"

"She said she didn't expect him. Do you?"

"No."

"I didn't think you did. Well, it's been charming, Jerry old man . . ."

"Did you convert her?"

De Berg's face was momentarily lost in the mottled planes of light on the water. Scanlyn bent closer. "I don't know anything about that," he said in a dark voice.

De Berg chuckled. "I don't think we ever shall, Totty. No more would I expect to understand the life style of the Lapps." He chinned himself to the edge of the pool. "Reza, will you take Mr. Scanlyn back to his hotel?" The stream from the hose dipped an answer. "You don't mind?"

"Even the Chairman needs his swim."

"Say I'd rather. I may stay an extra day or two, a working vacation. Perhaps we'll see each other again."

Scanlyn reached his hand down and De Berg took it, his skin puckered.

Reza was waiting at the car. He'd discarded the belt and club, and just before they started off he removed the beret. Scanlyn thought Reza was being very practical; he had a healthy respect for deputies himself. Neither spoke on the way back. The day was cooling slightly. De Berg would be leaving the pool, patting himself dry. He might put on a terry robe like Grace Buffre's, and in a celebration of fraternity and equality they might blend, shed.

As if it mattered; as if it would help.

SIXTEEN

The varnished rot endemic to the Hotel McKinley's restaurant spread to its rooms as well. They were small, furnished with pieces so anonymous it was impossible to identify them with any particular period, old without being actually worn, and there was such an overabundance of mirrors and chandeliers and glass tops that every corner was paneled with mediocrity.

Even the best suites were cluttered. John Stirby was distracted by the glitter and glare as he sat in an overstuffed chair which had no resilience at all. Across the way Harvey Timmins sprawled shirt-sleeved along a sofa. Though he was as big as Stirby, age had broken down the lines of his face and fat those of his body, and he seemed to fit perfectly into the atmosphere of barely restrained decay. But within the creases of decline and neglect there were unmistakable folds of authority, a detectable reservoir of power.

Timmins rubbed his stomach and released a gust of tainted air. "I swear the food gets worse here all the time." He let his eyes skip around the room. "And I can't say this old girl improves much neither."

"You should have come on home to dinner like I wanted you to," Stirby said.

"Well I would have liked that, Jack, and I'm sorry I missed seeing Maudie, but I'm getting to be too old a turtle for family visiting . . . particularly with that gang of yours." He seemed amused. "Those boys still wearing their hair halfway down their backs?"

"It's the style." Stirby fidgeted. "And that's all it is, Harvey, style. They don't have any foolish ideas."

"Oh, I guess I know you well enough not to think you're raising a gang of hippies."

"I can't fight the whole bunch—not and Maudie, too."

"Course not." Timmins sighed and sat up. "Not that I've ever been able to understand just what it's all about. Nor a lot more of what's going on. Why, I don't believe what's happened right here. I've been coming to this town on and off for thirty years, and now it's not safe to go out after nine o'clock. Nine o'clock, Jack, in the *capital.* What in the world have you fellas let it come to?"

"Damn little anybody seems to care, the way they run home every night. And with what they've got for public safety, there's only one group I know of is safe any more."

"We didn't have any problems like that when you were in the driver's seat back home, did we?"

"I like to think so." Stirby said.

"*Like* to? Why the difference between then and now is like night and day. Night and day. The crowd that's in would give their eyeteeth to have you back as Commissioner."

Stirby looked pleased and embarrassed.

"Course I know you wouldn't work with that bunch, not after what they had to say about you when they were working so hard to get themselves in the fix they're in now. And I'm glad to say it doesn't look as though they're going to be around much longer. People are fed up, I tell you. Fed *up.* Things are getting so bad they're going to have to call in the U. S. Army soon. The *Army.*" Timmins' cheeks puffed out and he rubbed his stomach. "Don't happen to have a cigar on you?"

"Don't use it," Stirby said.

"If I don't have them around I'm not tempted. Get thee behind me, Satan. But I sure get a yen. At my age you sometimes wonder if it's worth it."

"I hope I'm in that good condition at your age."

Timmins patted his paunch. "Not so bad, not so bad. But you're looking absolutely great, Jack."

"I still work out."

"You're smart to. But what in the world are you doing otherwise these days? That fatback organization they palmed off on you, what're they up to now?"

Stirby adjusted his cuffs.

"I've heard about some project or other," Timmins said, "and I don't like what I've heard, not at all. We had more than enough of that line, and we know where it's got us to. I never thought Prippet was very much, but I never recognized him for an outright fool. What are your folks going to think when they see you mixed up in this?"

"Damn well you know none of it was my idea, Harvey."

"Nor did I think it was. But there it is, prominent as a bare-assed pig for anybody who takes the trouble to look. I know where it's coming from, all right, and I've had my say there, too. But it's Prippet being fool enough to take it on that's going to make you look bad, Jack. Even giving you the benefit of the doubt—and your folks will, they're that much for you—they're going to wonder what you were doing as deputy in a bureau that was selling them down the road."

"I don't know about Frank any more," Stirby said. "Wherever he's going, it's not anywhere I'd like to be. We've been working on it, Harvey. Only I'm sort of caught in the middle now and need a little more time."

"There's not much." Timmins chewed his upper lip. "That Jew professor isn't getting you turned around, is he?"

"Not likely. He knows who's working for who."

"I don't doubt the association's been useful, but you might want to get rid of him soon."

"No sooner than they'll let me."

"As I say, not that things haven't gone along pretty good. He's gotten off a few sharp ones. They're crafty that way. But we might just be past that point, Jack, and this isn't any time to be hopping from one foot to another. Right now . . . Hell, it's not supposed to be out yet, but I guess I know you can keep your mouth shut." Timmins sat forward. "What would you think of getting out of this circus and coming back home?"

Stirby rubbed the arms of his chair. "You're that sure of that gang going out down there?"

"In the city? Dead certain. You could walk in backwards."

"A little more help from the state organization and I might never have had to walk out."

"Now Jack, we did what we could. There's times when you have to save your ammunition for another day, when you're forced to sacrifice a skirmish in favor of a battle. Not that I don't know how much those involved can get hurt. I thought we'd talked that out, that you'd understood there wasn't any way around it."

"I do, I do." Stirby put his hands along his thighs and looked away, but a portion of his image stood in the glass no matter where he turned. "There was a time when Maudie felt sour enough to think we were well rid of it, but I guess she'd see it as a kind of admission of who was wrong."

"She's a great girl." Timmins clucked and shook his head. "You both deserve it, you do. Makes me feel like Santa Claus. No sir, Jack Stirby, I'm not talking about going back to the city. You already proved what you could do there. It's onward and upward, as they say, and there's no man I know of who'd make a better lieutenant governor."

Stirby saw himself very still in every corner of the room.

"Yes sir," Timmins said.

"Damn, Harvey."

"Porterfield's a shoo-in. There's been enough gone wrong that people want somebody willing to take hold. Counting your folks, we'll be absolutely over the top, and that's why I'm telling you there's not much time. Why, the primaries are only eight months away and you know how these things are—lose a week's worth of ground and it takes a month to make it up. There's some think you're not the one, that we ought to have a man with less guts, but I tell them no, what's needed now is a man people know where he stands. We've got to have that, Jack. *Got to*, absolutely."

Stirby's knuckles were white on the chair's arms, and his head shot forward truculently. "That Frank," he said, "he's really trying to fix me."

"He's not doing you much good, Jack. You're the one likely to get flipped over."

"Does he know? About the lieutenant governor?"

"I don't know of anybody back home would think he was worth the trouble of telling, but if he asked, there's no doubt somebody down there would mention your name."

"There's ways to fix him, too. But it's more than that. It's going against Him. How am I going to get around *that?*"

Timmins had spread his arms against the back of the sofa, and now he stretched his legs and drummed his heels against the floor. "Whatever foolishness is going on now, He knows it's not going to help him any to have that other bunch controlling too many state houses, and that might just happen if it don't look like we're willing to give people what they want. There's nobody ever got anywhere without taking some chances, and He's going to have to take them as well as us."

"That sounds a lot like *me*, Harvey."

"I can't deny that, Jack, and I wish I could say I had an understanding for you to go ahead on, but getting this administration to say anything definite is like trying to catch hold of sand. Not that there's any doubt what they want. They can't make up their minds how to go about it, is the trouble. But I got the feeling you're not going to be bruising too many apples if you come out plain."

"You know I want to, and would if I thought it was wanted."

"There's no doubt it's wanted, Jack."

"But maybe not allowed."

"No, not that—at least I don't think so."

"It's my skin if you're thinking wrong."

"That's a man with guts we're going to put in, and I believe it's you, Jack. In addition to which, Porterfield's not the type to stay. He'll take his four years and move on. By that time Jack Stirby ought to be quite some figure in the state. I don't think he'd have to worry about having to take some piddling public-safety job. It's all there, but nobody's going to bring it to you—you're going to have to go out at least halfway towards it."

"That's the point where the limb starts to bend."

Timmins stopped drumming. The pouches around his eyes deepened and there was a hard glint within them. "If wanting to be safe's your chief ambition, Jack, then I think you'd better stay here. For a year, anyway, until He gets turned out or in or whichever way. And even then He may decide to change that shuck-all of yours into something else you just might not fit into. If that's what you're looking for, then go right ahead and no hard feelings. But there's plans to be made. I already told you I put my neck out by saying you were the best man for the job —and that's all right, too—but you're not the *only* one. There's some I could sell as easy as popcorn."

Timmins pinched one thumb and forefinger together and cupped his other hand beneath them in a gesture of carrying an overflowing bag. "That easy. And will if I have to. Now of course I'm not saying you won't be taking a chance of getting into some temporary hot water, and I'm not going to guarantee absolutely you're going to get in no matter what. We both of us know better. But if you come out plain enough so that your folks are satisfied, I promise you Jack Stirby *will* be on that ticket no matter what happens with this circus. And I think that ought to be good enough for anybody."

"It *is* good enough, Harvey."

"Then get up on your two hind feet and speak your mind."

Stirby gathered himself as though he were actually going to stand, but then he slumped back and his hands shuttled restlessly along the arms of the chair again. "Frank's going to raise hell," he said.

"Might at that."

"I guess I can stand it."

"I guess you'll have to."

"Here's to it, then."

Their soberly nodding heads were caught in all the bright surfaces in the room.

SEVENTEEN

It wasn't only successful lawyers in youth tones who rented convertibles. Most people who came to Las Vegas left their children and station wagons behind and were nearly young again in imitation sports cars with four-on-the-floor automatic transmissions. The men drove them grimly over the flat roads while the women held their hair.

Scanlyn rented the raciest model he could find because he thought it might give him a touch of the drag strip, a few strokes of youth, and then he went to his room and clutched the telephone like a man trying to chin himself. It was probably only wishful thinking on his part, but there seemed to be less sour pucker in Lorry Noon's voice, and she actually sounded interested in taking a drive and sharing one of those meals which he had given up trying to find a name for. It was she who suggested the lake.

They left the minarets and towers behind and passed through low hills enclosing other pannikins of scrub which could as easily have been the accidental site of a crystal pleasure city. Scanlyn was heavy at the wheel at first, but as the road continued to unwind in straightaways and slow curves he began to enjoy the car's toylike responses. He tried talk and found it torn away by the wind. The radio was better, a bridge between false starts and inconsequential murmurs. There was twangy music and local ads for products he'd never heard of, a low-keyed sell to people he would never meet.

Except for service stations and diners at major intersections the country was spectacularly empty. Old tracks wandered toward the highway, disappeared beneath it, and meandered away on the other side. He tried to imagine how immense those spaces must have been to anyone bound to the agonizingly slow turn of a spoked wheel. He wondered how many of the tracks were original trails which had crossed at some scratchy X, the wagons creaking toward a dry meeting and then angling off toward separate Dorados; prairie schooners perhaps carrying some dusty Ahab hailing insanely after news of his own white death on the flats. Scanlyn had grown too accustomed to the East with its history frozen into monuments. Out here the ruts of the past were still visible and the land seemed to be in transition, waiting for a final form to be stamped on it.

As he himself was in transit between arid poles. He looked sideways at the girl. Her head was bound in a gay cloth, her hair whipped into long Spanish curls at her ears. There had been moist pouches beneath her eyes when he'd picked her up, the residue of either sleep or practice, but now the skin of her cheeks stretched in a boneless plane to the point of her chin. She was colored gold by the sun and looked very young, while he sat clumsy and wrinkled, following a scaly nose.

The highway was ideal for those huge cars usually trapped in cities, and they rushed by at full power, leaving faint spirals of dust in the air. Scanlyn was into the swing of the road. He felt that he was at last on the way to something, his jaunty sloped hood eating away the miles. They began to climb slightly and then came to a saddle of road in deep shade unmistakably traced with moisture, a long cut which came out above a dam stretched like a curved white band. It held back a lake sawtoothed pale in the sun, blue under the hills' shadows, its base disappearing into a spumy gorge. He fought the wheel through a twisting descent, and they rolled onto a broad approach where cars were parked and people in odd hats leaned toward the scorched rainbow over the gorge as they watched the discharge jets far below. The lake had filled in between sheer slopes and was shoreless. There was a thin beard of green along the waterline but nothing on the hillsides except the knotted wood and tough spines which had always grown there. They crossed the dam in a slow wind-slap of stanchions. There was no sound or vibration from the power wheels turning within that vast fall of concrete, no indication of the whirlwind of energy being generated.

On the other side they slid back into the desert, and Lorry Noon directed him in a series of turns which took them back to the lake at a point where the far side still rose impressively but the near one was level enough to accommodate a variety of homes and docks. Powerboats swept ahead of long wakes and sailboats kited over the water in triangular puffs. She asked Scanlyn if he wanted a little action before they ate. He looked at her and she hiccuped, put a kind and slightly mocking arm on his hand and explained she'd meant gambling. He said stiffly he'd understood. She bit her lips and looked away.

The restaurant she suggested was fronted with glass and aluminum. A mild breeze carrying the smell of fresh water soughed through the dining room. There were a few people eating early, families evidently taking a last break before pushing on toward unknown motels hidden in darkness still hundreds of miles away. She led him to an open deck sheltered by a canopy whose tie cords hummed in the breeze. Water lapped below, and youngsters nearby swam between a beach and a float, dripping blue-silver when they climbed onto the raft.

Scanlyn chose a table near the railing, and while they were settling themselves he rehearsed the opening patter he'd prepared on the drive, but he was disconcerted to find her sitting with her face cupped between two hands, a bronzed heart with a wickedly full mouth and eyes which were measuring as much as looking at him.

"Like it?"

"It's very nice," he said, pretending to inspect the deck.

There was another couple, another younger girl and older man, one Scanlyn might turn into in a few years: the commodore in a double-breasted blazer, a scarf at his throat, his face the color of brick and his head massively freckled in a nest of dull gray hair.

"Yes, lovely," he said.

"Uncle Sam's bathtub."

He could see the metaphor. If the dam went they'd be left high on the slopes of a burned valley, the river a trickle far below.

"You've been out here some time, I take it."

"*Here.* It's not *out* here."

"Long enough to take on native coloration."

"Are you doing Indians now?"

He'd pull the plug, and the drowned settlements where red and white bone had rotted into the same silt would rise dripping like a Western Atlantis.

"The only thing I'm interested in right now is an ex-student who became a dancer."

She made a face and turned toward the water. He was still trying to think of something to say to recapture her attention when a shirt-sleeved waiter came to take their orders for drinks. She wanted a Coke.

"Liquor isn't the thing, is it?" he asked when the man had gone.

"Your head must have stopped working a while back, Prof. You sound as though you're still scuffling around trying to find handles. A fulfilling life, right?"

"I guess I haven't managed to get into that third level of consciousness."

"More of that moldy professor shit, you mean—some creep grooving on kids whose only system is they don't have a system. They're just passing through, but he's got to make a production out of it if he's going to keep collecting that check."

"When I was teaching I often had the feeling we were all moving in slow motion past each other, not touching very often."

"Did you? What finally happened—an electric bulb, pop, in the middle of the night?" There was the same shuffle of faces Scanlyn had seen at the party, this one flaring out at him. "Did you work out the equation, pedagogue equals pederast? Corn-holing kids for a living."

"That's stronger than—"

"You don't think so, Prof? All right, all right."

The drinks came. Scanlyn took a long swallow, grateful for the taste of the lime and tonic and the effect of the gin. She sipped and then threw her head back and narrowed her eyes.

"Would it be better saying most teachers crawl into rat-holes?" she said. "Very special nests you're invited into so you can have your veins tapped. But I'm still coming on too strong for you. They're spooks who lock themselves in their castles and inhabit any souls who wander in." She gripped the glass in both hands and looked down into it until the ridge along her jaw softened and disappeared.

"Did you really find it that bad, Laura?"

She took off the headcloth and held the corners so that it bellied in the breeze. "Only pure shit."

"And I was part of it."

"A specialist." She laughed brokenly. "No, worse—I thought you *weren't* part of it. The cool dome from the East. I mean, you'd been in the streets and written that book and you talked about legislation."

"I sometimes got carried away during seminars."

"That's beautiful retrospection, a real mystic look up the bull's ass. The Eastern guru with the crystal dome, all the hot circuits showing like the lines on a phrenologist's chart. I thought you were talking about the real thing, Prof."

"So did I. Do intentions count?"

"Sure."

She made a mouth, a *moue,* that might have been on the verge of becoming a blown kiss, Scanlyn a loved one in spite of all his frailties.

"Can we order now?" she said. "I don't want it rolling around like a cannonball while I'm on."

There was a choice of appropriate blue-sky fresh-air food, a snap in the late-afternoon breeze. Scanlyn began to feel that things were possible, that he could advance himself along avenues warmer than cash in hand, perhaps even revive the near-mythic figure he'd once been to her.

"So, from there to here," he said. "How?"

"Commitment to commitment."

"I don't understand."

"Well what's a poor girl to do? But you don't come in for all the credit, Prof. My father contracted a fatal disease . . . he turned on when he was forty years old. I don't mean he was a schmecker, but burns and bells and the whole bit. A great scene at first—Pop's liberated, he's with it. Except it didn't take long to see he had no idea at all of what he was turned on to. Like my father thought he could get it all together if he just bought the right vines. A lot of you didn't understand what it was really about."

Scanlyn was so tired of being grouped. He wished she'd use something like *thou*. The waiter brought iced shrimp, crisp lettuce, a biting sauce. He was hungry.

"And he even got by with it in business." She ran her tongue along the tiny fork. "He was in advertising, and they probably thought he was a prophet for the whole new world coming. Only it was too late for him to change his *real* life. He had a house and a wife and two kids and he was forty. Cement. You have to get what you can on the way because you only get one turn on the wheel."

"That should be enough for anyone," Scanlyn said.

She shrugged and swished her lettuce in the sauce until it looked like a cross section of a recently living cell. "If he'd been grooving on a new thing just to get a little action on the side, you know. They were all so jammed up that way—all the arrangements, all the switchies and group balling. But I don't think he was into that; there wasn't that kind of tension in the house. He sent my mother up the wall just the same, anyway. I mean she was almost forty years old too, and she wasn't about to do beads and a mini and look like one of those Hollywood dogs. And then he had to go get a bike. At first it was just something to fool around with, but he kept trading up until he had a real chopper and it wasn't just transportation to the office any more, he was gone all day Sunday too. He thought he was Captain America even before they made that flick. My father."

A wildly dressed figure roaring down the nearest escape road because he'd had a glimpse of the end of the tunnel and hadn't seen any light. Scanlyn was familiar with the sickness. But they had a right—he and the man whose name she'd changed—they had as much a right as anyone to their personal disasters.

"When the shoe is on the other foot . . ." he began. "Why should you young people feel the pinch so severely when one of *us* tries on boots?"

"Because you already had your chance and fucked it up. And when you're the age I was you expect somebody to be minding the store. I don't happen to be that age any more, so maybe I can see how with that kind of nothing work and living the way we did he might have been afraid of dissolving entirely. But that didn't give him any excuse to leave us behind like we were the garbage in his life. At first I was hoping it was only junk —*only* junk, if you can believe it. I used to go through their drawers and closets hoping I'd find something. I had a plan that we could turn him in for holding and get him committed to some kind of rehabilitation program where he'd sort of be in our custody until he was clean, and we could get him straightened out in the meantime. I was going to turn him *in*. How's that for a dutiful daughter?"

"A loving one?"

She turned her head so that her face was hidden by an inky cloud of hair puffed up by the breeze. "Well, Daddy didn't get himself all hung up on love," she said. "He just phased out. At the end they couldn't even talk to each other unless it was about the arrangements. I'd hear them, and it was like it was happening to four other people, not to us. And when he went, it was bango. Nothing about maybe coming back after he got his head straight. He took the bike and *went*. But what do you think he left behind—besides us, I mean?"

"What?"

"All those mod threads that got him started. He'd already

taken that trip. He's probably wearing leather now—or denim and a headband. My mother kept those clothes for six months before she got rid of them. We were still hoping, even though we didn't have anything to hang onto but an address in Humboldt County to send the papers to. After the decree was final we didn't even have that."

The breeze from the lake had freshened. The swimmers had disappeared, but sails were still bending and a water skier bounced over the stiffening ridges.

"I'm divorced myself," Scanlyn said.

"Congratulations."

"There weren't any children."

"That was considerate."

"I didn't mean that as a throwaway. It's only that divorce is so common now it's hard to see it in terms of tragedy."

The waiter brought steak with the fat crackling, potatoes running butter, dark greens. It was local fodder, and Scanlyn ordered a local wine to wash it down. He felt a grateful rumble in his stomach.

"He probably wound up in leather and a Nazi helmet so he could ball all those gringy sisters of the road," she said. "Or maybe he went fag. Sure it's common, it's part of the general disaster nobody's supposed to mind. At least I was away at Cal most of the time, but Billy and Mom held out in the house for a while. I think there was one period when she got a little desperate and put out any time someone tapped her on the shoulder. A great scene for Billy if he was on to it. They finally sold the house and now she does beachwear down at Balboa. Billy's at UCLA. I see them once in a while."

She held her knife and fork upright, like a child, and leaned forward. He was very conscious of her eyes, a smoky blue chipped by something deeper than memory.

"Right, it wasn't a tragedy," she said. "That whole life we'd had together was nothing but a big fart he let loose before he took off. That was some stone to carry. Because even with getting out of school and fooling around some afterward, you've got to think you're going to wind up with some one person, and probably kids. Why not? But if it can all get washed out so easily . . . So I had the idea to do something serious, something I could look back on, a time I at least tried. Which I thought would give me a sense of accomplishment, a little balance, if that someday-person decided to bug out on me the way Daddy had. It was a plan, a thing I could hold onto, and I was already into it when you came along with that seminar and really turned me on."

Scanlyn had been paying his way, listening with care and sympathy while he waited for an opening, but she wasn't cooperating. She was changing mythic Scanlyn, improver of lives, into a man who evidently made crooked ones more crooked, who could lead a girl out of the sorrows of a broken home straight into the joys of four-a-night box-wrenching with fifty-dollar tricks thrown in on the side. He filled his glass again. She'd barely touched hers.

"I mean you weren't just one of those mossy old creeps with chalk dust in his wrinkles," she said. "You looked so sure of what you were hustling, so full of brass. I believed."

"At that time . . . well, at that time I thought I was on the verge of changing my own life. I was probably somewhat in the same position as your father with his motorcycle."

"But that wasn't the message you were passing around. It was inspirational self-help, the bootstrap society if we all pulled together. If we jacked each other off, you meant. The message is"—she went uh-uh-uh—"the message is no matter what you do or how hard you try, you get to the point where the only way to keep going is to go out and get a new bike, right?"

Easy riding on the community sow . . . But she still had chances he'd already used up. Her bones were young and supple and could bend to any configuration. His grated together.

"Whatever my message was, it couldn't have brought you all the way out here—*here*, I mean."

"That wasn't the original plan." She chewed a piece of meat and squinted at him. "Sure, intentions count; it's only that they don't have any effect. I was going to do more than you had, I wasn't going to pack up my papers and go home every night when it started to get dark. This was about a million years ago when they were telling us the slums could be changed if we just moved in, if we showed those people we were willing to share all that shit we'd made them live in. All we had to do was spread a few gray faces around to improve the neighborhood. Hysterical."

"I opposed that program."

"Well that was really great foresight, Prof. I only wish you'd put a little of it on me. I had the impression that the heaviest thing anyone could do was share completely, not like a social lady doing Tuesday afternoons at a home for wayward girls. We were going to be different, we were going to light up the darkness as soon as we moved in. We'd show these people how to live better and more meaningful lives."

"Great white hopes," Scanlyn said.

"You know it. Exactly. I joined a GWH organization. We weren't going to live as poor as they did, of course, and when it got too gringy we could take a break and go back to where we got all this expert knowledge. Only lives didn't happen to be very meaningful back there, either, with people like my father running away or sloshing themselves blind or balling each other like if they did it fast enough they could make believe they didn't know what was happening. But that's where we got all this light we were bringing to the disadvantaged, that's the level we were going to raise them to. Real community sharing—beautiful."

Scanlyn felt like an old priest-confessor listening to a recital of his own sins. What was his next line—that with all its faults it was the only True Church? "It couldn't possibly have worked," he said.

"You forget I didn't have all that great foresight you did. Like I went down there with my duffel because I didn't want to flash any fancy luggage. But what kind of trash are you if you don't own even one suitcase? And the clothes . . . We had one Christy type doing bib overalls because he wanted to get closer to people who'd been trying to get out of bib overalls for maybe fifty years, and the only whites they'd ever known who wore them had been honkies.

"Or when you made a call—after you got an appointment, what the uptown office called soliciting an invitation—you'd wear something simple and find the lady of the house dressed up, so you were putting her down just by the way you looked. And then you were supposed to try to teach her how to scrape together a high-protein diet out of food-stamp mush, a diet you had to learn out of a book because you didn't have any experience with not getting enough to eat. I was twenty-two years old teaching some woman who'd had her first baby at fifteen how to manage. And that was a great bit. What was your wife on, the pill?"

Scanlyn was startled. "We didn't . . . it hadn't been perfected at the time." She seemed to be waiting for more. "The diaphragm was effective," he said.

"Sure, there are a million ways. And that was really beautiful too—the way we were supposed to demonstrate birth control. I mean the agency wasn't trying to keep families together, only to keep the numbers down, and so they sent around these little paddy bitches who had great experience in not getting knocked up—like me, you know—to run a course in practical fucking. Tips a mother could pass on when her daughters had to go out on the street."

"*If* they had to."

"You mean there was so much free stuff going around, nobody would want to pay for it. But if the neighborhood was halfway safe you could count on Whitey coming in to get rid of his hang-ups. Halfway—that means you could do street work at night if you happened to be standing under a light and there was a police cruiser parked across the way. And you'd be okay coming back from a meeting as long as the two biggest guys there walked you home. Otherwise the only time you had maybe an even chance was to lock yourself behind one of those tin-sheet doors after dark and get your community experience by watching the tube.

"My first roomie lasted exactly two weeks. She couldn't take rats—like the rest of us learned to love them, you know. The second one, Sheila, was tougher, also dykey, but she was company those nights when the smells came down and some junkie might be scratching at the door because he had the wrong apartment, and meantime some insane woman would be laughing up the airshaft . . . *laughing*, Christ knows why. I really needed somebody, and Sheila was all right until she started getting ideas. I kept her going on maybes as long as I could, but when it finally came to put-out time I just couldn't cut it."

Scanlyn sneaked a glance at the commodore. He was holding hands across the table, a sincere and foolish expression on his face, while his lady love merely looked bored. Scanlyn envied him.

"So then I got Carl," Lorry Noon went on, "also GWH. We had to keep it quiet because mixed pads were strictly against regulations—all of us were supposed to be Snow Whites no matter how much banging was going on around us. Carl wasn't a type I could come close to turning on to, but I thought it would be worth giving him a tumble now and then just to have someone around. No sacrifice too great in the true cause, right? Except Carl wasn't interested in anything I had. He was hooked on black ass. All day he did moral uplift and some kind of electronics training thing, but he had to write home for money to support his nighttime habit. And he had to bring them to our pad because he would have been cut every way but loose if he'd gone to theirs. So I'd plug into the tube and make believe I didn't hear him slurping away in the next room. The whores thought I was queer, and when they finished with Carl they'd try to turn *me* on. He'd get this smeary look . . . I think he would have paid to watch."

"In but not of that life," Scanlyn said.

"I had it in my head that a good girl only gave it away to one at a time. I had Jake then. He was into metal sculpture—junkyard stuff, and very heavy about it. I never knew if it was any good, but he was at least a great welder. And it didn't hurt that he had this neat pad in Ventura. On one side you could watch the hot doggers beating themselves senseless on their boards, and on the other the beards and beads thumbing their way to heaven. Jake admitted he occasionally did one of those

bed-for-a-bang deals, only he called it bloodstream communica-
tion. As long as they didn't give him anything he could pass
along, I didn't mind. Because my own bit was pretty much like
that. I'd go up on my day off and cry on his shoulder, and he'd
hold my hand and listen and sometimes even get excited
enough to try to put what I was telling him into a shape—like
Welfare Form 6015, you know. So I'd smell some wild thing
cooling off in the studio while we were making it, and I'd think
what good was that rack of twisted pipes, and Jake and I screw-
ing away under the silvery moon—what good was all that if
those people were still getting shit-on whether it was my day
off or not?"

"No one has been able to change it yet, Laura. We've all
failed." But *yet* was Scanlyn's operative word; her story rein-
forced his idea of Buffre as a wedge, or at least a splinter, and
only the first.

"That's a great revelation," she said, "but what do you do
if you're hooked? I mean if you can't quit because you're afraid
to find out what else you're not good at. I got so hung up I was
halfway to the needle—which would have been one more original and beautiful statement, and maybe I could have given
some caseworker a chance to save both of us. But I got lucky,
Prof, I got myself really straightened out. I'd been down there
ten weeks—not forever, the way I make it sound—when it so
happened there was only one guy to walk me home, and he just
wasn't big enough. I don't need to tell you the rest."

Scanlyn tried to keep his expression neutral, but he could
feel dismay tugging at his face.

"You knew what was coming," she said, "with all that foresight."

"I know what can happen."

"But you'd just as soon not hear it. It might get in the way
of that rip-off you're running."

"I'm not teaching any more," he said. "I'm less deceived
and less deceiving than I was five years ago."

"Four." She pushed her plate away. He gestured with the
bottle but she shook her head. "Do you think it's going to be

cheaper, the hustle with the drive and the dinner?"

"It isn't a hustle."

"Don't you want me to lay for you?"

Scanlyn wished he hadn't eaten so well. "So that was the end of the social experiment," he said.

"No?"

"It wasn't."

"I meant, no you don't want any? You might not if you get to hear it all."

"I might not. Can't you just tell me how you got from there to here?"

"That's what I've been doing. It's all one trip, you know, and the shrinks said talking about it might help. So I talk about it." She dealt him another face, this one a glittering queen of diamonds. "This Buddy was everybody's best buddy, but his own especially because he wasn't big enough. We were coming home from this meeting on garbage collection, trying to get the city to collect more regularly when half the problem was getting the garbage into the cans, and these three dudes began to shag around. Kids, they were real kids, fifteen and sixteen, but they were bigger than Buddy's best buddy, and when he didn't turn them off you could see a sort of light growing—the idea, you know, that maybe they weren't just being diddly, that something might be happening. And when I tried to cool it, Buddy was all mush-mouth assurance, giving me a lot of teeth and not helping any, and even when it was starting to get real nasty I let a cruiser go by because I told myself I couldn't put myself in that position, hanging onto the Man, and still think I was any part of what was really going on. Telling myself that and at the same time thinking maybe I'd been waiting for it all along, looking to get put down to the point where my ass wouldn't be worth more than anybody else's. But we actually got past all those alleys and to the front door, the bottom of the stoop. That's when old Buddy made up his mind. By then they were really jiving around and acting as though they were going to cop a feel at least, so Buddy got sort of a blind look and said goodnight and walked away."

She was talking away the lake and the slopes and the sky, unpeeling Scanlyn's memory until he was back in the constant sub-roar of voices and traffic, the rank smell of rot which bred everything teeming, whether roaches or rats or people.

"If I'd made a break I probably could have gotten up the steps, but I was still trying to act like a believer, like I couldn't run away scared and still think I was in touch . . . Like kidding myself I'd ever been anything else but out of sight out of touch, and so I was *talking*, if you can believe, going on and on while these really stupid dumb faces—and I don't care if it was environment or diet or whose fault it was—but these really animalistic faces got a sort of numb dazed look. The dancing part was over and now they were ready for action, and they probably thought I was really saying I wouldn't mind, community relations. But I had the idea I'd turned it off and started to go in even though there was this sort of crowding, and I kept talking until I'd talked the four of us right into the vestibule. And that was the end, right? Because one of the first things you learn in those buildings is how to be deaf. If you thought it was your mother screaming on the other side of the door, you'd turn up the volume on the set so you wouldn't hear and have to open up. So I don't even remember if my voice got any louder, only this sort of edging and pushing, and I knew where we were headed—where the junkie goes for his fix and the drunk stops to take a leak and where they usually find the bodies. At the back of the hall and under the stairs, where it always smells like shit and blood even if the super does get around to mopping it up once in a while."

Scanlyn poured the last of the wine and thrust his nose into the glass.

"By then I was ready to fall down and just let it happen, but if it's going to be rape you might as well get your money's worth, and there had to be all this grabbing and ripping, like you were taking apart a rag doll, you know, and then restuffing it. They weren't satisfied just putting it in, they had to shove as hard as they could, and talking all this gibberish, this Christ-knows-what language. That idea you're supposed to relax and enjoy it is very funny if you don't happen to be involved. And they were such goddamned kids they never stopped coming—they were shooting longer than they were fucking. One, two, three; and while one was wiping his dick in my hair the next one would get on. I don't think they even went soft between turns. Eight times—one of them must have been off his high-protein diet. And afterward I had to lie there while they were shuffling and giggling and all this stupid kid talk about making me eat it and cutting me until I almost wanted to ask if they were finished. Then I heard them go out."

She looked at him out of the still-glittering face as though cataloging his reaction among all the others she'd had. Scanlyn tried to remind himself that it had happened in another time and country, but he felt bleak.

"Carl was beautiful. I got myself together in a hurry because they'd been having such a good time, they didn't even think to go through my bag, and I was afraid they might remember and come back and start all over again. I practically made those stairs on my knees, but I finally got up to our floor and into the apartment and there was Carl just coming out of the john balls-naked, which was no great sight, and the bedroom door was open so I could see his action propped up on her elbows looking at me while I was trying to hold what was left of my clothes together, with that stuff running down my legs and in my hair, the three of us probably a great right-now triptych. His face sort of came apart, and naturally he did the great line 'What happened?' and the whore just shook her head and said 'Uh-*huh*' which said it just about perfectly, you know, the idea that if you ask for it long enough you're going to get it. 'Uh-*huh*,' and what else was new. The only thing I cared about was that there was enough hot water left in the heater so I could lay in the tub and soak it off me, out of me, with Carl screaming on the other side of the door. But not for long—he must have been on hourly rates. When I came out he was going to go for the doctor or the cops or anybody at all. He should have gone for the sanitation department."

Scanlyn wanted to look away from her grin.

The Best of Our Time

"But the whore knew what it was all about. She told me the only friend I had in the world right then was an ice bag. Naturally we didn't have one, but I put a few cubes into a plastic sandwich bag and tucked it between my legs and went to bed and cried and after a while I fell asleep."

Scanlyn reached across the table to take her hands, wishing his brain would go dead so that he could wear the same foolish expression as the commodore had.

"The shrinks tried to get me to say I really wanted it to happen."

He could feel a slight tremor against his fingers, as though he'd caught a bird. "I'm terribly, terribly sorry."

"Who cares, you know? What did it matter? Buddy called the next day to make sure everything was all right, and I had to practically crawl to the phone, but sure, everything was great; that's what he wanted to hear. And Carl lasted for about a week before he got too randy to play mother any more. He couldn't go quite so far as to bring it up to our place again, and he couldn't afford another pad, not and have enough left over for his life's work. He felt real bad about moving out, but we had a nice long talk about it and ended up real pals.

"So I got from there to here by putting myself in a situation you had foresight enough to avoid, Prof. That and my boobs weren't big enough. I couldn't go topless. I was thinking of silicone, but I thought the hell with that, turning entirely plastic."

"Laura, Laura . . . I'm so sorry."

"Me too. *That* was the end of the social experiment. I wasn't about to yell for the law and get somebody gassed, the way they did Chessman. And if I had blown a whistle it would've meant making a line-up, and that would have been super-beautiful because I'd also have had to admit I can't tell most of them apart. That was some commitment, wasn't it? Some involvement."

The harsh light went out of her face as abruptly as though an arc lamp had guttered, and when her head drooped Scanlyn could see a line of feathery curls along the back of her neck. He put his fingers beneath the fine point of her chin and got her head up, but her face was shadowed and difficult to read because of the changing sky. The sun had disappeared behind some distant ridge, and overhead a cobalt slate reflected indigo in the lake where a single boat moved under power, its sails furled.

The terrace was strung with plastic Chinese lanterns, and these came on now, the pale colors a failed illusion. The commodore and his lady crossed the deck, he carefully erect, she in postureless youth. They were still holding hands, and even though Scanlyn was caught in a ring where the sky was hard and the lanterns weak and the lake textured like a blot, he felt a momentary lift, a painful shrug of wings, because there were still times when things seemed worthwhile.

"I wish I had a joint," Lorry Noon said.

Her voice was not quite even and he wished her wish so that she could steady herself on the bubble breath of grass and perhaps separate both of them from everything she'd said.

"Is there some place we can buy it?"

"No way. You're all right in Vegas, but these local road runners are dying to bust anyone they even think is holding."

"How about coffee? How about a spectacular dessert to stoke up your sugar content?" He tried a smile. "I remember your saying you needed it for energy."

"You're a retainer, Prof." She shook her head. "What I need more is to come down. Is it all right if we go?"

He called for the check and emptied the dregs from his glass while he waited. She didn't reach back for his hand as he followed her across the terrace. The bar was filling with what looked like locals, the juke box beating. Scanlyn had the feeling that he'd slipped a time link again, that he should have been arriving with his night still a promise.

The dam was rimmed with gray and seemed to have gathered early darkness as well as the waters of the lake, the spume from the gorge tinged lilac by a stray beam from the sun. Outlines in the desert were no longer burned dim, and there was a remarkable clarity which gave Scanlyn the feeling that he was driving into a looking-glass twilight, that he might reach a magic point where both their pasts would be left behind. But he drove on without encountering a threshold of any kind. When the light began to fail he switched on his low beams, looking for the first sign of the plain's one fiery city.

EIGHTEEN

I t was nearly a double entendre, Allenstein's compre-
hension lagging until he caught the echo of his secretary's careful enunciation: Mr. *Rance* Tufton was at
her desk.

Allenstein looked at his watch. "Mr. Stirby won't be back
for another hour or so."

"Yes sir. Mr. Tufton wonders if you have a few minutes to
spare."

Allenstein had, and in fact there were few people in the
capital who wouldn't have found time for Rance Tufton even
though he was a fairly recent administration acquisition and his
exact position in the structure hadn't been defined. Tufton had
come to town to the beat of high-level gongs and drums, bringing with him the pungent atmosphere of coal, gas and oil interests from the near-West and Border States.

Allenstein's office had never looked shabbier to him. He
thought about clearing his desk, putting on his jacket and shaking the dust from the flag standing in the corner, but then
decided that Tufton wasn't likely to remember still another
smooth man in an anonymous room, and he left everything as
it was. Tufton floated in beneath a wing of silver hair, so impec-
cably turned out that the surroundings became a few degrees
more dingy. Allenstein was reminded of those rich Homecom-
ing Day alumni who were cooed over by department heads,

plucked by the dean. Tufton had that same faintly amused look of familiarity with the uses of wealth.

"I don't think I've had the pleasure before," he said. His handshake was firm, his eyes keen, direct, and promising nothing.

"The pleasure's mine, Mr. Tufton. I'm sorry John's not here to see you."

"A shame the way these public ceremonies cut into a man's time." Tufton only pretended to glance at his watch. "I thought he might have gotten through a little early."

Allenstein felt a click, as though the dial of a safe was being turned. If Tufton knew Stirby was the chief speaker at a ceremony that day, he must also have known when it was scheduled to begin, and that Stirby couldn't possibly have been free yet.

"I had a nice talk with Frank," Tufton went on, and there was another click, protocol satisfied so that the visit could appear completely casual. "He's got a good deal on his mind these days . . . that project you people are working on."

"It's a touchy operation."

"I've always thought the best way to get what you want is to go right up to the front door and knock, but then I don't have much experience in the way of things here."

"I think there are times when we're not sure just where the front door is," Allenstein said.

Tufton smiled at his folded hands. "Not always easy to find, is it? Though I've heard that this office seems to have a pretty clear sense of direction."

"We're only a unit in the Bureau, Mr. Tufton."

"Well, I suppose we're all units of one sort or another, Mr. Allenstein. Establishing identity seems to be one of the most difficult things to do here, but you and John appear to have managed that. Evidently your work has a very special appeal."

"I hope so, if only because we're unlikely to keep working unless someone finds us appealing."

"That's a practical viewpoint, but then I've heard you're a practical man. Pity there isn't something like tenure here." Tufton looked genuinely concerned.

There was a final click, and Allenstein sat back. "And nobody makes allowances for the resources we deplete," he said.

Tufton looked from under his brows. "It *is* thankless work in the main. One often has to search to find any rewards in it."

"I'm sure they exist."

"Yes, I'm sure they do. But we have to be careful in our use of those resources we mentioned. Now I'd say the stand John's taking certainly has its merits."

Tufton began to take on the outlines of a firing-squad commander. "I don't know if it's as much a stand as a statement of principles," Allenstein said.

"Indeed he's a highly principled man." Tufton chuckled. "Though I must say it's somewhat surprising to find anyone with a background like yours quite so dedicated to those principles." His eyes widened. "You don't mind my being candid?"

"Knock away, Mr. Tufton."

"Not at all, and in fact I'm distressed to have you construe my remarks as criticism. In my opinion we can well do with that sort of background, with a little of the intellectual atmosphere which our esteemed opposition made out to be their special province—intellectual *and* practical, that is. What I've said badly, Mr. Allenstein, is that I admire your flexibility, the way you've been able to work with such a thoroughly established personality."

"I've done what I can."

"And done it well."

Allenstein strained his ears for the implied *too well,* but Tufton went on. "John's become a distinctive part of the landscape, someone you can take a bearing on. Our unwashed friends aren't ever going to convince *him* that the times they are a changin'."

Allenstein didn't need convincing, only an extra second or two in which to think. He swiveled in his recently-oiled chair, dropped a pencil, picked it up, and drew a deep breath. "But they are," he said.

"Well of course they are, and always will, though I doubt there's as much movement as appears on the surface. But there's a continuous flow, sometimes slow and sometimes fast but always moving . . . and rarely backward."

"In those terms that distinctive feature in the landscape sounds like an obstruction, Mr. Tufton."

"If a man insists on standing where he will he has to expect to take the consequences. But not an obstruction, Mr. Allenstein. While I might not agree completely with every aspect of John's position, I well know there are many who admire him for it. It's a point of view several people in the administration think should be visible."

"But not so vocal?"

"On the contrary. I'm inclined to believe it should be even more obvious."

Allenstein rocked gently in the chair, trying to get his balance. "Is that a strictly personal opinion?"

"As short a time as I've been here, I do know that is one luxury permitted very few of us."

"That's true," Allenstein said, "and that's why guidelines are so necessary."

Tufton stretched his leg and regarded an elegant shoe. "In our zoo back home we've got monkeys who can ride tricycles, but then so can most four-year-olds. While I'm a firm believer in leadership, I don't think creative thinking has to be abandoned. But I can see certain difficulties in this situation. Let us go back to that idea of having John's stand become even more forthright. We in government are expected to satisfy a variety of expectations, and there's no reason why those people entirely in agreement with John shouldn't be given the strongest possible assurance that someone here represents their viewpoint."

"And we in the Bureau haven't been given the impression that's what's wanted—at least not by Frank Prippet. I'm sure you've discussed this with him."

"Frank's certainly more familiar with John's philosophy than I am."

"And Eric Krug? I'm not fishing, Mr. Tufton. It's just that I've been led to believe Krug's an interested party."

The other looked bland. "I'm not at all sure what Eric's responsibilities are, and in fact there are times when I wonder about my own. But we haven't crossed tracks yet, and I don't believe we're meant to."

"That leaves John pretty much on his own."

"He seems to have been happy with that position in the past."

"There *are* those changing times."

Tufton leaned forward. "Put it that there's still a need, say an audience, for an attitude like his. Then I say let's have it stated as strongly as possible. Let's give those people such a good John Stirby no one will try to set up a copy."

"And Flipover?" Tufton looked at Allenstein alertly but didn't answer. "The administration *is* behind the project, isn't it?"

"I don't think either of us believe it would have come into existence otherwise."

Allenstein felt he was losing touch, that not only the conversation but its possible consequences were moving out of his control. "Mr. Tufton, a little while ago you questioned my dedication to John's principles."

"I meant to express my admiration."

Tufton's look was open, neutral, and held no invitation, but Allenstein could see no choice except to tilt. "I'd like to be as candid as you've been. I have serious reservations about the attitude John's taken toward Flipover."

"A matter of conscience, Mr. Allenstein?"

"Call it a matter of Allenstein. *I'm* not opposed to Flipover —or to any other administration policies. I can bend with the wind when necessary, but I don't think John's engaged in anything but a holding action of strictly limited value."

Tufton pursed his lips.

"And even accepting your statement that there's an audience for his performance," Allenstein went on, "it's not one I'd like to be permanently identified with."

"Knowledgeable people are aware of your sentiments."

"I had a reporter in here the other day calling me a hack for a honkie—which I may have become, but I don't like the reputation spreading."

"Reporters . . ."

"That may be so, Mr. Tufton. Nevertheless, I don't think that sort of definition is going to do me one bit of good."

Tufton sighed. "An *eminently* practical man. And I like your style, too. I'm afraid we've let ourselves get made out as frumps when there's no reason we have to look like the good gray folk, no reason we can't shine while we're about our work. That *was* admiration I was expressing, Mr. Allenstein. You've done very well with what is not in any terms the most pliable material. I shouldn't wonder that your performance would be even more remarkable if you had a different grade of stock to work with."

"I'd certainly welcome the opportunity to demonstrate that."

"One might very well arise, but I think we ought to concern ourselves with the immediate present. You'd certainly want to finalize your obligations here before turning to any new fields. Leaving loose ends behind doesn't give the best of impressions."

"It's the impression I'm now giving that has me concerned."

"I can appreciate that." Tufton nearly twinkled. "Of course, I don't think John Stirby needs any directions from you and me to find the road best suited to his talents. And in fact I don't even see that there would be any point in letting on that we had anything but an amiable chat today. If John's just allowed his head, I'm sure he'll have no difficulty in arriving at the position which seems to be indicated for him at the moment."

"A position I'm not in agreement with," Allenstein said. "Not that I think that will shake up too many people, Mr. Tufton. And I certainly don't expect to be encouraged to make a public statement, but how about a discreet memo?"

"It has been my experience in this city that even the most discreet memos somehow find their way into very strong daylight."

"Then you're leaving me in an official position of—"

"It's not your official position that's brought me here today," Tufton broke in. "As I said, there are people both aware and appreciative of the real nature of what you're doing. They realize the value of wit and balance . . . and of teamwork."

"Working for a losing team isn't my idea of a promising career."

"The future tends to arrange adequate rewards for the man who has a proper outlook, Mr. Allenstein." The look of concern slipped back on Tufton's face. "There's another factor here, you know. It's very likely that without some modifying influence John may find pressures, both internal and external, too great to resist. He may be carried away to what I might term unacceptable excesses, and carry you right with him. As you have already made clear, there's the danger of being tarred with a mutual brush in a situation like this, and no matter how much you might disassociate yourself from him after the fact, I doubt that your reputation would recover entirely. No, Mr. Allenstein, when I suggested that John should be allowed his head I didn't mean that he ought to be let run wild. For however much longer you may be associated with him, I think that it would be in your very best interest to continue to smooth his way, to keep those rough edges trimmed to tolerable limits."

"And the hell with Flipover."

"That project is not our direct concern at the moment." There was a touch of asperity in Tufton's voice. "And in any event I don't think that we ought to overestimate the influence of a few random speeches, no matter how ringing and well turned some of the phrases might be. The program you're talking about wasn't simply pulled out of a hat, and it isn't likely to be all that vulnerable to the actions of an essentially minor official."

"I think I hear a creaking in that velvet glove, Mr. Tufton."

Tufton held up his hands. "They're absolutely bare-knuckle." He looked at his watch. "How the time does go. As I say, thankless work in the main, but I'm here to do what I was asked to do. I believe we all are, don't you?"

Allenstein pushed off on one foot and spun around completely in the chair, landing with both arms on the desk, his smile tight and his eyes slightly unfocused behind the glasses. "Sure," he said. "We all are."

NINETEEN

By the time Scanlyn dropped Lorry Noon off he had a rancid clot at the back of his throat from too much food and wine and from the cold leftovers of their joint failure.

She lived in a string of open bungalows set in a horseshoe around a small pool, the open end screened from the desert by panels of colored plastic glazed and pitted by the scouring of the sand. As Scanlyn helped her out of the car he was reviewing the next ploy, the tentative probing which would ease him through the door or send him away with a half-promise or with nothing at all, the move he didn't think he wanted to make but felt would be expected of him. Taking a ring of keys from her purse and holding one between thumb and forefinger as she jabbed it at him, she saved him the trouble by asking if he wanted to come in. Her eyes were narrowed in bitter curiosity and there was no invitation in her voice. He suspected she might bleat her strange laugh and slam the door in his face if he said yes, but it wasn't fear of that refusal which sent him into a windy explanation of how another brighter time would be better for them. He had to see a man, to rinse away the taste of defeat before he could bear the thought of two losers grappling to match torn remnants.

The keys swung once, twice, and then she shrugged and told him to suit himself. After she'd gone in, Scanlyn stood for a few moments watching the last bruised spot of light leave the sky; then the window air conditioner came on with a rattle and blew him a long stale raspberry touched faintly with female smells.

Traffic in town was in full cross-flux between the end of day and beginning of night, and it crawled through a scattering of police whistles. On the boulevard it moved so slowly that the figures on the signs raced past the cars. He still had the top down and could feel the evening gathering into a coil, hear the first pulses of laughter. Hotel walls were programmed in a tesselation of bright windows, behind them a rage of dressing and undressing in preparation for the good times certain to be at hand. But Scanlyn's thoughts were colored. If he was ever going to raise his own worth he had to flip Buffre into the opposite balance pan, to coax him up the ladder and onto the rack for his own and everyone's sake. And there was no time.

He drove as far as his hotel, then made a nearly ritualistic turn back toward town, a charge filled with blue troopers and yellow bugles, and went grimly through the downtown area where nothing mattered and no one cared, through the suburbs which looked safe and cozy once again. A stream of dim buttons flowed from the hills, grew brighter, glared, then passed in a roar of open exhausts. He found the turn and was on the secondary road, his beams gray on its surface while the night stretched toward a ragged fold where ridges met a sky so heavily dusted the stars seemed to dim each other.

He came to a track, hesitated, then turned onto it. He'd gone nearly a mile before he realized his error, and by then there was no way to swing around without catching his wheels in the sand, so he drove on until he came to a clearing where his lights picked out the splintered poles of what had been a small corral. There was a house of adobe and sagging palings, its rusty corrugated roof shuffled by the wind. Scanlyn backed and twisted and stalled the car, a four-on-the-floor sport captive in the land of the wagon rut, and he smoldered between rage and despair not only at his own predicament but at the fact of that clearing, that relic of a desperation which had forced people to forsake shade and water to come out there to catch and keep something in the corral, to find themselves caught by the house. Except for the crackle of the dead engine there was no sound, no trace of wind, and the only thing moving in the headlights' beams was the drift of dust from his maneuvering.

His hands were trembling, and he felt that he was on the verge of dissolving into a long howl. He started the car and fled, and back on the road he drove slowly and heavily as he tried to recapture his sense of high purpose. The nighttime desert was overwhelmingly bleak. During the day there was a promise of life, a chance that irrigation and the power of the sun could force blooms, but night had a feeling of age beyond the new history he'd so recently become infatuated with. Those life forms hadn't been able to survive, except on their bellies: what chance was there now when everything was so much more complicated, when everyone was wrapped in see-through envelopes which deadened touch? The desert was like a charred repository for every failed dream and experiment. It was the future arrived, a wasteland of isolated Xanadus where the last revels were being held. He felt a wrench of sorrow for the world caught in that rolling doom.

And yet . . . and yet a spark here and there could stay the dark. If he was able to jog the decomposing pile even slightly he might be able to set off a tiny reaction. He was a sour-throated man in a silly car and his life was marked in increments of failure, but he hadn't quite lost his sense of the way things should be. He began to feel buoyed by his own need; his present purpose was as good as all the others had been, as manageable an illusion as any.

He pressed down on the accelerator, gave a tentative tap to the horn and nearly went past the gravel track, braking and turning so quickly the sky moved in an arc. The car slewed and bounced, but he clung to the wheel and soon there was light ahead, a yellow window which looked fresh from a painter's brush. Then he could see a funereal glow from the pool, a cone of sparks from what must have been a charcoal brazier in the yard. As he pulled up, his lights slid over a row of figures gathered in the driveway. A single eye flared like a jewel. When he stopped the car a flashlight beam wobbled toward him and voices began squalling until De Berg's rich tones floated his name. The flashlight went out and someone shouted toward the yard that Dink shouldn't burn the grass.

They tumbled toward Scanlyn as he got out; the Buffres and De Berg and Reza, then a dumpy figure wearing beads, a softball jersey and long knotted hair, and another one trim and clean-shaven in dungarees and a work shirt. He recognized Barney Zimmer, the imp in rat's locks who'd been prominent in a failed daisy revolution for peace and pot. The other, the lean image of sincerity and intellectual devotion, was David Rindell, whom Scanlyn had last seen on television solemnly warning that the day of the banks' destruction was on hand. Both were De Berg's people, post-trial exhibits of a successful defense. Scanlyn glared when the lawyer took his arm and said something pleasant. De Berg had no right to bring them here, to indulge himself in a strut of phrases. Zimmer and Rindell were as old and useless to their times as Scanlyn was to his.

He broke away from De Berg and tried to talk to Buffre, but the night and Buffre's lowered lids combined to shade his eyes into half-scoops gleaming only fitfully. The hard planes of his wife's face bobbed over his shoulder, and Reza was protectively near. Scanlyn found himself isolated between separate triangles of black and white. He shivered, chilled by the drizzle of cold light from the stars. "None of us have any more time," he said. "We've all wasted too much."

"This is Mr. Washington, you mean?" Zimmer said. "The creep Jerry was talking about?"

"Good evening, Mrs. Buffre."

"He's got wooden teeth," Zimmer said.

"We've got to at least start to talk seriously right now, tonight," Scanlyn said.

"This is too beautiful, a talking dinosaur."

"Totty's all right," De Berg said.

"*Totty?* Like in potty?"

A girl drifted from the yard, long streaked hair cutting her face into an oval. Her jeans were skintight and her denim shirt so loose that it was impossible to distinguish her breasts among the folds. Scanlyn's link to time hadn't merely slipped; it had broken and left him permanently a background figure in a rerun of last year's news.

"It's okay, hey . . . no bust?" she said. "You want me to put more franks on?"

"This who's coming to dinner, Tussy?" Zimmer said. "But who asked him to? Did you, Jerry? Naw. Dave?"

"Not me," Rindell said.

"I'd love to see how he gets the mustard stains off those teeth, but it's the wrong night. Come back tomorrow. You lost your hair ribbon. You lost your horse." Zimmer did a little jig. "You didn't bring Martha because Jerry doesn't have a phone. He's got a shithouse but no phone."

"Would you like something to eat, Totty?"

"You said you'd stay out of it if there were no legal problems. Then why did you bring those idiots here?" Scanlyn turned to Buffre. "You don't need De Berg any more, and you never needed these clowns."

"You're allowed to leave," Zimmer said. "We don't want to keep you from dropping dead. Or maybe you want to turn on. You want to be a *living* talking dinosaur? Clump, clump. Straighten his meat for him, Dink, send him back happy. Hey, I can tell he's the real one because he's got the same immie eyes as the guy on a dollar bill."

"That wretched shit of yours is old, Zimmer—*old.*"

"He looks enough like Leary that I'd think he was if I didn't know Leary was on Mars. He used to be the man in the moon before they extradited him. Do you want to turn on and do a fly-by, Mr. Washington? Did you ever think of posing for quarters?"

"Can't you give me a half-hour?"

Buffre's wife snorted and folded her arms and looked over her shoulder at nothing.

"Wouldn't another time really be better?" De Berg said.

"All right, include him if you have to," Scanlyn said, "if

you're worried about the legal points, but he's got nothing to do with it any more. It's you and your wife and everyone still living in the dark."

"Not *you*," Grace Buffre said.

"See if he's got a rubber head, Reza, like his pig friends think all of us have."

Scanlyn turned. "Tell him how the fun and games marched the rats into the river, Zimmer, how pot helped straighten people shooting four bags a day. And when they didn't have enough to eat Rindell cheered them up with a circus . . . Blow, baby, blow."

"Dink does that."

"Hey, Barney," the girl said.

"That's a failed tactic," Rindell said. "There are too many of us for divide and conquer to be operative."

"Too many of *you*, Mrs. Buffre? Would you like to trade places with this young lady and do a black version of their road show with your husband as Rindell and Reza as Zimmer? The children can stay—"

"Do you recognize, do you happen to be familiar with this creep?" Zimmer broke in. "He's stuck in the tar pit is what it is. He's bellowing for company. He doesn't want to die alone. He wants us all to go with him, and he'll even shoot us to save the trouble of making up our minds."

"It might come to that," Scanlyn said.

Buffre's face went flat and Scanlyn waited a moment, perhaps two, time a stop-frame, his hand extending through until it took Buffre's arm, the fingers a silvered claw against the night-blackness of the other's skin. A warning cracked across his mind but he ignored it, prepared to go further, to tug when he felt Buffre's muscles bunch as though he were going to pull away. They stood for a moment between trespass and retaliation, and then Scanlyn felt a tremor in his hand and brought his lips so close to Buffre's ear he could see the pattern of nubby hair around the helix, a tiny mole near the lobe.

"There's no time left."

"Is he kissing or just blowing in your ear?" Zimmer

said. "He's coming out, it's gay lib."

"Bring your wife along," Scanlyn pleaded.

"She already heard enough," Buffre said.

"But it isn't any of De Berg's business. You can discuss it with him later, tell him anything you want to."

"You're giving me the right."

"Do you want to take the car?"

Buffre raised his arm slightly and Scanlyn let his hand drop. He followed when Buffre turned toward the yard, the others frothing behind them.

"We're not going to shoot Zimmer," Scanlyn said. "We know he's really harmless; he's practically become a diversion. But you and your wife and Reza are a burden. We don't know what to do with you because we don't *need* you. There are enough people to do the work at the bottom, and they would if you hadn't made such a monopoly of it, if you hadn't turned it into *your* kind of work. That's when you can find it—and when you can't we have to support you. There's no room for you, Buffre. Save us the price of ammunition. Build an ark and take all those so-called brothers with you."

"Aah," De Berg said behind him.

"Ask your old friend Jerry; he'll tell you I'm right."

"I've told him you were just like all the rest."

"Do you hear that? You're *him*, an object. A dead weight . . . Get off our backs, man, disappear."

Buffre turned and stood at the end of a table strewn with beer bottles and half-eaten sandwiches. The coals in the brazier were graying, the grill edged with petrified drippings. "Why don't you go home?" he asked.

"Why don't *you?* It hasn't gotten any better since you've been on the road. Go all the way back to where you came from. Did your mother move because she didn't want to see you turn into another one of the county bucks? Is that why your father left her? You can't stop running because you never learned to keep your mouth closed, but none of it has done any good. Massah is still dying in bed, probably while a brother's fanning him—or more, a real half brother."

The whites in Buffre's eyes seemed to boil and Scanlyn saw his arms swell and bunch, tried to set himself not to flinch, hoping at the same time that the front plate would give rather than any real teeth. Then there was a twist of fingers in his hair and his head was jerked back, his jawline raked briefly, and he could hear her panting, feel her breasts digging into his back. Her hand was locked in his hair and he was twisted sideways, crook-necked and staggering like the laboratory assistant in a horror film, while she muttered what he could easily believe might have been Swahili dredged up from some memory as dark as her rage. Then De Berg was pulling at her and Reza half unsheathed his club. Zimmer and his crew were disinterested spectators, Buffre a scowling tribal judge transported to a sur-burban barbecue session. Scanlyn's eyes misted over in what might have been pain or laughter and the faces became long wet streaks as he finally spun free. De Berg released Grace Buffre and tugged pettishly at his paisley neckcloth.

Scanlyn touched his fingers to his jaw and brought them away trembling and flecked with blood. "That's what we need," he said, "what we really need—more direct action."

"I can't be responsible—" De Berg began.

"I know that. Neither can he. There isn't anyone—"

"You had that, you already had that long enough, didn't you?" She stood with one hand thrust out, the fingers bent like live roots, and Scanlyn wondered if there were pieces of his skin under the nails. "Responsible to whatever kind of chains you put us in . . . the same ones no matter what name you gave them."

"Hey, you can't go talking like that," Zimmer said. "Nobody gave you permission. Keeping quiet is one of the rights he's handing out."

"Totty, I think—"

"Don't do me any favors, Jerry."

"That's what he wants," Buffre said.

"George—" De Berg sputtered.

"I want somebody to take responsibility for—" Scanlyn began.

"You want quiet." There was the beginning of a rumble in Buffre's voice. "But we decline to oblige because the idea has finally come through, it has finally been beaten into these solid bone heads of ours that there never was any plan to bring us into the big house. Not eventually, not ever. We won't get any closer if we let you polish our skulls with baseball bats for another two hundred years. There just isn't a final bleach on the market."

"That's right," Scanlyn said, "so now you have to—"

"Nooo." Buffre curled the word into a suppressed chuckle. "No, we do not *have* to do anything because that one-tenth of the law you can't quite take away from us is possession. We kept pushing until we worked ourselves right up into the front yard. That's where we are now, watching you run around trying to keep the walls from falling in and the roof from coming down on you. And losing." The rumble had turned into bubbling, like tar. "What was already rotten as soon as you built it. What has blood for the mortar and bones for the foundations. And when it comes down, you are not going to get us to help clean up the mess. A little selective collecting is what we'll do, our own dust, which is all that's left of the beginning. And that's what we'll begin with all over again, what we'll wet down with the tears you never even allowed those people to cry, and out of that salt and dust—"

"Good God," Scanlyn said.

"—out of that salt and dust," Buffre went on, his voice nearly humming, "the fruit is going to grow, the pulp and juices to sustain us, the seed for new fields. Which we will water with our own blood, feeding new life with those old sorrows until they're all used up, until that last bitter pit of what we let ourselves get made into is swallowed and turned into waste to feed those new roots. And meantime you won't learn anything even if you get shut of this present mess. You'll go back to building another slapshack, hammering each other up to the beams to try to get them to hold. Each other and whoever else you coax in. But not us. This time we won't happen to be available. We'll be busy growing a fence of ourselves higher and stronger than anything you can put up. So it'll be your eyes looking out of that crazy house, rolling in the jungle of old laths and broken bricks, while we'll be so strong we'll be able maybe to afford a tear of pity every once in a while."

"As long as you stop crying for yourselves," Scanlyn said. But weakly, too dismayed by Buffre's gospel tones. The surrogate he'd put all his hopes into was so badly flawed that he divided even this small group. Grace Buffre and the bodyguard were still nodding slightly to currents the rest couldn't feel. De Berg looked embarrassed. The others stood unmoved and speculative.

"Well, you know . . ." Zimmer said at last.

He left it unfinished, shooting a sideways glance at Rindell. The girl's arms were folded and she was looking at her feet. Scanlyn could see them all slowly drawing away from each other, being pulled into the separate spheres of any of those millons of stars.

"I'd like to go inside," he said to Buffre.

"Oh, Totty . . ."

Scanlyn glared at De Berg. "Just let me have a couple of minutes and you can all go back to whatever you were doing before I interrupted."

"What is it now that nobody else is supposed to know anything about?" Grace Buffre said.

"Please join us, Mrs. Buffre. Whatever your husband does certainly concerns you, but not anyone else here."

"It's you who's the one—"

"A couple of minutes?" Buffre interrupted his wife. "If that's all you want let's get it over with for good."

"Hey, I know what," Zimmer said, "the death-defying love leap."

"Aw, Barney," the girl said.

"You think the board's not high enough?"

"What do you think he's got to show you that you haven't already seen?" Grace Buffre asked.

"I'll try to handle whatever it is," Buffre said. "Come on in if you want to."

She didn't answer. Buffre gave her a long look, then turned toward the house. Scanlyn hurried after him. There was the unmistakable odor of marijuana inside.

"You'd better put that air conditioner on," Scanlyn said.

"Hardly worth it for a couple of minutes."

Buffre leaned against the kitchen counter, his arms folded. Scanlyn watched him adopt the amused and contemptuous face of Baad aass, and began to tingle because he'd had too much of a day to be diverted by the cool dude or *macho* or whoever. "You must be out of your mind to let them use grass here," he said.

"Not my house."

"Which won't keep you from being picked up for being 'in the presence of.' But that's the least of it, those two retarded adolescents and their community bang. You've got some clever lawyer, letting them park here while you've only just gotten out from under . . . some legal whiz that he'll risk getting you nailed by the state or even the county, let alone the federal people. I know his services are free, but I don't see how you can possibly afford them."

"We manage," Buffre said. "And that's about a two-minute lecture."

"The least of it, I said. What I'm really interested in knowing is how often you take a fit like that, how often you're so overwhelmed by the sound of your own voice that you don't realize you're not saying anything."

"To you, friend."

"That's true, but then there's a limited audience for be-Jesus exhortation. You might even have to go back down to the Delta and look for a Sunday afternoon picnic crowd. I don't know what you can possibly be thinking of—another wagon train? Can you still hitch a mule?"

"You wouldn't know—"

"And don't give me soul," Scanlyn said. "It doesn't stretch that far. Right now it won't even stretch from one end of any city ghetto to the other."

Indifference slipped from Buffre's face. "I *read* it," he said.

"I read that great book you're so proud of, and you wouldn't know. You wouldn't know what stretches where."

"I know what hasn't done any good, and that no Holy Roller is going to begin to put it all together. If you're looking for a broader market, why don't you get yourself a cloak and hire a bunch of fags to dance in the background?"

"Oh my, how we do offend. Getting too uppity, doing things without getting permission first. Those days are *over*. You want to get it through your head that nobody's waiting on directions any more."

"I am," Scanlyn said. "And from *you*."

Buffre's eyes closed so that only a smoldering light shone through. He sucked in his cheeks.

"If preaching's the best you can do, then they're smarter back there than I thought," Scanlyn said. "Then they've sent me out here to bring back a prize exhibit every racist can chuckle over. Wasn't that your voice I heard on those tapes? That person had something to say. That person is the one I want to put in a position to be heard."

Buffre threw his head back and smiled broadly.

"Is that so funny?"

"Well, you're so strong to get me into the game, and here you are worried about what tricks they're pulling on *you*."

"I never said it would be easy."

"Now that's real information you're putting on me, how hard it maybe could get."

"That preacher act won't—"

"I do a paddy radical too. Or a prince of Africa. Or off the pigs. I do whatever I can to fuck you up."

"Then do it from a position where you can be seen."

"Yeah."

"That's not yes."

"It's yeah, like get yourself put in another box, let them run around you like you were a maypole until they've got you all tied up."

"You can beat them, George."

The first name slipped out so naturally Scanlyn was a half-stutter into what he was going to say next. He stopped, suddenly aware that his head of steam had run out, that the situation was falling away from him.

Buffre raised an eyebrow and shook his head, one corner of his mouth curled in what might have been amusement. "Well you know," he said. "I might just be thinking about that."

"You are." It sounded terribly flat to Scanlyn, and when he tried to gather himself to be brisk and assertive he stumbled again. "Then you'll have to get rid of that circus . . . and Reza, too." Buffre looked as though he were going to snap. "I mean the uniform—that one, anyway. You might be able to keep him as a chauffeur . . . you'll probably have a car assigned."

"Yassuh."

"There's only one attitude possible. Absolutely straight, everything—the way you dress, your wife . . ." Scanlyn blinked while he tried to find the source of that blunder. "Wait, please. I meant that you can't leave them a way to put you down."

"No way at all."

"Of course they'll try. They'll find ways. But then you'll be the victim, you see. It's they who'll look bad. Follow the leader and—"

"And get to be fat cat too? Steal my share?"

"They might give you a chance to." Scanlyn was no longer sure of what he was saying. "A very sensible move, set you up to be caught with your hand in the till—the unregenerate chicken thief. That's the way it would come out. And there was once a time . . . Once it was all right, there was something to be gotten out of seeing someone outside the club come in and rip them off, not doing any good but simply rubbing their noses in it. But that won't do any more. You'll have to be absolutely clean in order to be able to speak out, to blow the whistle whenever you can."

Buffre locked his fingers and gave Scanlyn a long calculating look, weight and counterweight. He flexed his hands and examined them as though he were critical of the weave of fingers. "You mean only perfect," he said, "do what's right. The reason you don't get that preacher is he's not just passing out

instructions, the way you're used to. He's putting himself in
with the people he's talking to." Buffre paused, and Scanlyn had
the impression he was being allowed to catch up, to move into
a small and recently created space. "That's not news, that
they've got the guns and aren't much worried about using
them. I could find myself feeling grateful if they do me the favor
of not shooting me, even give me a chance to get a fingerful of
the honey if I'm a good old boy. Why, I might even get to like
looking down from up there where they've got everything on
their side."

"Use the opportunity to get as much done as possible."
Scanlyn said it without thinking and heard a sort of prating in
the echo. Intimations were gathering and he couldn't ignore
the weight of the hammer in his hand, found himself groping
for another nail.

"It's if I can't," Buffre said. "If I come to being not that
smart after all . . . and try to make up for it another way."

"Why, I . . ." Scanlyn began bluffly but trailed off, that new
space widening into distance until he was afraid he was beginning to shrink.

"Like, what happened with you?" Buffre said.

"Happened?"

"That you're still there."

"But I . . . somebody has to . . ." A builder of ovens, a
manufacturer of napalm. "You've got to understand that I truly
believe a change in direction, in approach, no matter how mis-
guided the motives . . . that it could bring about . . . not that I
hope for anything like real understanding, but if an area of
adjustment could possibly be developed." Scanlyn wrung his
sweaty hands. "Accommodation?"

There was a hiss of breath between Buffre's set teeth, and
Scanlyn hoped the sound was more charitable than critical, that
Buffre was trying to revive him, but there was no time to form
a conclusion, Buffre's indrawn whistle barely beginning when
the kitchen door was slapped open and Grace Buffre entered,
stiff and accusing. Scanlyn felt his face twist into some form of

wheedling, but she didn't look at him, not out of contempt this time but because she didn't see him, the glare of rage directed toward her husband instead, the sharp twist of her head driving him through *What now?* and into understanding, galvanizing him to a complementary stiffness and a rush into the yard with Scanlyn behind them.

He'd seen blue movies; once in an ugly New York loft converted into a studio he'd even paid to stand in a crowd of distraught men and watch one being made, the actors bobbing painted serpents' heads toward each other, only able to simulate while the real thing, the damp odor of leaking seed, spread slowly through the audience. There had been something pitifully honest in that statement of group need, the voyeur entering into the double fantasy of himself as one of the artificial couplers. But here under the starlight, bracketed in air currents Scanlyn could feel against his own skin, the action on the diving board was simply coarse.

Since Zimmer was shorter than the girl she didn't have to raise herself, and they stood flatfooted in a pale disjointed X, her lean thighs clamping him, his toes curled to grip the rough surface of the plank as it oscillated slightly. They met in a cautious, nearly coddling movement which gave the effect of puppylike pubic nuzzling rather than sexual thrust, and Zimmer's hair moved like a crown of soft nettles, hers in a metronomic swing, while Grace Buffre's arm shot out in a rigid invitation to witness what everyone was already staring at: Rindell a little uncertain beneath his assumed cool, De Berg rubbing the edge of his hand across his upper lip, Buffre's face edging toward a new and different contempt. Scanlyn tried to seize the moment, to hash together a deft and fatal comment, but he was pulled into identification with those two unlovely figures locked in a revelation of the dream of all dreams. There was a faint roaring in his ears, as though the desert breeze had grown into a hollow forerunner of the doom rolling toward them all.

But there was still work to be done, particularly when

Buffre had budged ever so slightly, and Scanlyn fashioned a phrase cunning enough to smear the love faction and was about to let the venomous gob fly when there was a choked sound from Zimmer, *Now* tangled in the strained cords of his throat, nearly lost in a gargle of saliva. They waited, eyes even sharper while for what seemed minutes nothing happened, the diving board slowing until there was only a sort of combined trilling of wood and rubber and metal. Then the girl's buttocks spread in jerky parturition, the cleft none too clean, and the single figure, the upright backed beast, trembled and wobbled its way to the front of the board and went over with an animal sound, disengaging midway in a minute spray which the starlight converted into a handful of discarded beads.

As soon as the heads disappeared the watchers let their eyes roam anywhere but toward each other, feet shuffling backward so that by the time the joint splash reached the sides of the pool all but Reza and Rindell were moving toward the house, black and white now a simple checkerboard quartet, and when Zimmer's dripping head appeared, the girl sleek taffy next to him, his quavering *Hey!* was directed at their backs. Grace Buffre whirled and stopped, her eyes boiling toward the tips of the cypress, the three men in a sheepish bracket around her. Scanlyn gathered his various sticks until he'd smoothed his line, barbed a new delivery, and then was unable to say anything because her look washed directly over Buffre and he held two pale palms toward her, a self-protective pleading gesture to which she gave a snuffle nearly lost in the suck of water as someone came out of the pool.

"I tried to dissuade him," De Berg said, and her hot pitch spilled over him. "My dear Grace, it was really more childish than anything else. In spite of their antics, they're—"

She turned, lost in the shadows of the house and only briefly silhouetted at the kitchen door before she was gone.

"It must be in the eye of the beholder," Scanlyn said.

"Please, I think there's been enough for one night." De Berg was visibly distressed.

"No sloppy seconds, or thirds? What would *I* get, at the end of the line?" Scanlyn asked.

"That was a drag, Jerry," Buffre said. "You're making him" —a nod toward Scanlyn—"look good."

"Another illusion," Scanlyn said. "We're—" He heard the pad of feet and saw Zimmer loping toward them, still naked. "We're finished."

Then Zimmer was beside them, streaming, his sex shrunken. "You think that beats crossing the Delaware?"

"Him, too. Taps all the way down the line. You're the only one left, George."

"You want to try your luck, Mr. Washington? Or can't you get your oar straight?"

"Barney, I think you should get dressed," De Berg said.

Zimmer showed his teeth in a grin meant to be fierce, but Scanlyn could see years, flesh sloughing off, the skull behind it. There were voices from the pool, Reza and Rindell and the girl in some sort of contretemps. She'd put on her shirt.

"You're the only one who hasn't really tried yet," Scanlyn said, still working on Buffre. "And unless you do . . ."

There was a yelp and the girl came running toward them, the tails of her shirt fluttering away so that the scraggle of moss seemed to be borne upward, separate from the rest of her body. She caught the shirttails around her and stood next to Zimmer with one foot on the other, lashless, her hair damp and kinking. "That crazy"—she looked at Buffre—"that crazy Keystone Kop is giving us heat about the grass. Tell him he's got no right, Barney."

"I've got to go," Scanlyn said. "And I mean *got* to while I'm still in possessiion of a few faculties. Someone else ought to have a turn. You can call me—"

"A lot of things," Zimmer said.

"That's right, but it doesn't matter." Scanlyn took Buffre's arm for the second time and found the muscles slack. "The only important thing is what *you* say. Are you afraid of trying because you see what an unbelievable mess *we've* made of it?"

"Barney."

"Yeah, Dink."

They walked away with their arms around each other's waists, Zimmer's buttocks silver against the green-black of the grass.

"That's the literal ass-end of that last hope of yours, Mr. De Berg." Scanlyn released Buffre's arm. "Remember that when he's trying to tell you what to do . . . or when your wife is. We're all very busy helping you."

"I think I should talk to Grace," De Berg said. "I'm sorry about the upset, George, but it can be all right, you know, when there's less of a mixture. She'll understand."

De Berg's moccasins were stained, his hips too wide for the luridly striped trousers, and the kitchen fluorescents picked up the gray among his curls.

"Do you think she will?" Scanlyn asked.

"I want you to spell it all out," Buffre said. "I want to hear it absolutely clear, just what it is, and who's going to be in charge, all that."

"Of course. And the financial arrangements."

"That's right. All of it. When can I get it?"

"I could fill in everything but the names and the final figure tonight."

"Oh, man—you know?"

"Okay, not tonight. But you'll be leaving soon, won't you?"

"There isn't any set schedule."

"The day after tomorrow then, to make sure I can get it all? They'll want to know what your intentions are, but there's nothing definite I can tell them, is there?"

"I might even want to see it spelled out on paper."

"Then call me the day after tomorrow. And if I happen to be out for any reason, you can leave a message."

But Buffre had stopped listening, his head turned toward the group wrangling at the pool. Scanlyn had been dismissed. He didn't care. He was tired of pat exits, of asking to be remembered to wives who despised him. He simply walked away.

The seats of the car were filmed with moisture. There was

a chill in the air, and all four voices carried from the pool, a muted rumble from within the house. The engine kicked over immediately and drowned them out. His lights sent a red-and-white flare into the darkness as he backed, his high beams glittered along the gravel. The wheels spun a shower of stones into the air as he roared away, but no one watched him go.

TWENTY

Howard MacFarlane was normally contemptuous of any place serving food and drink in an atmosphere lacking a sense of well-rubbed wood and flesh, time suspended in the drawl and rumble of contented voices, but he absolutely detested the Bull Run cocktail lounge. Its Civil War décor was preciously safe, dead ground even within the contrived neutrality of that artificial city. Neither Old Glory nor the Stars and Bars were hung. Wall lamps fashioned like miniature drums carried the badges of regiments which had never existed. There were replicas of period rifles over the bar, carefully greened bas-reliefs of field pieces embedded in the walls. Barmen wore short military jackets decorated with senseless gold scrolls, and the waitresses' blouses and caps could have been either Boston or Atlanta, the stars spotting their long transparent skirts from either flag.

Bull Run's customers identified with the colloquialism rather than the battle, and the lounge was a plain of babble, filled with signs and countersigns, hands patting backs or laid reassuringly along coat sleeves. Every move was a gesture of extraction. The only echo of thunder was in the accomplished bass voices plying all lines of least resistance, hustling and genially allowing the hustle, a bloodless confrontation of middlemen. The lounge had come to be the meeting place for lobbyists who worked for people balancing one kind of power and bureaucrats who worked for people balancing another.

It was a mark of the Bureau's dim luster that MacFarlane had only been there twice before, and neither occasion had been an attempt to obtain preferential treatment, only a blunt probe for vibrations from some sensitive area whose periphery the Bureau just happened to touch. But when Sam Bascule called MacFarlane and suggested that they get together at Bull Run, Prippet was enthusiastic about the meeting even though they'd never heard of Bascule and weren't able to turn up any information on him. MacFarlane went because keeping such dates was one of his recognized duties as Prippet's chancellor, concertmaster and second banana; Prippet sent him because having a man from the Bureau seen at Bull Run might raise others' opinion of his own influence.

MacFarlane hated the smell of the place, a mixture of slightly turned bar fruit and expensive shaving lotion and deodorant-treated perspiration. His nostrils were pinched in disapproval as Bascule delivered the intense sincere smile and overlong handshake customary in the lounge, and he had to suck in his belly to squeeze between the table and the walls of the booth. Once he'd ordered and admired the waitress' legs he gave Bascule a long glum look and decided that his hair was too sandy, his skin too raw and his lapels too wide. Bascule insisted that MacFarlane call him Red because everyone else did, and after a solicitous inquiry about the amount of water in MacFarlane's Scotch and an exaggerated pucker to indicate the dryness of his own martini, he laid out his credentials verbally, shuffling names not generally well known but typical of those being dropped all over the room in accents from Yankee astringent to country-boy rollicking.

"Everyone asks to be remembered to Frank," he said.

MacFarlane grunted. The people Bascule had mentioned hadn't ever given any indication of remembering Prippet.

"He's got some real friends, Frank. Even tucked off in a pocket the way he is now, they keep an eye on him." MacFarlane supposed that he was by implication a mere patch on the pocket. "It's that steadiness, that staying quality. Damned few with his kind of record, Mac." Bascule ignored MacFarlane's quivering jowls. "And there's more than surface . . . depth, too." He chewed his olive thoughtfully for a moment, and then his eyes widened as though he'd found illumination in the gin-soaked fruit. "He could move, Frank."

"I'd say he expects to," MacFarlane answered.

"*Move*, Mac, I said."

"I got that."

"You sure? I don't take second to anybody in my admiration for the faithful-servant type, but better not to have to wait around to be one of the few called and even fewer chosen. This could be prime time for Frank. Get on the mark, get set, and *go*."

MacFarlane fumbled his pipe and pouch from separate pockets, his hands hidden beneath the table while his body jiggled in what could have been taken for suspect activity. He looked down into his lap. "Go where?" he said.

"Let's think about pulling levers instead of strings. Let's give John Q. a chance to see what a good man looks like."

"Let's who?"

"John Q. Public, Mac."

"I also got that."

MacFarlane tamped the tobacco and shook a few loose crumbs into the ashtray. He paused with the pipe in one hand and a cylindrical lighter in the other. "Who's doing the letting?"

"There's no one contrary."

Bascule caught the waitress' eye and held up two fingers. MacFarlane flicked the lighter and there was a minute roar, then a jet of flame. Bascule drew back. MacFarlane, faintly cross-eyed, applied the jet to the bowl of the pipe and was momentarily lost in a blue cloud.

"That thing ought to work great on bunkers over in Nam," Bascule said.

"It lights pipes."

"You're lucky to have any eyebrows left." MacFarlane glowered. "He can go, Frank. Where is up to him. Once he gets started. Gets started, Mac. He's got good will in abundance."

"There's always an abundance of horseshit."

"I knew you'd been around, that you knew the score." Bascule winked at MacFarlane. "Horseshit can be had by the ton, but you've got to have people to get behind the brooms and move it along. Money. Buttons and bumper stickers, telephones. An organization. A nucleus. No way if there's a lack of money. All right, say there isn't."

"Why isn't there?"

"Because of citizens for, ad hoc committees, whatever you're able to shake together. Grab the people who know a good man's hard to find. An old song, but never truer. I don't mean there's a fortune. Seed money, front stuff, enough for a setup to attract the real thing. Get those sweepers working."

MacFarlane's pipe had gone out. His breath whistled into the stem and a puff of ash rose. "You're not registered as a lobbyist," he said.

"Not me. I'm staff. We've got a regular man here—Charlie Drummond."

"Who's *we?*"

"Educational devices."

"Teaching aids? Books or something?"

"Talking books, if you want them. Education through recreation, learning through play. The happy child is a willing learner. Our equipment makes his world warmer and brighter. You couldn't find anything cleaner, not these days when anyone civic-minded gets bad marks for dirty thoughts. Frank would care about that, I know."

They sat back while the drinks were served, then turned to watch the waitress walk away. Bascule made a guttural sound and looked into his glass. MacFarlane relit his pipe.

"He can go as far as he wants," Bascule said. "But he's got to get started. Other people have to knock down back doors, climb into second-story windows. They break legs. But I know a place, Mac. And the boys have no objection if it's Frank. How does Congress strike?"

"You'll have to ask him."

"You do that. A seat that's been like grandpa's rocker for forty years. The incumbent's running. Which could be a problem, Mac. You could never beat the incumbent in this seat. But I happen to know he's only running to hold it temporarily. He's got a big move coming after the inauguration dust settles. He's going up almost to cabinet level. So think about this seat as a stepping stone. Or an express elevator for a guy who really has what it takes—like Frank. Are you with me?"

"Where's the seat?"

"It could be in Honolulu. Who cares? A special election next year and all the time in the world to get ready for it. Meanwhile holding his current job while the old pay check keeps coming in. Is it beautiful?"

"Where is it?"

Bascule put a fist to his forehead, smiled and shook his head, then nodded at MacFarlane as though assuring him that what he was about to say was, incredibly, true.

"Frank can commute. He can campaign every night and take a trolley to work in the morning. It's in Philadelphia. Could that be more beautiful? Right in your own backyard. You can see it from your treehouse. And they tell me you're going back to the firm. You can help him. All those friends and admirers. And special friends like us to get you off the ground. Congressman Prippet. For a start."

"Exactly who has no objection to Frank?"

"Don't you think Red knows enough to count his coconuts before he starts to beat the drum? Call Tom, Dick and Harry. Call Larry, Curly and Moe. And I know you will, Mac. You've got that fish eye on me when all I'm trying to do is help change your pumpkin into a prince."

"That's not the way the story goes."

"I know how it goes. You don't want me to call him a toad."

"What I want to know, Bascule, is why you picked him."

"Because the seat's going to be empty and he's in prime time and it's your backyard. Get Philadelphia on the blower, check with Hollinghead. Did you think I didn't know what I was talking about? Who I was talking to?"

MacFarlane tapped his pipe in the ashtray. "Educational devices."

"A million beaming kiddies behind you. What greater power than a child's love? They'll be contributing their pennies because they love Uncle Frank and want to see him win."

"Philadelphia firm?"

"Not *a* firm. A consortium. Countrywide affiliation of the finest manufacturers in the business. The best applied executive skills. No bad-guy dirty initials like NMA, AMA, CIO. Dirt from a sandbox? Never."

"There's got to be something."

"A public service for the man kids love to love."

"What do you want, Bascule, legislation?"

"Keep looking at the wrong end of the horse and you know what you'll get a faceful of, Mac. Do you have another source for money? Your boy wouldn't draw anybody even if it was steak and free beer at two dollars a plate."

"There's always money."

"Also a lot of very interested locals. Nobody hates Frank now, but they're going to as soon as he declares. A little stiletto work behind closed doors. Nobody knew what happened when the lights went out. Get those brooms moving, get that organization set up ahead of time and there won't be any way to go except with Frank."

Bascule twirled his toothpick, eyed MacFarlane, then popped the olive into his mouth and bit down viciously. "The party's not going to help," he said. "Not for a seat in a district that's in the bag. And in a post-election year when everybody will be broke? I don't think you'll want to try to get started on local money. Go scratching for it and you'll wind up with dollar bills attached to rubber bands. Every time somebody wants a favor he'll pull the snapper. Local money can become very visible, and Frank can't afford a slip. He's so prime he's almost overripe. If he makes his move and doesn't cop it, goodbye."

"He's never said anything about wanting to run."

"Then you ought to talk to him, Mac. He's better off moving under his own power than he is standing there with his hand raised and his knees crossed. Teacher might give him the Italian salute. He might think the safest thing would be to snuggle in right where he is. Then if the wrong man happens to be wearing that silk hat in January, he'll be back chasing ambulances . . . A figure of speech, Mac. We know you run a class shop."

MacFarlane put his glass to his mouth, then his pipe, then the glass again.

"Those kiddies would love to buy you another drink," Bascule said.

"I don't want one."

"Be worth it just to watch that waitress' ass."

"Not to me."

"See? No drinkee, no stickee. That's what we want . . . cleans."

Bascule caught the girl's eye and signaled with his middle finger.

TWENTY-ONE

Scanlyn lacked the bite of nails along his spine and thighs, but he felt like a fakir as he stretched out in bed in a state of near-suspension. The telephone had at last become an instrument of opportunity rather than a mocking ornament, and yet he couldn't bring himself to approach it, couldn't bear the thought of moving even vocally into that circuitous world which would be filled with pauses and sly evasions as soon as he asked solid questions.

He lay racked on sheets and a mattress and went through flaccid mental gymnastics on human perversity. The apple turned brown as soon as it was bitten into. Since he'd succeeded in changing Buffre's outright distrust into something better than suspicion, he should have been experiencing a trickle of juice into his stiff joints, Mercury finding another breath or two, flourishing his tarnished caduceus as he came down the stretch. But he stayed in bed, keeping the telephone away until the clock had wheeled enough to coincide with lunchtime in the capital and he was released from having to call for another two hours. Then he rose to rinse curd from his mouth, wash dust from the creases in his cheeks and comb his hair until the sodden thatch crowned an aging adder puffed with sleep and time and life, each spike of beard glinting.

There was a joke in it somewhere, there had to be, but he wasn't able to locate it as he fingered the loose skin around his blemished eyeballs, couldn't find the humor in his forced and discolored grin. If there wasn't a bubble or two in the phlegm, a comedy in striving toward dubious success in even more dubious ends, then there was something infinitely sad about the entire process. He was accumulating rot, in decline and nearly old, for no good purpose. And this time he couldn't conjure up the project as a be-all, think how things might be without it, because he saw too clearly how they were with it.

He opened the interior drapes and was startled to find the sun replaced by a woolly ceiling which sheared the tops of the highest mountains and gave Las Vegas an autumnal cast. Scanlyn was grateful not to have sunlight pricking his weary tissues, grateful that wool was reflected in his eyes and drifting into his mind until thought became embedded in it. He stood flexing soiled toes in the artificial fibers of the rug, declared the season closed, and slowly rocked himself into a wholesale grayness so dense that the telephone's first ring penetrated only dimly. He moved his head toward it as though he expected someone else to pick up the receiver and take the message. The second ring found him in slow motion, the third with his hand on the chill slick surface while the vibrations moved along the heel of his palm and caused the hairs on his arm to rise. He lifted the phone, looked at the squawks coming out of it, then put it to his ear.

He wondered dully why Lorry Noon had taken the trouble to try to find him, if it was a substitute sun or father she was looking for between the slats of her blinds, and he could nearly see his words entering the mouthpiece like cold gray smoke. He wasn't quite sure of his answer to her *What?*, and he had to process the *Prof?* from the other end until it became *Prof-Prof-Prof* in a diminishing cackle filtered through the earpiece. Suddenly he felt a tearing need for her, wanted her so badly that the edges of the wool began to frizz. The clouds of Las Vegas were like a gigantic waffle lid curling the borders of their lives. The word *breakfast* swam up and Scanlyn thought for one green-bright instant of lunch in the capital, found *breakfast* again, and said yes.

The Best of Our Time

He showered, watching minute particles of his person disappear down the drain, and then hacked through the clumps of stubble, pulling the skin taut as he dug after the follicles which made up the sheen of dull pewter. When he'd finished, there was color in his face, tired rose overlaid with the pale varnish of just-turning sunburn. He put on a shirt and jacket but no tie, stuffed a dotted pouf in his handkerchief pocket, and in the mirror still rimmed with steam became a nearly gay apparition peering into a frosty window, as young as he'd ever be.

The same car was available at the rental agency. This time he drove with the roof buttoned tight, the windows closed, locked into the hum and rumble while the sky stretched like an inverted field of dirty snow. In the downtown streets people seemed to be hunched against the lack of sun, drifting through arcades where their faces took on a blue-white glow. At Lorry Noon's motel the pool enclosure was deserted, the short stretch of sidewalk which began and ended in nothing empty except for a child who stood crying against the wind.

Scanlyn pressed a button and heard sluggish chimes, felt grains of sand settle against his scalp, tried the doorknob and brought his hand away smelling of rank brass. He touched the button again and there was a muted yelp from inside, the knob rattled, and she was there in blouse and slacks of dark-blue silk, her hair pulled back, eyes nearly the same color as the cloth, sea water deep-sinking and pulling him after it until the door's closing exchanged the sound of the wind for a clock ticking, a pot bubbling. He could smell coffee.

Her face was only lightly made up, but there was a red twist to her mouth when she made an opening remark which he apprehended vaguely, his answer mechanical while his eyes slid away from her and picked over furnishings worn and chipped by any number of successive lives, the room musty with constant occupancy but giving no hint as to who might live in it. He was momentarily disjointed until he found her again, blue swells shifting, eyes narrowed under soft lids he wanted desperately to press his mouth against. She mentioned eggs, and he followed her into the narrow Pullman kitchen where among the smells of coffee and melting fat he detected perfumed soap, unguents tinged by almond, a slightly acrid female essence, and felt his hands trembling with anxiety to have all those separate sources steaming beneath his palms and fingers.

Blue turned, bent until he was sure he could detect the swatches of coarse muscle banding her rump, the slight falling away then recovery as breasts settled in place with a nearly imperceptible quiver. She reached high for something, and through a gap in the cloth the intricately figured oval denting her belly winked at him. One of his eyes clicked in response, the other dropped to the hidden tangle of roots at her joints, and he had to turn away and press his rising anguish against a wall while he pretended to see something in the whorls of sand skimming the barren yard.

Then they were eating. He could feel the smoothness of egg and the coarseness of toast on his tongue, feel juices gather in his gullet. His gums tingled from coffee; perspiration dewed his armpits and fogged his crotch. The thoughts he tried to squeeze out were lost in a throbbing sensory apparatus, and Lorry Noon was constantly shuttering her eyes and tilting her head. Conversation was congealing along with the leftover eggs when she lit a cigarette and exhaled a cloud unseeded by hallucination but carrying enough bitter fumes to pepper his nostrils, the hairs whipping out a sneeze so forceful that his vision became speckled. She turned into a tear-streaked blue figure on the other side of the table, then allowed him the deadened pantomime of her laugh while he trumpeted into a fold of linen, blotted his lashes, and found he must have blown something free.

Next he was pleading for forgiveness, understanding, a reaffirmation of faith, Mr. Prolix on his elbows rather than his knees, grinding crumbs beneath the knobbed joints as he tried to include her in his expiation. Her eyes bloomed like smoked periwinkle, the rims fuzzy with the effort of trying to absorb the few nuggets of sense in all that gabble, *What?* breathed among his broken weaving, and *What?* again as he tried to explain the quest for Buffre being for her sake as well as for his own, for all of them who'd believed they could mitigate desolation simply by participating in it.

He felt a sweaty heat along his temples even as his lips elasticized nonsense, saw her recognize, accept and ignore it all in one swift intake, Scanlyn as a sack of debilitated lust not worth her attention at that moment. She was too busy trying to catch something in that medley of inane phrases, forcing him out of corners he talked himself into. Understanding flared, died, then flared again as she prodded him past another devious turning, and he thought she was about to present one of her laughs, but then she sat back and folded her arms so that they cradled her breasts. His eyes went humid.

"You mean? . . . I don't believe. You mean you're trying to get this hot cheese to join that waxworks?" she said.

"I don't see how else we can expect to—"

"You're still selling shit, Prof."

"Do you know, I'm a little tired of having everything made so reducible. Stamped and classified, the lower the better."

"If you can't smell it, your nose must have gone dead."

"After that sneeze?"

There was a flicker like the reaction of a photocell, and for an instant he looked in, only to find no one looking out, gone too quickly and leaving a surface patched with slightly rancid articulation.

"The same old dodge," she said. "A little color for contrast. And so what if he buys? You think you'll be getting anything if he says yes?"

"I hope he does. We need him."

"Sure you do. A real representative specimen. College, right? What in—philosophy, ethics, *business* administration? Doing paddy campuses, I bet. Couldn't you find a real one?"

"George Buffre is the most real thing anyone has ever tried."

"Oh hey, wow, groovy, neat."

"Laura, I can appreciate your experience in . . ."

"Can you, Prof?"

"All right. I can only approximate—"

"Can you approximate Silver?"

"I don't understand."

She moved slightly away from him, perhaps from Las Vegas itself, sidling toward an entirely separate time and world. "Silver was a player," she said flatly.

"A player."

"A pimp, a pimp."

She took another cigarette, but didn't light it, passing the tube between her fingers instead, the pink of her nails moving back and forth in a stroking motion which brought such a fresh flush of heat to Scanlyn's temples that he began to worry about exhibiting sweaty ears.

"He was a little bonus in that course I was taking, the one I thought I was *giving*—on how to save the world," she said.

"I see."

"Sure you do."

"At least I'm trying to."

"You're what Silver would have called a curiosity. He had a really great voice."

"Aah."

"You remember where we left our Little Nell, don't you?"

"I remember, Laura."

"But you'd rather not. It takes you mind off playing with yourself." She waved the cigarette at him. "Then you shouldn't have started prancing along the old salvation trail again. Everybody included, even if they don't want to be. Or didn't that ever occur to you? And you're trying to do it with a facsimile that doesn't even come close to being reasonable."

"I'm sorry," Scanlyn said. "They didn't give me a line on any pimps."

"A line on Silver." She gave him six separate thumps, uh-uh-uh, uh-uh-uh. "No way. He was the one who got all the lines. He knew where everybody in the whole world lived. Let him take charge for a couple of days and he'd have you so plugged into yourself you'd never do Straight City again. You didn't go looking for Silver; he found you if he wanted to. He was the one who ran Carl's whores, and he knew more about us than we did. That's why he came around."

"Aren't you playing with *yourself* now?"

"What's the matter, don't you love Little Nell any more? Don't you have room in the boat for her? Nobody else did either, not even Great White Hope. Good old Carl must have spread the word . . . about me being spread. They wanted me to take a leave of absence until I got my head straight—or my works. With Mom and Billy, I suppose. Or maybe with Jake; he could screw me back to good health if laying a gang bang was his pleasure." She snickered at Scanlyn. "I ate out of cans and lived in the tube for a week after Carl left."

Her expression became pebbled with the same glitter he'd seen at the lakeside, and he tried to turn her away from the wrong kind of tit for his tatty ideals by murmuring something about understanding without having to have all the details.

"You mean you're looking for a different kind of head job," she said.

"As far as I know, I was only invited to breakfast."

"But maybe I need a little help with the rent, too."

"All right."

"You're just one big total love-in. What you ought to be doing is running one of these life-line deals, collecting other people's shit over the telephone. Silver would have gone totally ape over you—he could have rented you out by the hour."

"Does everything have to break down to a trick, Laura?"

"It did for him, with the Johns hating the whores because they had to pay, and the whores hating the Johns because they could be bought. And if you couldn't see the joke, you were dead."

Scanlyn sighed for the sense of humor he lacked. "And so you had yourself a million laughs," he said.

"Flatbacking for Silver, you mean?" Her face nearly burst into coruscations. "Why wouldn't I—who else really bothered? GWH wasn't offering anything but prescriptions for numb pills. And I could see myself living with Mom, her trying to get into my clothes so we could do mother and daughter. When Silver came through that door . . . He had the whore do the talking to get me to open up, but he was the one who came in. Very slender and small-boned, not menacing at all. Arab blood from Madagascar, he said. But right then he might as well have been King Kong or the advance man for a whole street gang waiting in the hall. I wasn't seeing too straight and I might have gone out the airshaft window if it hadn't been for that voice. Missy. Rueful and slightly amused, you know, as though he knew it all. And he did. He said he'd heard about my trouble and wanted to offer his protection—the warm shadow of the raven's wing, he called it. Cool. And what could it matter, what could he turn me into that I wasn't already? If I was lucky I'd wind up some sultan's hump in Saudi Arabia. If Silver *hadn't* come around I might have gone out on the street just to make a point."

"You *might* have."

"Wasn't it about time for Missy Nunenburger and her duffel to transfer to real graduate school, move in with a one-name stud who looked like the vizier from some court gone to dust a thousand years ago? Better than talking to the rats or Johnny Carson."

"I don't need explanations, Laura."

"You don't? I thought you were so anxious to know how I got here."

"It doesn't matter."

"It does to *me*. Some of us aren't lucky enough to be running around playing bagman for those ugly, ugly friends of yours. Not that you're ever going to collect anything worthwhile."

"Maybe not."

He felt an ebb, saw himself drowning in the sea-blue of her eyes, the pupils opening nearly enough to admit him and then shutting down again as she made a slightly negative gesture with her head.

"I hate to spoil your jollies, Prof, but Silver never did run me. Not that he'd have had to stomp ass to get me moving—pointing a finger or raising an eyebrow would have done it. I simply wasn't up to it when he first came around. And I still don't know what he had in mind; he'd never tell me. He said the only thing he found worth the least consideration was what people did, not what they intended to do. Himself included. So I don't know whether it was curiosity or he was policing his district or working up a pitch, but when we did the Nunenburger story it was like slipping a couple of gears—we sort of went off somewhere else. I think he had trouble keeping his face straight when I let fly all that shit about family and school and service, but afterward he got that rueful look I told you about, like it might be dumb but it was sad, too. A sad gas, or what he called a waste of substance.

"It was like he started writing on me." She seemed to be drifting toward a different voice, one she'd had in another time. "He was the stylus and I was wax—and no phallic image intended. I didn't move in with him because he didn't ask me to, didn't even want me to be seen on the street with him because that would have put a mark on me, a kind of challenge to all the other studs in the neighborhood. Not that anyone in his right mind would try to grab anything of Silver's. So I stayed right where I was and took lessons. At least half of it was that. So much history gets lost down there. I had the feeling he thought he might be able to save some of his own if he could teach me to parrot it—what I'm doing now."

"Pretty pol," Scanlyn said in a cracking voice.

She looked at him with distaste. "The message doesn't come through in any of the books like yours. The sense of what's left when all the flash gets ground away. People squeezed into the bottom don't have much they can waste on ritual. It's a more real life, a sort of compost pile generating the kind of heat we don't have any more. As though we'd used it all up trying to sterilize everything we touch."

Yearning for any sort of touch at all, Scanlyn was hoping she'd stop, but she went on.

"Silver had to be right with it in the way he dressed because half a player's reputation is what he carries on his back. But what he spent on his vines didn't put him out of it, only gave him definition. The way he looked and acted we could have gone out in any neighborhood in the city. Put a few people cross-eyed maybe, but we could have gone. Except that Silver knew who he was and where he wanted to be. Wearing some gorgeous outfit didn't stop him from bringing our dinner over in paper bags. Some of it was pretty funky, but at least it was what everybody else was eating. Shared experience, if you want to call it that, belonging in a way we've forgotten.

"Even the whores . . . Whores are wild with money. They'll squeeze out the biggest possible score and then hand most of it over or throw it away, like the game is to get as much as they can for giving nothing. Silver probably stomped on anyone holding out, but that was standard procedure in the trade. Anyway, he had this one old girl working her way out of the life, Verna, saving to set up a beauty shoppy. That was the way she pronounced it. Only she wasn't looking for a location in some half and half *good* neighborhood. She was going to open up where people knew her well enough that they'd probably call the place Verna the Whore's. And that was all right with her because it would be her accomplishment, no matter what kind of storefront hole it turned out to be, and it would have been lost if no one knew her history. That was important, everybody knowing who you were and what you did. None of this coming home in an armored car and pulling down steel shutters against the world every night."

"Only against the junkies," Scanlyn said. "The way *you* had to."

"I happen to know Silver never did any dealing, not even in grass. And if a whore was holding when she got busted he wouldn't have anything to do with her. He used to say he was selling nature, not vice. And that was *our* great idea, wasn't it, to replace nature? Because it sweated and stank. But what were we going to substitute?"

"I want to replace poverty and rats and stunted childhood," Scanlyn said.

"Show them how they can make it if they wear the right clothes or say the right prayers. Selling what had people your age coming apart and kids mine running as fast as they could.

When you stop for two minutes, you know, when you see the whole sick scene insisting blacks want in and doing everything possible to keep them out . . . wow."

"You know it's more than that." He was seeking accommodation for his words rather than his person now, but her face was expressionless, Cassandra's mask in desert gold. "I want everybody to have the same chance," he said.

"At what?"

"At not having to go whoring, for instance."

"And this super-jig of yours is going to fix everything."

"He'll do as much as your version."

"Silver never pretended to do anything for anybody but himself. He was *his* own version, and all there was to life was what he tucked into his pants every morning. He gave me a couple of weeks of his time because he was probably using me in a way too, but I want to tell you I was so grateful he could have tucked it into me any time he wanted to."

"Were you looking for quality or quantity?"

"Is that what's been holding you back, that you're worried about coming out short? Forget it. If size was that important, they'd already have fucked us out of existence."

"You'd know more about that than I would."

"That's beautiful, the beautiful liberal dome getting himself in an uproar because he's worried about a rising on the plantation."

"They rose against you, Laura."

"Me?" She looked startled. "What's that got to do with—"

"With me . . . it's got to do with me."

His eyes filmed and he had to look away, but in one corner of his vision the blurred blue figure stiffened and then slowly collapsed until it was like a piece of cloth thrown over the back of the chair.

"There you go," she said, "that's what happens. You talk because you have to, and it always turns out that one party starts to unload on the other. Nothing personal, Prof, you're just handy."

"I want it to be personal."

"Okay, sure."

"You didn't make it up?" he asked in a tight voice.

"Make it up?"

"You might have, just to get back at me."

"Make the whole thing up, the whole *thing?*"

"I wouldn't blame you."

"Jesus Christ."

"I may sound like a fool when I talk about my work, more so to you than anyone else, but—"

"And you really want to believe the whole thing was a put-on, that Little Laura has been waiting all these years for you to drop by and send her to the land of joy? You want me to tell you you're hurting me? I'll cry a little. Anything else? Do you want me to do pigtails and socks?"

"I must . . ." Scanlyn attempted a smile but it dribbled across his lips. "God." He struggled to minimize the whine. "I can't handle anything any more."

"Really? Such a curiosity."

"There's nothing special about that, is there?"

"You bet your sweet ass there isn't . . . and not about your blubbering over it, either."

"Everything I try goes wrong."

"Ah, itsoo baby."

"It *is* blubbering." Scanlyn tried to hold it back.

"Everybody's favorite music."

"I had it once, you know, the courage or stupidity—the will, anyway, to try to change things. And still do, I think, but there doesn't seem to be anything to apply it against."

"You're a continuous wonder. Like, you're just discovering the part where it begins to go downhill, when in fact it's been downhill all the way right from the beginning."

"I still can't believe that."

"Whether you believe it or not won't change it. But don't worry, Prof, you'll manage to talk your way through. I've never met anybody better at running his mouth."

"If we can't talk to each other . . ."

"What's the difference if we can?"

"But there is something." Suddenly he felt sly. "Beyond all the things we never quite say." It was like slogging around a track without beginning or end, perpetually passing familiar markers. He took a breath to freshen his blood. "As you said, we waste so much in ritual. We should reduce things to the sublime, not to the absurd." She seemed about to laugh. "I believe in sublimation."

"Hallelujah."

"In something that matters very much to me."

"You do, huh?"

"In *your* sweet ass, Laura." He felt audacious and triumphant. She looked at him as though he'd made the most commonplace remark in the world. "I do," he said lamely.

"That changes everything." Her face was barely lit as it hung over the ruins of the meal. "Everything that Silver wrote on me. And that big deal you're trying to pull off. We can forget all about them."

"If that's the life they want, let them have it."

"I didn't say they wanted to keep on living in shit."

"Of course not. We'll fix that."

"Sure we will." She hooked a finger and thumb around the top button of her blouse, and Scanlyn felt a sort of sizzling at his temples. "We still care, but we're out of it right now."

"Haven't both of us done everything we could?"

The button slipped its loop.

"Right." She eased another button free, and when she leaned forward there were two golden oriental eyes along the border of her blouse. "You're looking to drown your sorrows, Prof."

"*Ours* . . . together."

"You'd be surprised at what they get for rent here."

"It doesn't matter."

"Like the song, right? Grooving on a Sunday afternoon."

Time collected in a rush. Sunday. Then he wasn't delinquent; he couldn't have called the capital and he was free to worship at the altar of his choice.

"I want to, too," she said. A pink-white crescent was edging into the sun-and-sand color below her neck. "From that first time I saw you I've wanted to."

Her voice was frayed with obvious deceit, but Scanlyn was able to thatch the tufts in his ears and found his deafness compensated for by sharpened vision, a heightened sense of touch. "When we first met . . ." It was too enormous a fabrication; cutting light flashed from her eyes. "That might just have been during the best period of either of our lives," he finished gamely.

"It's not coming again, for sure."

"With you, I can feel that excitement all over again."

"It's all coming back," she said emptily.

She was near enough now so that he was able to elbow the plates away and reach over to take her hands. The nails moved against his wrists and his pulse thudded when he thought of a gap a generation and a table's width distant.

"It wasn't actually so long ago," he said desperately.

"Not really."

"And there's no more difference in our ages now than there was then."

"Less, in fact."

Eliot Emeritus on the comeback trail, the campus stud, lover of lonely women, figure of shadowy power. He shifted his legs to ease himself, and when he half stood to lean toward her he was caught beneath the table's edge by an operative fulcrum which guided his mouth against hers.

Scanlyn ate his breakfast a second time, buttered tongues more slippery, the rough underside of hers flavored by a residue of toast and eggs. And there was a tickle at the back of his throat, the onset of an ache in his jaws. Symptoms of laughter. He must have found the joke after all. That was why his eyes were filling.

TWENTY-TWO

The capital's little dying on Sunday might have been a rehearsal for a time when it would be nothing but an archeological curiosity, its ornate buildings the tombs of a civilization which had struggled desperately to maintain its image of wealth and power. On Sundays there was no hint of the internecine fury raging between the huge departments and agencies. Windows were blind, interiors vacant except for guards and warders and occasional archivists burrowing their way through subterranean passages, and only the temples were left open. There was a holiday air. Family sedans replaced official cars, buses were parked like ranks of sleek roaches, and thousands of visitors formed vividly colored serpentines.

It was Frank Prippet's city in any form, at any time, but on that particular day the haze of sunlight was magnified to a golden shower in his eyes. The summons had come at last, an invitation to one of Eric Krug's legendary Sunday brunches. The doors of inner circles were about to open, the silences of inner councils about to be made clear. He barely noticed the ache in his calves as he strutted past the sweep of lawn and the immeasurably grand wings of the white building which had once sheltered him long enough to have his hand shaken by a President. He muttered a senseless jingle about the good old days becoming the good new days, saw himself in dark suit and quietly figured tie, most of the gray touched out of his hair, as a figure of at least ministerial proportions. And privileged. While the tourists moved in a slow and carefully supervised stream through the main gate, Prippet was allowed to enter through a slot in the fence. The guard at a side door found his name on a printed list and passed him through respectfully; the young man assigned to escort him looked serious enough to be carrying a gun. They went through corridors furnished in a two-hundred-year-old medley of time, a sanctuary sealed off from the hum and shuffle and drone of voices on the other side of the walls.

The young man opened a door for him and withdrew. Prippet's jubilation dipped slightly. He had expected walls of Colonial blue or red, white trim, neo-Hepplewhite. Instead there was faded yellow stucco, rattan pieces with worn cushions. What had once been a good rug was nearly worn through. Glassed doors overlooked a garden, but the view was blocked by a lattice overgrown with faintly sinister wisteria. He felt a damp silence, heard his clothing rustle, his bones pop. When he arranged himself on a sofa facing the interior door he discovered his hands prissily in his lap, and flung one arm across the sofa's knobby back instead.

He knew the pose was a trifle formal, but the occasion demanded dignity. Investiture, he was sure, and more binding than any scout's oath. A simple word, pressure of hands, an understanding between clubmen. Running for Congress was all very well, particularly when the outcome was so secure that he wouldn't have to expose himself to electoral whims, but real satisfaction lay in being touched by an executive wand, in being selected when there were no visible rules governing selection. A sour man would have said it was about time; Prippet had a philosophical shrug ready if any apologies were made. Krug had invited, after all, not beckoned. He was probably aware that he was dealing with someone who had options. Prippet wouldn't rub Krug's nose in it, but he did intend to make it perfectly clear that in taking the assistant directorship, he was turning down another opportunity—if the A.D. was all it was. There was every indication it might be more; there were voices on the wind, rumbles of sweeping change. He'd have to be careful not to show surprise, deference without humility. Whatever it was, he had it coming to him.

The glass doors scraped open and he turned his head sharply, his arm curled along the sofa in a parody of guilty embrace, chin nesting coyly in his own shoulder. It was a gardener, and Prippet made a face until he looked past the dark glasses and discovered an unmistakable resemblence to Eric Krug. He was wearing a baggy corduroy jacket, a shirt with an open neck, stained yellow shoes. In his hurry to rise Prippet made the error of turning into the sofa, one arm flung out stiffly as though to hold Krug away. Then his knees became twisted and he had to make a complete revolution, a dervish unspiraling, before he was able to get to his feet.

He straightened his tie and pocket handkerchief when Krug turned his back to shut the doors. "Ah, Eric."

"Humidity," Krug said. "Like Africa." He kicked the door. "Everything stuck."

"It probably should be planed."

Krug's head swiveled. "To fly?"

"It's a tool . . . for wood." Prippet made fists as though gripping a plane, and Krug drew back slightly. "You'd have to take the door off, of course."

"Then the flies come in."

Krug gave the door a final kick, brushed his hands and settled at one end of the couch. Prippet sat at the other. "Well, isn't this pleasant," he said.

Krug nodded speculatively, and a doubled Prippet bobbed up and down in the dark lenses. "Are you hungry?" Krug asked.

"Oh yes."

Krug pressed a buzzer on an adjoining table. He removed the sunglasses, then sat back and pinched the bridge of his nose, the skin of his eyelids wrinkling around not entirely clean nails. Using his fingers like tongs, he pulled his head forward and with his eyes still closed fumbled in a pocket for his regular glasses. He put them on, took a breath, then gave Prippet a broad smile. "So," he said, "the time comes."

"Well Eric, they say that all things come to he who waits. Ha ha."

"A funny saying." Krug's smile disappeared.

"It isn't meant to be, not exactly. I only mean to say I understand the necessity for patience. You often have to wait your turn for your share."

"Do you know something?"

"What?"

"No, no. Something about why we are here."

"I guess you'd call it more intuition than knowledge. After all these years . . ."

"I could not believe it otherwise. When someone says security, we know exactly what that means."

"I'm sure you do."

"Without security there is no freedom to act."

The beginning of Prippet's reply was lost when the inner door opened and a grizzled Negro wearing a houseman's jacket entered. He walked with a high careful step, as though he had to give each joint time to articulate.

"Good morning, Alvin," Krug said. "What is it today?"

Alvin's lips were wrinkled, colored like the juice of a dark berry, and Prippet couldn't understand the rasping reply.

"Cheese-cheese or cheese-strawberry?" Krug asked.

The answer came from a deep old furry place. Krug tilted toward Prippet. "Cheese Danish or plain? Or roll and butter?"

The head as stark as an anvil turned to fasten on Prippet. "Plain will be fine," he said.

"For me, croissants. Sugar?"

"One, please."

"He brings the whole bowl."

Krug dismissed the Negro with a nod and watched his ghostly cakewalk to the door. "From the time of William Howling Taft," he said. "He was the twenty-seventh President."

"So he was."

"Astonishing."

"He was also Chief Justice of the Supreme Court," Prippet said.

"I mean Alvin. Astonishing. But now . . ." Krug made a little settling gesture and beamed. "Good news."

"Ah ha."

"You are expecting *something*."

"It's only that sense developed over the years, Eric."

"You are sure?" Krug looked roguish. "A little bird has not been flying too close to my window? A tell-bird?"

"Eric, I'm sure you know I would never solicit . . . I have never wanted to know anything you weren't prepared to tell me."

"I am prepared now. To tell you to be happy. This troublesome business, this Flipover, is finished for you. We have more important things for you to do."

"I've felt . . . That's very gratifying to hear."

"It is what you have been waiting for to come, like the saying."

"And waiting willingly."

"We finish this . . ." Krug made a chopping gesture with his hand.

"I wouldn't want to leave anything unfinished, even if my new duties have priority. I'm perfectly willing to follow through on Flipover—after hours, if you'd like."

Krug thought for a moment. "Why not?" he said. "Begin today. Immediately."

"That soon." Prippet smoothed his lapels. "No rest for the wicked, ha ha."

"Do you think he is so bad? I have the feeling only that he is out-of-date." Krug smiled and closed his eyes. "Not *with it.*"

"I, ah, suppose not."

"Call him today, yes. Tell him."

"Oh I will."

"But still you do not wonder why. That makes me think."

"Well, if that's what you'd like me to do, Eric." Prippet was fighting the impression that something was missing, the finger of God not quite touching his. "I don't want to seem—" he began.

"The business of the risk," Krug broke in. "You are thinking of it, I know. That I said there was nothing to be gained without it. But only up to a point, my friend. There appeared to be too much risk, and we began to be not absolutely sure. Not absolutely, you understand, although the idea was sound. So we decided, and it was done like lightning. Astonishing."

Prippet tried to look impressed.

"One minute there was nothing, then in a day and a little it is completed, certified, the entire poll. They are like lightning people." Krug peered at him. "You didn't know this?"

"A poll."

"They ask a little people and know what everyone thinks."

"No . . . no, I didn't."

"It was a secret, absolutely. With no one to find out. And the information is positive. No one cares this way or that way. This black man is so unimportant it would be better not to bother. And in another fact, there is just a little bit of caring that he should not join us instead of that he should. Interesting."

"Yes. Yes, it must be."

"And you also, of course, avoid all further risk. The warrant, we give that. It is our donation, finished. He goes as he pleases. And if there is more upset, an entirely new thing begins. To those who maybe will complain, we explain that there is a technical error, a new review is necessary. They forget. If there is a leaking of any of the business, we do not confirm anything. But we can tell one part unofficially to observe how we tried, and we eye-wink the other to say that they should know better." Krug clapped his hands. "Arranged."

Prippet was staring at Krug and trying to put a variety of thoughts together, but the only clear one he had was that Krug hadn't even bothered to shave.

"You have an excellent idea," Krug said, "to call Scanlyn today. Tell him he must stay long enough to prepare a . . . a disengagement. Not too sudden. What we can avoid, we avoid."

The door opened and the houseman backed in, turned in

a stiff but practiced gesture to close it again, kicking his way tremulously toward them, his back bowed under the weight of an all-silver service. He performed a curious maneuver somewhere between a split and a curtsy, stiff-legged as he slid the tray onto a table. Prippet looked dully at the elaborately embroidered initials on the napkins. Alvin had brought two croissants but only one Danish. There was a series of tiny popping sounds as he crossed to the door and slipped through it.

Krug poured coffee for himself and bit into a croissant, the crumbs flaking his chin. "You are pleased," he said.

"I'm to understand that the entire project is dead."

"Like the nail in a door. For us it does not in reality even exist any more. There is only your part to terminate. Quietly but quickly, so that you are ready for the new business."

The very small hope which stirred in Prippet was nearly a conditioned reflex. He poured coffee.

"This time, no risks for anybody," Krug said. "If anything is mentioned, it will be to say what a public service you are performing. It will be seen, my friend, your concern that there should be care and protection. People will be touched deeply in their hearts."

"I presume we're talking about an operation for the Bureau, Eric."

"Yes, certainly—*your* Bureau."

Prippet nibbled on his pastry. It was surprisingly good, and he was hungry. He finished it and wished that he had another. Krug had begun on the second croissant.

"Did that bastard Stirby have anything to do with killing Flipover?" Prippet asked.

"Him?" Krug was startled. "He has nothing to do with anything. What he says now cannot matter, and if he says it against the new business, he is putting his boot in his mouth— with holes in it, so that he will be biting his own toes."

Prippet twisted his napkin into a ball and clenched it between both hands. "I was asked to make a commitment to that project, Eric."

"You did it very nicely. He appreciates."

"And I appreciate that, but I would have liked to see something more concrete come out of it."

"All the credit is to you."

"I would hope so, after all the work I put in."

"But of course, my friend. And now there is new work, new recognition, a new opportunity to catch the eye of importance."

Prippet had a sudden urge to spit in Krug's. He watched him purse his lips to release a puff of gas. "I do hope it has more substance than the other," he said.

"Substance, emotion, everything. Let me tell you . . ."

Krug removed his glasses and wiped them with a napkin. As he launched into a description of the Bureau's new specialty his voice was the same but his eyes had collapsed into those of the imbecile mouse. Prippet took advantage of his momentary blindness to stick out his tongue at him. And then, as he began to link the sometimes eccentric swing of Krug's words, the light dawned and grew gradually brighter until it was a hard cold glare at the end of the tunnel.

If advance information was any indication, Bascule of Bull Run indeed had connections. And Krug didn't seem to know anything about him. Prippet used a silver spoon to add sugar to his silver cup. No doubt rank had its privileges, but a man who had options had unlimited prospects, and a man who had Bascule behind him had options.

TWENTY-THREE

Back in his own room Scanlyn lolled through the evening after, a euphoria of decompression where he tried to remember how long it had been since he'd held anyone really young in his arms. And she'd nearly been real, too, a definite transition in moving away from the littered plates in that overused living area and into a bedroom where there were hints that Laura Nunenburger might be wrapped around that purse he was so anxious to ransack. There were no carnival dolls or college pennants or metal-framed photograph of parents who blessed everything she did and by extension everyone she did it with, but the books and pictures must certainly have been hers. He took the touches at face value, afraid to look too closely because he might discover a total person and be forced to recognize the gap between the love poems of his youth and the stark biology of what was about to be served up. Better to concentrate on unwrapping, turning back the coverlet, getting to bed before molt set in.

If she lacked the abundance necessary for go-go bouncing, there was enough for his hands to fit around, places free of creases or wrinkles or signs of wear. Except perhaps interior. A little roomier there than he'd anticipated, certain contortions needed, knees stiff and toes arched. But she knew when to help, and they found the proper heave and fall until he was able to stand on his own head and spit out the stale glut, less than might have been expected after so long a fast.

Scanlyn sighed because the old accumulator had lost so much capacity, the old supply line become so clogged with rust. And yet life stirred even in the mechanized draft of the air conditioner. His lazy kisses became a spate. He busy-lipped a snail's trail to the grotto, old habit perhaps, or some dark act of contrition to absolve the tongue of its lies, feeling a hazy reservation about being eye-high to what had been such a public accommodation. But when he got right down to it he didn't find any traces of anyone else or even of himself; all the fluids were hers. He did discover a responsive button and was able to bring everything to a distinctly saline boil, so that she jumped, bucked, then lay back with a guttural rumble like a tide receding.

Time passed, turned into time for turnabout, play which might have been one of the features of rent collection, the agent servicing the pull which opened doors and kept the wolf away. When she said she didn't do it with everybody, Scanlyn didn't care whether or not he believed her and simply lay back, seeing the ceiling dimly, wondering if the vertical shuttle would leave him ringed in the color of her lipstick, then forgot everything while what felt like a rosebud danced him fizzing. It was more than practiced, done with what he had to admit was expertise, a sword swallower gulping down fires as well.

They drifted into gummy sleep, got up to take a kinky shower together, though not enough so to arouse new expectations. Afterward, dry and slightly fragrant, he passed a few minutes when he thought what she didn't do for everyone might include waiving compensation for the sake of old times or even simple affection. It was a very few minutes, only as long as it took her to notice and correct his direction, more than a hint conveyed in her eyes and gestures. He left what he thought was proper on the plastic mantel of the artificial fireplace, and she gave him a big sloppy kiss.

As anticipated, it had been a grapple between losers, with no way to judge who'd had the best of the three falls, but that unpowdered puff had dusted his tensions slack. The poets might call it ecstasy and the scientists read it from meters—Scanlyn wondering how well a silver electrode substituted for an enameled finger as love's suppository—but whatever the name of the response, it had sprung him from self-sequestration. He was back to feeling enthusiasm for the project even though Lorry Noon had rattled him into seeing what she saw. He hadn't the advantage of her alternatives, couldn't dance his cares away in public or jiggle them quiet in private—and both for profit. The work couldn't be worthless as long as he did it in the best possible way, and tomorrow, when he placed a call to the probably bilious-colored instrument Prippet used as a hot line, he was determined to demand explanations, tables, charts, and like a mad navigator suing for the queen's jewels, lay them all at Buffre's feet.

Then, as the lumpy quilt of clouds became stained an inky blue, he had his second phone call of the day. Still suffused enough to be picking over the tailings of old dreams, he thought Lorry might be calling to offer a few only slightly acid words, and was distinctly annoyed that Prippet had presumed to break into his day of rest. But his thoughts gathered quickly enough for him to decide he might as well take advantage of the opportunity, and he ticked off his needs in a voice deliberately made crisp to contrast with the mewling at the other end of the line. Prippet asked if there was anything more he had to say. Scanlyn's no was frozen, imperious. Prippet then laid out the facts of life in a few dozen words which effectively fused the cable connecting them, Scanlyn left in an acrid haze of melted neoprene and oxidized copper. When he sputtered, Prippet gave him the Ubangi dead rubber lip of officialese. Scanlyn said he wouldn't stand for it, and received a mean invitation to sit. He hissed at the pauper's wit but understood that he was being *told,* and no mistake possible. Prippet's tone had all the confidence of a man running an errand for the king. He let Scanlyn know what he was expected to do, and hung up.

Scanlyn was left holding the dead phone while something drained from every pore and orifice, the panicky flight of the

Holy Ghost from a disintegrating vessel. Not to him they couldn't—do it. Not leave him so little. He nearly strangled the telephone while he tried to force a high-level squeak out of it. But there was nowhere Eric Krug could be reached or was expected; it was Sunday, after all. He wondered how he could possibly have mistaken the day, how he'd missed hearing the mechanical rocking of bells in some simulated adobe mission tower that morning. Missed the mantillas draped over minis and hip huggers, the creak of plastic boots as pink knees bent, the string ties looped like Peter's double keys.

Now he stood watching the electric prayers of Las Vegas' vespers. Only the demented would be looking for salvation; the practical were asking God to bless their luck. And who would speak for Eliot Scanlyn; what would he find to say to Lorry when he kept their date at four o'clock the next morning? Body language wasn't likely. But if he did happen to find inspiration the rent was at least paid. *House* rent; he didn't know about the other. Better a light supper, a little wine and fun-fun, the high point his exhibiting the rug they'd pulled out from under him. He'd weather her laugh, admit his errors, expunge all the formulas he'd ever believed in. Choke a little, cry a little, as he clapped the erasers together afterward. If he wiped twenty-five years from his brain he could be as young as she was. Lobotomy; lift his mind rather than his face, an amnesiac coming out of a quarter-century fog. Who am I?

No, they could not, *would* not be allowed to do that to him. Up Prippet's dry whistle with his faggy-toned instructions. Scanlyn would ease Buffre down, all right, in the same way he'd ease a shell into the breech of a cannon. He'd load, ram, lock and leave Buffre to his own inevitable percussion. Perhaps even canister shot showering those living saints of the Chamber of Commerce. His eyes were stinging again.

The phone rang, sonic drought replaced by a flash flood carrying everything before it. This time it was George Toussaint Buffre piping a cool voice. There were a couple of things he thought they ought to get straightened out before Scanlyn tried to put the deal together. A merger of bankrupts. Scanlyn kept his voice even, winding up internally for the table spinning he and Buffre would accomplish in tandem, but when Buffre suggested that Scanlyn come out to the house he was indignant. They'd meet right at the hotel. Separate but equal revenge was out of the question.

Scanlyn put on a tie to spruce his wilted pouf and went down to the lobby where he was indistinguishable from the other good cannibals observing the Sabbath. He wished all the men chancres, the women toxic discharges, then had a chill moment wondering what he himself might be incubating, safe from hoof-and-mouth disease only because his feet were the one part of his body which hadn't been exposed. But at *her* rates? She could afford the world's best gynecologist—or guarantee luxury clap, bejeweled spirochetes. If it came to a choice, he preferred the latter because he'd be dead before they had time to reach his brain.

All those people. If the day or the season didn't matter, if every palace had the same tables and the same whores, what was the point of the staggering variety of their arrivals and departures? And if he had tried to expose the futility of it all, if he'd torn his clothing, riven his cheeks, and stood on the nearest table and shouted every truth he was reasonably sure of, they'd have listened attentively while they gathered a little guilt to spice their bland sinning. Not that his act would have lasted longer than thirty seconds even if he'd scraped his bag of truths clean. Woe to the leader or shaper who created situations with no elements of profit for any of the principals involved. Excepting landlords. He tried to remember if it took a week or ten days for gonorrhea to show.

His puling was the only discordant squeak on that roundabout, his thoughts preachy because he was too purged for even visual lust to be more than a reflex tic. He was overreacting, and when he saw Buffre come through the door dressed like Caliban looking for a place to happen he felt a distinct lurch. Buffre's velvet bells were split to show crimson insets at the cuff, his chest covered in beads and shredded leather, and he wore a medallion the size of a small dinner gong. Scanlyn was outraged at the cool-dude dress-up after all that talk about looking as straight as possible. Which didn't happen to matter any more, but which did matter until Buffre was told it didn't.

Scanlyn extended his hand gingerly, had it ignored, and turned the gesture into a quizzical tug of the ear while he looked around the lobby as though searching for a quiet place to talk business. If he could give the impression that Buffre was some sort of entertainer and he an entrepreneur. He took Buffre by the arm, felt him pull away, then tried to steer him with his palm, only to end up stroking the air when he slid off. Perhaps everyone would think they were demonstrating a dance step. Scanlyn ground his teeth, at last succeeded in talking, and nudged Buffre down the corridor and into the casino, where Scanlyn extended an arm as though revealing the white man at his most secret and revolting ritual, praying for money. Buffre took it in without any visible reaction and himself seemed to be ignored in spite of what Scanlyn thought was an ear-catching swish and jangle. He couldn't believe that Buffre was capable of dressing like that on his own; he must have borrowed the clothes from De Berg.

In the cocktail lounge Scanlyn chose a table because barmen were unpredictable and waitresses seemed willing to put up with anything. The eye the nightingales were giving them wasn't nearly as cold as he'd anticipated. Sizing them up—and what imagined yard of flesh was Scanlyn being measured against? He sneaked a look at Buffre to see if he was indulging in the old plantation fantasy of the lady of the house looking for an earthy cultural exchange. He felt shame, clenched his jaw further, was nevertheless relieved when the waitress seemed to be color-blind as she served the drinks. With his nose nearly buried in the glass he congratulated Buffre on his astuteness in suggesting that they get together that night, the meanwhile feinting long enough to keep him away from whatever was on his mind until Scanlyn had a chance to oil the tumblers of his own. Oh, the pity of it all, Scanlyn slightly wounded but terribly sincere as he explained to George, the name rolling easily in their new fellowship of betrayal. He more than explained, rewriting the entire history so that no base motive for personal gain could possibly be attributed to his part. Scanlyn was the well-intentioned simpleton. Buffre looked at him as though he were still waiting for some kind of news, and Scanlyn pressed on to fuss with the background until it was perfect, then unreeled the snake in all its violent colors, pleaded for understanding, and signaled for another round of drinks.

This time Buffre didn't look at or through Scanlyn but fixed him with a probe which mushroomed behind Scanlyn's eyeballs until they were pinned to the dark face looming over the carnival dress and out of the blurred background of teased hair, pinkness and near-nippled breasts, out of the clink of chips and ice, the wailing of players, the blare of show music. It was the direct examination of a man wondering if the person he was looking at had the least idea of himself. And then Buffre made a gesture of supreme weariness and disgust.

Whereupon Scanlyn breathed his scheme into a pinwheel.

"You're going to fix it," Buffre said after listening.

"We can create a terrific stink out of this."

"Create one. Like you have to."

"Use it to profit, then. Not only for ourselves, George—for everyone. Not that there's going to be anything in it for me . . . not after I swear to all the details. But you might even be able to make some money by selling the story."

"You think so?"

"Get them by the shorts, make it hurt. The way De Berg says."

"And that's all it would come to." Buffre pushed his drink away. "No."

It was an unacceptable answer. If rough justice was going to be accomplished, they needed each other.

"Like Abel needed Cain," Buffre said.

Scanlyn couldn't be that easily discarded, an unplayable piece of paper, a worthless IOU. "Will you tell me something?" He paused. "But that's silly, to expect an answer before you know what the question is. Will you tell me if you'd have taken the job?"

There was a glimmer of pain in Buffre's eyes.

"If all the proper conditions could have been arrived at," Scanlyn said.

"Come *on*. You never had the least intention—"

"If."

"What does it matter?"

"To me . . . personally."

"It does?"

"Very much."

"Then you go figure it out." Buffre gave him a small, impenetrably black smile.

"All right." Scanlyn felt on the verge of a new set of tears. "If that makes you feel any better. But what are you going to do to get out of that kitchen you're in?"

"I quit that job."

"Figuratively speaking, George."

Buffre made invisible lines on the table with his stirrer. "Maybe I'll check out that rumor that a so-called political process still exists."

"Are you serious?"

"Maybe I had that in mind all along."

"You'd run for office?"

"I just might."

"Not in those clothes."

"Hey, no?"

But in the proper ones, dressed for the occasion . . . There were sprays of light. Scanlyn saw assassination from within the palace, black thumbs on the jugular. Oh, it would serve them right; it was even better than the original idea. And Scanlyn could . . . He looked into his empty glass for a role he could fill.

"If I'm going to be wearing a collar—" Buffre began.

"Don't doubt it for a minute."

"Then I'll pick it out myself so I'll be sure to know who I belong to."

"George."

"Yeah."

"It's a great idea. You can do it. And I'd like to help."

Scanlyn got a withering look. "Please. I have a plan." At least he was getting one. "I think I can get the project back on. I'm sure I can."

"You think I want that *now?*"

"Of course not. Even before I'd told you about this new development, I'd thought about making a strong corrective move—you know, using a little leverage. But I know you wouldn't want it that way, my forcing them to accept you. And in fact you wouldn't have been nearly as effective if I'd had to use pressure to get it through. But I *can* make it happen."

"Well go right ahead."

"I will . . . and then we'll turn it down."

A spectacular twist, two shotgun blasts right to the head, one barrel for him and one for Buffre. All he'd needed to get back on his feet was those two drinks. He pointed to his glass when the waitress came by. Buffre shook his head.

"You see it, don't you?" Scanlyn said. "I won't let on I've said anything at all to you, just go in there and really sell them on the great mistake they're making. They'll listen, too. I'll go tonight, see the man tomorrow. I can be back tomorrow night with everything we need—guarantees, documentation, anything you want. Save them until you're ready to announce, and then we'll make it all public. You had an invitation to sell out and turned it down. Though I don't think we should bring in the first part, about leaving the country. That wouldn't be fair." The phrase twisted Scanlyn's tongue. "I mean it would be better if you didn't show any malice. Refuse with dignity . . . you have another, better road."

"I've got more than one other."

"Of course you do. This is only the best."

When the waitress brought his drink Scanlyn decided she was really a very sweet-looking girl.

"Look, I don't care *what* you do," Buffre said.

"I can appreciate the way you feel, George."

"I mean I don't *care.*" There was a touch of weariness underneath Buffre's anger. "I had enough of people putting me in their plans. I'll work out my own."

"I know, I understand. I only want to help, to work with you."

"No thanks, man, no thanks at all."

"George."

"You are a mother, one sucking mother."

"I don't think I deserve that." Buffre looked stony. "There are no strings at all to this. I'll wrap up the package and then you do what you want with it."

He tried to look reassuring, a combination of smile, wink and body English which sent him twitching. Buffre's eyelids moved up and down slowly, wiping the image.

"One thing," Scanlyn said. "You have to promise not to take the job."

The eyelids stopped, and instead of the slot or scoop Scanlyn was usually allowed he was treated to full round, dark centered in dark and spinning away.

"What?"

But Buffre seemed to know the answer, his face beginning to crinkle in lines oiled by a hundred years of secret smiles.

"Not take it," Scanlyn said. "If you did, it would spoil everything."

"Oh yes." Buffre let out a long hoarse whistle ending in what sounded suspiciously like a hiccup.

"It's the only way."

"I promise." Buffre held his lips straight, threw his head back and looked at the ceiling. "I do promise."

Scanlyn studied him for a moment, drank, then glanced at his watch. "I'd better see about reservations."

"Yes, yes."

"And I can be back tomorrow, late. Say the same time, in the lobby? I'll leave a note at the desk if there's any change in plans."

"Yes, yes, yes."

"This is what we should have done right from the start. I don't know why I didn't see it before."

"Like I said, I had the idea."

"I wished you'd told me. We could have saved a lot of time."

"Not knowing which way you went, you know."

"Well, I'd better get going now." Scanlyn tilted his glass.

"Maybe I'll stay and finish this." Buffre tapped a nail against the drink he'd barely touched.

Scanlyn couldn't find the waitress, so he left a bill on the table. "This ought to cover it."

"Don't worry about it."

"Tomorrow, then."

"Right."

"I know we can do it, George."

He held out his hand and Buffre hesitated only an instant before taking it. "Well you go get 'em."

He gave Buffre's hand a last squeeze, then stood to find the air rarefied by bourbon. But he could handle it, off again to a world larger than cards, dice and slot machines, sweeter than the clouds of perfume from the overdressed line waiting for the dinner show, and far more important than the ham and boob Sunday suppers represented by the butterflies' circling.

The girl at the travel reservation counter told him there was no direct flight to Washington, perhaps with a hint of reprimand in her voice for someone who might be connected with the public weal wanting to arrive at his desk Monday morning still unmentionably stained. But she could get him to Chicago —changing planes presumably earning an indulgence—and from there to the capital. There was a seat open in first class, on the Champagne Buffet, she told him in a slightly thrilling voice. He thought that just might be good enough.

There was no answer when he tried to call Lorry. He went around to the revue lounge and found it hadn't opened yet, then arranged for flowers and a note asking for forgiveness and a twenty-four-hour raincheck. At the desk he collected his attaché case and paid his bill but told the clerk to hold the room, chuckling over the good story it would make later, Buffre's first campaign headquarters in a tower built on sands of propinquity. Upstairs he changed to the straight-cut suit he'd arrived in, decided he could get by without shaving. In the full-length mirror, carrying his case, raincoat over one arm, an Eastern hat on his head, he was something to be reckoned with. The slight sag he was beginning to feel gave the proper touch of gravity to a face which otherwise might have had too much holiday smirk. Little did they know what was coming their way.

The sickle of cabs at the hotel driveway was like an automated production line; out came a couple quivering with age, eyes defiantly bright, and in went Scanlyn. The walls of mad light on the boulevard penned him for a few minutes, then peeled away to leave him under a tunnel of sky illuminated only by glareless lamps hung on overhead brackets. The airport tower floated like a ghostly green box, the main building arranged in onyx rectangles scrawled with neon. The cab rank was busy, people arriving and leaving as he had, as he was.

He checked in at his airline and declined to surrender his case. There was time for a drink he didn't really need, buzzing slightly before he'd even taken off. He sat at a bar open to the concourse and marveled at the scrambling procession which changed form but never substance, an oddly complementary feedline to Las Vegas' rigid form and lack of content. He'd have to get Buffre out of there as soon as possible. A million plans to be made, the meanwhile his stomach growling and the bourbon a shade too sharp. By the time the announcement of his flight came through the gabble on the loudspeakers he'd sipped the glass dry.

There was an edgy moment at the gate when Scanlyn became confused with the combination of his case, finally able to get it open and show them he was carrying nothing more threatening than fraud and deceit. He stepped between the sensors of a machine which inspected the metal in his mouth and on his wrists and in his pocket. Afterward he felt less secure because he was reminded that some desperate loser could have blocks of plastic strapped around his waist in a mad plan whose terminus was Lebanon or a million dollars swinging from a parachute evaporating into the night. And there seemed to be losers enough coming aboard with him, glum sports who'd left what they'd brought and were bringing back nothing they could exhibit; others with a speculative look, gauging their chances in the next assault; couples who seemed to have come on the Weekend Special, THREE WHOLE NIGHTS AND TWO DAYS, TRAVEL + HOTEL + BREAKFAST + PLUS. Even people with spent children—and why not, when the dream of luck could be made into a family outing leaving Chicago after work on Friday, arriving for the last dinner show, and back in time for work Monday morning still bedazzled?

But now it was over, and they were loaded into the rear as though they were no more than ballast to keep the forward compartment in trim, their hostesses harassed drovers. Scanlyn's nearly did curtsies, welcoming him to the Buffet in throaty tones which implied a dozen mysteries. He tossed the attaché case negligently into the overhead rack, sat down, thought a moment, then recovered the case and stowed it next to the seat where he could keep his foot against it. He didn't want to begin his dramatic demands with an explanation of how he'd lost ten thousand dollars and some of the best specimens of work of major government artists.

The last of the herd was prodded aboard and a curtain lowered to screen them off. There had been more than one seat available on the champagne fantasy; Scanlyn's compartment was only half full. One of the flying houris wanted to know if he'd like something to read, shuffled sophisticated amusements printed on slick paper. In the rear they were probably fighting over *Life, Reader's Digest*, perhaps racing forms. He was asked to buckle in, the stewardess making a half-flutter suggesting she would be only too happy to help, tee-hee. The rear-mounted engines began to whine and the plane lurched toward the runway, its wings like silver paddles floating above the ground. Everyone sat a little tensely while power built up, and then they were slung down the strip and rockily airborne. Las Vegas fell away to a blaze, diminished to a spill of bright pebbles, then a glowing spot. Scanlyn wished them all luck and a good, good night.

Now smoking lamps were lit, the belts in careless disarray.

He felt like Caesar in one of those old epics screaming with color; let the procession of haunches, ribs and steaming joints appear, let them try to tempt his jaded palate. He was given a split of domestic champagne, forgettable pâté and caviar. The wine was cold and he was thirsty; a second split appeared. Remotely Spanish *gazpacho* was served. The buffet proper was non-succulent ham, roast beef and chicken, a two-fifty delicatessen platter from yesterday. But there was champagne in deed as well as word, Scanlyn only having to empty a bottle to qualify for another. The stewardess shot him a sidelong glance at the third, and he stared her down. Cheese sandwiches and soft drinks in the rear, but everything which extra fare could buy for the front-running cavaliers. When he was offered a second portion he said yes and made a sound like a cork popping. He ate too much too quickly, but got some slight relief from a few vinegary gas balloons. Champagne was better than bicarbonate. He had another bottle, coffee and a chocolate-colored pastry masquerading as a mousse. After the litter was cleared away he wished he had a cigar, then realized he might be just a little drunk—and perhaps not a little.

His head fell forward and nearly encountered his stomach. He let it slide toward the window. Was there a moon, a Judith? Kat? He felt his lips quiver, suppressed a giggle. The man in the Noon. Whoopee. But faint, expiring. He settled comfortably. The tiger eats, slakes, rests against the next day's hunt. They were so high, traveling along a band of stars. He smiled and closed his eyes, floated even higher, then away.

Chicago was a dirty sunrise over a lake planked in ancient gray wood, Washington the soiled ribbon of the Potomac winding past an Arab-looking city of white stone stained by rain. The tiger's stomach was still distended, his stripes had turned grimy and he had a fierce headache. Scanlyn was the only creased and stubbled example in a contingent of snappy early birds wearing his hat and raincoat, carrying his attaché case, solicitors who'd stumbled awake in the Midwestern dark to get first pull at the federal worm. They did a quickstep across the apron together, coats flapping and hands to hatbrims as though afraid they might be recognized, then were absorbed into the crosscurrents of what seemed to be a large part of the world hurrying along the main concourse.

In the men's room Scanlyn inspected the leaden growth sprouting on his cheeks and chin. There was an electric shaver guaranteed to have been sterilized by ultra-violet, gamma, beta, and perhaps even death rays, but he didn't trust its villainous look. He washed the face he wished didn't belong to him, tried to pull the wrinkles from his clothing, and looked hopelessly for signs of that senior statesman he'd seen in his hotel-room mirror. There was no time to go to his apartment and change because he hadn't any chance of seeing Krug unless he caught him before he was locked into his schedule. As for his chances after that . . . The eastbound flight had been a reversed time pleat in which he'd traveled more numbered than real hours and in the process lost the campaign manager and king-maker in various descents. Even an oblique look at his prospects sent what could have been a bag of shot shifting around his insides.

He took a few knees and elbows in the scrimmage around the taxi stand, gave up and settled for the airport bus. Downtown he stood trying to flag a cab while the fine rain found its way into every opening and spread a ring of damp around his neck and ankles. Now that the peak of the rush hour had passed and the clerks and secretaries and other fill no longer cluttered the streets, black cars of state whispered past, men in the rear seats looking out with keen blind eyes. He finally had to catch another bus, a low-pressure steam cabinet crowded with passengers who had the guilty look of being late. They were his people, in a hometown which was staffed rather than lived in, and he was only one more of the unnumbered among the numberless. Even the crowds he was part of were constantly changing their make-up; he was just one more bent and streaming fragment in a group hurrying to a honeycomb designed expressly to produce a blizzard of paper which dimmed outlines, stuffed vulnerable chinks, lay in protective drifts around the walls.

He revolved through a door and into the huge entrance hall of a labyrinth where even the Minotaur might have become lost. Scanlyn knew his way down the synthetic corridors, past the dozens of offices whose white shingles helped the people inside to know who they were. Eric Krug was hidden within a maze of glass partitions, and as Scanlyn moved from receptionist to receptionist he was often on the verge of colliding with his own image. At last he was brought to a young man with brutally short hair, inspected bleakly, and told that Mr. Krug was not available that morning, that day, and very probably not all that week. The secretary pushed his glasses up the bridge of his nose with an index finger, a gesture which might as well have had his thumb anchored, his other fingers spread.

Scanlyn sighed for the days when the government had had motion, personality. Now it was nothing but a conspiracy of palatines. He kept his voice kind as he asked to have his name taken in on the off chance that *Eric* might have a moment to spare for something rather important. This produced a frown, a rattle of knuckles against the top of the desk, then a second evaluation. The secretary nodded curtly, went through the door, came out looking suspicious and said Scanlyn had exactly five minutes.

Krug's office was a classic of simple American grandeur, done in authentic antique just-folks suggesting that money wasn't everything—there was power, too. His single photograph was enshrined on a glowing Colonial table, the President with an arm around Krug's shoulder, his beaming cheek close to his. Scanlyn couldn't find enough charity to envy either man. Krug looked small behind the huge desk; Scanlyn knew that he kept an embroidered footrest beneath it so he could screw his chair up to maximum elevation and still keep his feet on something solid. Now he sat with his hands linked across his stomach, eyes watchful behind his glasses.

"So, Eric," Scanlyn said. "So."

Krug smiled faintly and waved at a chair. The window behind him gave on a closed court where there was a miniature garden of dripping ferns, a backdrop as quiet and timeless as a rain forest.

"You're making a mistake," Scanlyn said.

"You should do as you are told, Totty."

"I did—and had Buffre biting. He shows all the symptoms of having the fever, Eric. You'll be able to use him."

"You are that concerned that we should? Or that you will be able to get something back. But it changes, and now he is not useful enough."

"Because of a quickie poll? I can't believe you're that unsure of what you're doing."

"Who is ever sure? At least we are probable."

"And on the basis of something like that you're willing to risk a reaction?"

"From *him?*"

"If he gets the ear of the right people it could be very embarrassing."

"The wrong people. The miracle would be for him to find the right people. And it is supposed to be your part to avoid too much reaction."

"I'm only afraid he's going to blow up."

Krug wiggled his fingers in the air. "Little pieces."

None of them were big pieces even when they were whole. The machinery had grown so gigantic that no one had enough stature to jam the most minute gears. Scanlyn was on the edge of an enormous doubt, but he had a few last promises to keep, and tried again. "This isn't going to do my credibility much good."

"They forget," Krug said.

"You could make them remember, Eric. You could gain a lot of credit for the administration if you simply made the gesture. There are people who'd give you the benefit of the doubt if you brought him in. Show them you're at least willing to make the pretense of being open-handed."

"There is no pretending now. All the considerations have been given, and no is the only possible correct answer."

"It's a mistake."

Krug leaned across the desk. "Do as you are told, Totty. Go back and tell him what terrible people we are, that he would not like to be with us. Tell him he is better off making bombs to blow himself up. Tell him you only stay with us to be a spy inside. Be nice with him, that you are not the one most hurt."

"I didn't know you were that concerned, Eric."

"For you."

"You're right that he could tell quite a story." Scanlyn paused. "And he has De Berg for collaboration."

"Better you leave the passports forged from no one knows where with me, and the check—now uncertified. Who has them could be arrested."

"I could tell quite a story myself if I had to save my neck."

"What would you save it for?"

Krug's expression wasn't unkind, and Scanlyn had to accept the question as fair. If he had too much to say, he'd destroy any value he had. And if the project wasn't reinstated, nothing he had to say would have any value to Buffre. He'd found the other side of that edge of doubt, and the real fall was beginning.

"It should not be made necessary to tell everybody your action was unauthorized," Krug said. "Not unless this Buffre becomes foolishly loud."

Lorry Noon was right. It was downhill per second per second, but not through fresh white powder and piny air. Down the slag heap of inconsequence, a yellow wind whistling in his ears.

"You are clever with talk, Totty," Krug continued. "Manage this so you are not too damaged and we will find something where it is not so necessary to be credible, something not too important. You do not look well. It is many years, and you should have easy work now."

The quiet of the office had created a sound lag, words confirming Scanlyn's realizations seconds after he'd arrived at them. "Not too important," he said. "You mean make work."

"There is always something needing to be done."

"An obscure corner whenever I get in the way. Would you prefer I resigned?"

Krug gave him an avuncular smile. "How could you be in the way?"

Scanlyn struggled to find an answer but only grew angry. What he'd intended merely as a half-threat suddenly seemed like the only possible course. "Never mind your preference. I think my own should be resignation."

"But how foolish. Another gesture?"

"There isn't any audience that I can see."

Krug turned in his chair and waved at the ferns. "They fall into the ground and make coal," he said. "And the little animals in the ocean, they make an island. We drop what the birds drop and something grows out of it."

"Something absolutely worthless."

Krug shrugged. "That is to be seen. The work at least is not worthless, with the salary. And for you in only a few years, the pension."

Scanlyn was stunned. Had it been so long, was he so close? And the closer he came the tighter the tether would become. "It's not work I want any part of."

"Nobody wants to do. Then who will?"

"Someone else."

"But as well as us, my friend?"

"I hope not." He opened his case, took out the envelope and gave it to Krug. The last few grains of Las Vegas sand fell on the desk. "Not because I'm worried about being arrested," he said, "but because I'm no longer entitled to have them. I don't work here any more."

"You are really serious?"

"I don't have any choice."

"We would keep you, you understand. It is not that important to us."

"I understand perfectly."

"To become a teacher again? *That?*"

"I don't know."

"Or write a book of memories of government. People read it after you are dead and wonder who you were."

"I think they wonder how anything at all has survived this

long." Scanlyn put the case in his lap. "I'll send in a formal letter."

"It is foolish."

"But necessary."

"And that Buffre? Better you should finish, so that he does not go shouting to everyone with all your lies. A quiet ending, at least."

"I have to go back to pick up my things anyway. All right, I'll tell him."

"You are not such a terrible fellow, Totty. There are commissions, consultations."

Scanlyn was at last able to say what everyone had said to him. He wanted to have it sail forth with dignity and clarity, but what came out was nearly a mumble. "No."

"As you wish." Krug's expression stiffened.

"Exactly."

He stood, adjusted his clothing. Krug did the same, not much taller than when he'd been sitting, and they looked at each other. Then Krug put his hands behind him, and Scanlyn locked his on the handles of his case. The ferns dripped a moment or two longer, Krug raised his eyebrows, and Scanlyn left.

The secretary glanced at his watch and gave him a very unpleasant look.

The clerk at the desk of his apartment-hotel greeted Scanlyn in the usual way. His room looked as it did every day when he came home. He didn't know how he'd ever be able to weigh his nearly twenty years in that city, when at their end his presence or absence was still an equally negligible factor. He sprawled in a chair and listened to street sounds which were more like the buzz of fretful voices than a metropolitan clamor.

He was bound to miss it all—the wrangles and pettiness, the constant scrabbling for better perches, fawning for the ears of men of the moment. He would miss the judicious doubts, the heavy silences, the eyes which saw only what they wanted to. He wished that he could muster a heavy sense of drama terminated, that he could feel as dense and lightless as a star after supernova, but in fact he was light-headed with what might have been fatigue, the aftermath of drink or just simple relief. He had given it all over to someone else to do or try to do, his responsibility not shirked, only passed on. There would be any number eager to pick it up, and not merely enthusiastic amateurs who believed they could change things. Nearly everyone believed that. They arranged meetings and formed committees and wrote petitions, came from all parts of the political spectrum, wore tennis shoes and hardhats and beards; and all believed that both government and life could be improved. The national myth sizzled in their bloodstreams. But the man who would continue from the point Scanlyn had left off at—or from the point he had failed to pass—would be very different, a true believer whose greatest faith was in his own ability to mold the world to fit his vision of it.

And Scanlyn was not so played out that he was prepared to say it couldn't be done. He was willing to believe it was possible, that all things were possible. Anyone who cared to should be allowed to make his point. As long as it wasn't him. After years of public service to his own ego he was at liberty. Teaching, perhaps, or maybe another book. It needn't be important, only sustaining. The race was over—if there had ever really been one, if it had ever been more than a series of qualifying heats, the final field never assembled—without his ever having really been included in it. He'd always lacked some element of what it took, the breath or muscle or spunk. But that didn't matter now. He only had to go at the pace at which his deteriorating sinews took him. It might be a longish way, and it would certainly be downhill, but it didn't have to be a violent drop.

There wasn't any need to rush toward a particular direction. He could begin at any speed. He had to go back to Las Vegas to collect his things, to tell Buffre—to tell him to do what he thought was best, whatever mattered to him. Scanlyn cared, but remotely; someone else would have to provide the passion. He'd even lost his spite, discarded the idea of the beaten breast, the catch in his voice, as he made the whole rotten mess public and flashed a light on the night crawlers. It wouldn't have been news in any event. They fed with such a tearing sound, it had to be apparent to anyone who cared to listen. Let someone else stamp upon the spade and take corrective action.

He was at liberty, and though nothing was free, it was at least available. No one had to be alone as long as his level of tolerance was low enough. There were worse prospects than those he and Lorry Noon might face, two losers dancing sporadically on a single leg—as long as what money he had to spare lasted. And what if she learned to tolerate him without it? He felt a silly flood of warmth at the idea. He was romanticizing again, and next he'd be tinkering with love, What a chain of hiccups that would bring from her. *I love you*. But what if she stopped laughing long enough to look closely, to see how naked and filled with need the old fool was? She might be touched. They were father and daughter of the same experience, after all, partners in the same failure. A shared joke was better than any other, salvation bearable *au-pair*. It was possible that he could *make* her laugh, and when he did he was sure he'd find the vein which had been trampled down but was still waiting to be tapped, pure quicksilver. There was nothing to lose if he discarded all the old combinations and played a new number coming out—and there just might be a fortuitous bounce.

Scanlyn looked at his watch. She'd be home by now—perhaps not alone, but home. And perhaps she'd be alone, with the scent of his flowers filling her room. He heaved his grimy person erect, rubbed his eyes, shook his head to clear it, went to the telephone and dialed long distance.

TWENTY-FOUR

T he Monument had turned nearly black under the rain, and Frank Prippet's face stood out distinctly from the background, an unlikely pale bloom. He shuffled his papers with a vicious snap while the staff at first waited patiently, then grew restless when he remained buried in the wisdom-gathering process. The room was blue with Mac-Farlane's pipe smoke, and even Stirby appeared to be on the verge of slumping by the time Prippet seemed to be satisfied that a certain psychic transference had been accomplished.

He fixed them with a frosty glare. "Flipover has been canceled," he said, "and while it's being phased out . . . Yes, John, I thought you'd be pleased by the news. You've made your feelings clear enough even when there was some concern that they might prejudice our overall effectiveness. But we all understand your absolute compulsion to make your views known, and we know that Lew is equally compelled out of loyalty. So I'm sure you'll both be relieved to know that your self-indulgences haven't been a factor in bringing about the cancellation. I'm sure you wouldn't want to feel guilty over jeopardizing an operation everyone else was so committed to."

"Damn well I'm glad it's over," Stirby said.

"And I'm glad to tell you, John, that the decision was an executive one based on developments which are currently privileged information. If I'm ever authorized to divulge it, I will. But you don't need all the details to follow the line we will all take if we're asked anything about the project; this Bureau has never had any conceptual or operational responsibility for Flipover. Which is in fact true, of course. That line happens to be official all the way to the top of the ladder. You're free to disagree with it if you don't mind having your fingers severely stepped on."

"I don't know anyone dumb enough to want that tin can tied to their tail," Stirby said.

"If intelligence was the prime motivation here, I think we would have avoided a certain amount of friction. But let's move on." Prippet rattled his papers. "None of you will have anything to do with Flipover's phase-out, so we should be able to count on everyone's participation in our new assignment. I can't see any conceivable objection to it, but if any of you happens to find one through some incomprehensible quirk, do your campaigning on your own time, and outside this office. I insist—repeat insist, not recommend—that whatever staff support work is assigned, it be carried out absolutely within the guidelines established. The bulk of the decision-making will be executive, and Mac and I will handle it, so I don't think you'll find yourselves called on to make any compromises. Just do what you're asked to, and keep your soapboxes out of the office. Understood?"

"Check," MacFarlane said.

Allenstein cleared his throat. "Right."

"Our new program will be a chance to perform a real public service. I want it utilized to the utmost. It may seem peculiar, but what we're actually doing is responding to a situation created by radical organizations. If radical isn't too mild a word . . . I mean pressure groups more interested in making noise than constructive criticism. They've got their teeth into something I thought even *they'd* have the decency to stay away from: children. I've always felt that childhood is one area of national life which ought to be safe from self-serving meddlers, but the spoilers aren't deterred by the same sensibilities the rest of us feel. Right now they're taking out after people who've dedicated themselves to children's welfare for years."

"Is this that baby doctor again?" Stirby asked.

"If you can manage to wait until I'm finished, John, you might get most of the picture. These groups are after people who are so responsible they hire expert consultants and employ the finest research facilities. And not just to keep children happy, but to make play rich and educative. They're under attack only because some few, some very few, of their products are being misused due to a definite lack of parental supervision. They're being accused of risking children's safety for personal gain."

"Crap," MacFarlane said.

"Mac's right. I cut my finger on a piece of paper this morning." Prippet held up his pinkie and they craned to look. "You can't see it from there, and certainly it isn't serious. We've all had paper cuts, haven't we? I don't think that brought any of us to the decision that paper was dangerous. We didn't hold the manufacturer responsible because we mishandled his product. And yet this is exactly what these nuisance complaints come to. Let it be perfectly understood that we're not for one minute going to ignore them. We're going to investigate each and every one. Ample funds for testing and research will be made available, and if we come across the rare instance where we're able to verify a case of some fault in the mechanical process of production, we'll make certain that it's corrected. But not in such a way that the spoilers will find out and be able to jump on these people and smear them further. We do have the authority, make no mistake. And we will apply it impartially . . . but discreetly. Understood?"

"I can't say I do," Stirby said.

"What I'm trying to make clear, John, is that I can see a chance for this Bureau to play an educational role of its own, helping children by bringing parents back to the responsibilities they've been neglecting. If something as simple as a piece of paper can be dangerous, think of any object in the hands of a child who hasn't been properly instructed in its use and who isn't being supervised. The threat to safety isn't in the products under study but in the permissive atmosphere in which they're

used. It's up to us to issue guideline advice and recommenda-
tions. Is that clear now?"

There was a moment of silence while MacFarlane
scratched his chins and Stirby creaked.

Then Allenstein stirred. "I'm not absolutely with you in the
area we're talking about," he said. "Is this some kind of recrea-
tional or playground equipment?"

"Every state has regulations covering public facilities,"
Prippet said. "We're not trying to infringe on their authority.
This is a wide-band operation covering educational devices of
every type."

"Talking books," MacFarlane said.

"You mean these complaints are about kids getting paper
cuts from books?" Stirby asked.

"I don't mean anything of the kind. I said wide-band;
everything a child plays with."

"Like toys?"

"If you must put it that simply, John. Do you have an
objection?"

"To *toys?* Hell no."

"This isn't a frivolous challenge, John."

"Nor did I say it was." But he was grinning broadly.

"And what is it you find so amusing, Lew?"

"I was, ah, thinking how pleased my own kids would be to
know what I'm doing. I hope we get to bring home some samples."

"For testing?"

"Well no, Frank."

There was a strangled humming sound in Stirby's throat.

"I don't think we should compromise ourselves by accepting samples," Prippet said.

Allenstein's smile broke at the edges and a brief whinny
escaped.

"There is nothing funny about this," Prippet said. "I'm
warning you . . ." But his lips twisted in an irrepressible rictus.
"This is no ha-ha joke."

The office filled with snorts and snuffles and quavering breaths, each laughing not only in relief but at the others, savoring his own secret. Howard MacFarlane wheezed until he shook loose a deep rumble just as an errant ray of light broke through the clouds and touched the tip of the Monument.

TWENTY-FIVE

I n the evening the rain stopped.
At Aquarelle there was a smell of wet metal from
the railings of the terraces, and the huge umbrella the
MacFarlanes sat under gave off an odor of sodden cloth. Mac-
Farlane wore a belted safari jacket and a blue yatching cap, his
wife was shingled in lilac chiffon, and they watched the capital
settle into a polluted aquatic twilight.

"I won't miss this weather," he said.

"You just never let yourself get used to it. And I don't see
where Philadelphia's that much better. Cold." The gown rip-
pled with her simulated shiver.

"Gets hot, too."

"Well there you are."

"But not this humid."

He pushed his glass forward and she poured a cocktail from
a hammered-silver shaker which whirred a fragment of "How
Dry I Am."

"I told you I'd give it one term," MacFarlane said. "That's
enough for anybody."

"You know I appreciate that you came here at all, darlin'.
It's just a pity it wasn't under circumstances a little closer to the
level you deserve. A man with your connections . . . he talked

you into something, I can tell you, getting you tied down at what's not nearly your potential. You are simply too generous is what it is."

"Wouldn't have if you hadn't been so anxious to come."

"Because I expected something a sight different than it has been. People here need to believe your position has the merit of their respect."

"I think you mean they need to know if you can be used."

"Well I would like to ask Mr. Frank Prippet to throw the first stone if he can find himself without blame in that department. We were painted some pretty pictures which turned out to be different from what they were represented." She settled in her chair, and the dress fluttered like a colony of angry moths. "At least maybe now that you're finished all that silly business with Totty Scanlyn we can relax a little."

"You can never afford to relax in this town."

"*We* can't. I ought to know that after three years of watching other people have all the fun, going around looking down their noses just because you happened to be too good-hearted."

MacFarlane sniffed.

"I suppose that means they don't count, Howard, they don't measure up to that Main Line crowd of yours . . . which only seems to be able to talk about how they've missed the train entirely what with the railroad going bankrupt. And then there's that bicentreniarial thing that's not even going to be held for another five years."

"Bicentennial, Gloria."

"Whatever they call it. Philadelphia reminds me of that play we saw with all the Scotch dancing, except those folks only had to wait *one* hundred years to come to life." The shaker ground out its dry lament. "Even with what we've lacked I would prefer to be here where there's at least something worthwhile to talk about and do."

"You'll be busy enough, Glory. We'll put you on one of the committees for Frank."

"Go around pushing on doorbells, I suppose."

"We'll hire people for that. You could be in charge of giving coffees during the campaign."

"And have all kinds of trash coming into the house?"

"Not necessarily." MacFarlane looked unhappy.

"But Howie, what you're doing is getting yourself all involved again for that man's sake in what I doubt anybody else is going to think matters very much."

"It could be important."

"A *congressman?*"

"Try to do business with one of them and you'll find out how important he thinks he is."

"Not a freshman."

"Frank's different. He knows his way around."

"Around you, he does."

The music ground down as they emptied the shaker.

"None of this is for publication," MacFarlane said.

"When is it ever?"

"I'm serious. Talk could do a lot of damage right now."

"I under*stand.*" The scales of the dress quivered. "You know I want to do anything I can, darlin', to help *you.*"

"It can't hurt. There's a connection or two in it."

"I just can't see how you think it's worth all the fuss."

"This might only be the beginning. He's not too old."

"And not all that young either." She sipped her drink. "I suppose we could open up some kind of teensy canteen. It might be a little fun at that."

"Good idea."

"And maybe all us girls could wear cute costumes . . . or straw hats at least, skimmers with our own special colors. Like red, white and blue."

"That's a good combination."

"Prippet we're for you. If you think it's only the beginning, Howard . . . like how long would it be before he could run for something else, governor or senator or something?"

"Not even two years."

"Well that's encouraging. What we ought to have is a slogan, to rhyme with his name. Frank's . . . blank?" She giggled. "Now you know I didn't mean that, it was just fun. Frank's . . . a real Yank. That's more like it. Or Prippet. Prippet's with it. How about that?"

"Pretty good," MacFarlane said.

"Why don't you shake us up another little batch and we'll do some more."

MacFarlane looked at his watch. "Getting late."

"Just a half," she said. "And then I'll get us something scrumptious together."

"You can bank on Frank."

"That's *clever*, darlin'."

"Make Frank your plank."

"Oh my. It's a pity we have to start off so far down with him, Howie. I bet if we put our minds to it we could get him elected practically anything."

"One step at a time."

"I'd be just a silly old girl without you, wouldn't I? You go on in and whip us up a little more source of inspiration and we'll see what else we can do." She threw back her head. "MacFarlane's my darlin'."

His jowls quivered as he got up, and when he went through the doorway his shoulders were shaking. Just then the rain began again, a fine drizzle which sounded like a hand brushing over the surface of the umbrella. MacFarlane's wife pulled her chair in closer, inspected his glass and drank what was left in it. The illuminated federal buildings in the distance were smudged and indistinct.

"I lawn," she said aloud. In the deepening gloom the dress moved like a dark and choppy sea. "Why, he could be *President*."

The room which John Stirby called his study was windowless and so small that he wasn't able to take more than a few steps in any direction. Even then he had to edge around the furnishings, a cheap metal desk enameled the color of sand, and a swivel chair and a bookcase, also of metal. The bookcase was sprung and buckled, and the figure topping Stirby's bowling trophy was aslant, preparing to loose his discolored bronze ball down a tilted alley. The walls were bare except for a nightstick and badge mounted on a plush shield which had lost most of its nap.

It wasn't a quiet room either, and distorted sounds from the rest of the house filtered in, but it had a telephone on a separate line which no one else in the family was permitted to use. Stirby had just finished using it to talk to Harvey Timmins, and now he was trying to think, a finger in each ear to block out the throbbing rock music one of his children was playing.

Timmins had been pleased to hear of Flipover's cancellation, yesiree glad they didn't have to worry about dragging that dead cat around any more. He couldn't see how the Bureau's new specialty would hurt, not unless Stirby got himself shot up by some wooden soldiers. Then his voice was slurred by an artificial chuckle and he said it didn't look as though it was likely to do them much good either, and it was a damn shame because that shuck-all Stirby had gotten himself saddled with hadn't come up with something with a little more meat to it. They weren't looking to go from the frying pan to the fire, but if Prippet was going to run the show the way Stirby had described, there wasn't going to be much of a chance for anyone else to get his licks in. If he was too quiet his folks would get to wondering where he'd disappeared to, and it wouldn't make Timmins' support of his candidacy much easier either, what with those knotheads at home who'd wanted somebody else in the first place. Timmins could hold his own people in line even if it had to be by the trotters, by God, but those others would be steaming their brains trying to think up a foolish scheme to catch other fools' eyes.

Timmins had paused, and even with the phone clamped to one ear and a finger plugging the other, Stirby had been sure he could feel the music vibrating in his sinuses.

The man they were going to run for lieutenant governor had to be a figure of authority—and Timmins had no doubt that

Jack Stirby was exactly what the doctor ordered—but what they had to have was a strong figure even during what might be called the warm-up period. Timmins knew there was no way to actually take charge of anything, not with the way the gang in that town kept *any* good man down, but there ought to be something could be gotten hold of. Timmins' breath had whistled for a moment or two, and then he'd gone on to say that one thing damn sure was that where there was smoke there was fire, and it looked to him as though Prippet had been given some kind of garbage to bury—which he would very likely manage to do assways, if Timmins knew his man. If that fool was so bent on telling everybody everything was all right it could only mean something was awful wrong. The first thing they ought to do was find out just what that was.

Stirby had felt as though he were treading water while he listened to the rasping sounds and what might have been the click of teeth on the other end of the line.

Timmins was trying to remember if there was anybody back home involved in making kids' things. If there was, they hadn't given any noticeable party money, so it didn't appear as though there was any worry about stepping on toes there, at least. What Stirby had to do was get hold of something strong, whether it was toys or whatever the hell. In fact, that wasn't such a bad angle—protecting the kiddies. If somebody was breaking the law they shouldn't be allowed to hide behind some cheapjack bureaucrat. Let them know Jack Stirby wasn't the man to let family interests get lost in some two-bit shell game. Of course, whoever it was told Prippet to cover up a stink might not be too happy to have Stirby digging it up. It didn't matter what Prippet got caught at, but it would be better if the government itself wasn't embarrassed. No point in making hard feelings if it could be avoided. He was sure Stirby would find a way to do it right if he just thought about it.

That was exactly what John Stirby was doing, and developing a headache. The music stopped abruptly. He took his fingers cautiously from his ears, then ground a knuckle into his palm as though trying to break down the substance of his conversation with Timmins. He cracked an ankle against the chair and swore because there wasn't a place left in the world big enough to turn around in. With Flipover dead he ought to have been able to coast awhile or even to crow a little about having been on the right track all the time, but they wanted to put him right back in the nutcracker. When he wanted to speak up for what was right they sat all over him, and now they wanted him to stick his neck out for something he didn't give two hoots about.

There didn't appear to be any way out of it. Harvey Timmins was nobody's fool, and whatever he thought ought to be done was probably correct. Even if Stirby had had contrary ideas, he was in no position to argue. Timmins had been the one who'd picked him up when that bunch of liberal wet nurses got him fired, and now he was supporting him for a big job, one Stirby was absolutely sure he was the man best qualified for. He was lucky to be on Timmins' team and he'd damn well better play by Timmins' rules.

He sighed, picked up the telephone and dialed. The line buzzed several times before there was an answer.

"I want to speak to Mr. Lumney," Stirby said.

"Who is this, please?"

"Big Jack." Stirby had insisted on a code name.

The line went dead for a moment. "I'm sorry, ah, Big Jack, Mr. Lumney isn't available right now. Perhaps you could call tomorrow."

"If I have the opportunity. And if the matter will wait."

"Could you give me an idea of what it is?"

"I'm only authorized to talk with Mr. Lumney."

The line went dead again, and then Lumney came on. "What is it?" he asked crossly.

"I would have preferred to call at another hour," Stirby said, "but I am not always at liberty."

"I'm on my way to bed," Lumney said.

"I regret you were not able to effect any action over that last subject we discussed . . . that certain fugitive. But that type doesn't ever change its spots, Mr. Lumney, and I don't have any doubt but that the opportunity will arise for you to put him where he belongs."

"You mean you called me up to talk about yesterday's fish?"

"I certainly did not, sir. I wanted you to know that my Bureau has begun an investigation which may turn up some very interesting things. We're going after people who make toys."

There was no response from the other end.

"We are just beginning," Stirby went on, "but I already have very strong indications that—"

"For Christ sake."

"No more surprised was I, Mr. Lumney. As I was saying, there are strong indications that there is an organization involved whose name I do not happen to have at the moment, only the initials, and even they are not absolutely clear. What I am afraid of is that certain aspects of this investigation may become suppressed, though you can be sure not through any effort on my part."

"What organization? Is it subversive?"

"Well I know we can never be too cautious in that regard, but what I had more in mind was enforcement. Certain standards are likely being ignored."

"We don't handle standards enforcement unless we're directed to," Lumney said.

The music began again and Stirby had to put a finger in his ear.

"I intend to take whatever I find directly to the public," he said. "And I'm sure that's going to be plenty. I simply wanted you to be aware of the situation in advance, Mr. Lumney."

"I don't see any situation, Stirby."

"It is only just developing, and I wanted to assure you that I will keep you current with events as they happen to occur. There's certain official parties—or at least one party—who I believe is going to make an effort to camouflage the facts, and I am not of a mind to allow that to happen. Our children are entitled to all the protection at our command."

"Look, it's late. Why don't you leave a message when you get something more definite?"

"I'll certainly do that, and I don't expect that it will be very long before—"

There was a click. Stirby frowned a moment, then slammed down the receiver, edged his way around the furniture, tore the door open and bellowed into the house to shut that goddamned thing *off*.

Lewis Allenstein scraped the leavings from the plates into the sink and listened to the garbage-disposal unit throb and suck like a living gut. His wife came into the kitchen and put her fingertips against her temples.

"Is she all right now?" he asked.

"She's just never really accepted the change, Lew, and seeing Dave and Myra got her started all over again. She can't understand why they couldn't have brought Mindy with them, and now she misses Mindy and misses home and misses—"

"*This* is home."

"I know you keep saying that."

"You'd better start to believe it."

"It might be easier if I knew anyone who really lived here."

"The Allensteins do." He gathered the silverware and began to rinse it. "Now that we've got a maid I don't know why you can't get her to stay a little later when we have someone for dinner. Can't you pay her triple time or something?"

"She won't stay out any later than nine, I've told you. She's afraid to be out alone after that."

"I wonder why."

"Probably for the same reason I wouldn't like to be." She began to load the dishwasher.

"But I don't know why what's-her-name should have to worry. Phronia, is that it? With all I hear about soul brothers and soul sisters, there's no reason she should be afraid of getting mugged in her own neighborhood, is there?"

"You've been writing for that big dummy too long, Lew."

"All right, Bea. But couldn't we at least leave this mess for her to clean up in the morning?"

"She'd be talking to herself all day tomorrow. It's practically done, anyway."

"The maid tells you how to run the house?"

"The maid was not my idea. I never said I wanted one."

"Do you have to put down *everything* I try to do for the family?"

"Do *you* have to feel so threatened every time anyone makes a comment? I simply don't need a maid every single day. I'd rather do some of the housework myself—it's more rewarding than having coffee with a lot of other dislocated women trying to pump their husbands' jobs up while they tear everybody else's down."

"They're no worse than the tea gang at Nowhere U, are they? Are you forgetting all that orange pekoe you poured? Didn't seeing Dave and Myra bring back the good old days?"

"They don't look too unhappy."

"Would you rather be doing what they're doing?"

"I didn't say that."

"What *did* you say, Bea?"

She closed the door of the dishwasher and pushed a button. There was the sound of a miniature cloudburst from within the machine. He went into the living room and lay on the sofa. His wife came in and began checking the ashtrays.

"I did that while you were upstairs," he said.

She slumped in a low chair on the other side of the room. "Anyway, it was good seeing them again," she said.

"Far, far away."

"What?"

"Maybe from the other side of the moon. I had a feeling of remoteness, as though they were talking about a strange place I'd never heard of."

"The other side of the moon isn't so strange any more, Lew. Washington's a better example of what you mean."

"Like Dave sweating out Assistant Head of Department. What is he talking about, what does it matter? What would it matter if they made him *Dean* of that diploma mill?"

"I don't think we'd be here if they'd made you Assistant Head of Department."

"I was grateful when they made me an *instructor*, Bea, but

that was back in the days when I couldn't see the anthill for the ants. How about a nightcap?" She shook her head. "Me neither. They're all anthills, and the country's full of them. I know they serve a certain function, but by comparison . . . Like I can picture a guy here, not any great somebody, who could close most of them down simply by signing a piece of paper. Withhold funds, cancel research programs, revise accreditation—who knows what? He puts his name at the end of a directive and they're out of business. That's what matters, real muscle—clout."

"Like what they clouted you with."

"Not me. A certain Francis Prippet may have been pleasured with the shaft, and maybe Stirby had to take a couple of inches of leftover."

"But not Allenstein."

"He's alive and well and living where the action is . . . and likely to get better."

"We're back to living in that meantime. We've never been out of it."

"You can't say I didn't try when I was supposed to be trying, Bea. I had to practically put my head in The Creature's mouth to keep him quiet, but I can guarantee you that nothing he said or did got Flipover canceled. It was a good project, a good idea, and I wish it had gone through. I honestly do. Give some of these heroes a chance on the trapeze and they won't be so anxious to criticize. But I'm not going to lie to you and say I'm not happy to be out of that box. This new thing is a lot safer."

"Alive and well and living where it's safe, as long as you don't go out after nine o'clock."

"*That's* my fault too?"

She closed her eyes. "It was for such a little while it looked like something was happening," she said. "This whole hive of drones, and those dumb charts you kept bringing home. And then it actually looked as though there was going to be a change and you were going to help pull it off. But it was for such a little while."

"Do you really think Buffre would have made such a big difference?"

"Something has to, Lew."

He stretched his neck and arched his toes, a prone shrug.

"Only *one* Allenstein is living here," she said.

"The one who brings home the daily bread, slightly flavored with his sweat. And there are times when that's bitter, I can tell you. Am I getting something so great out of all this? A snazzy sports car, a fancy bit of stuff on the side? Big things like a maid I thought would help you out."

"Don't make it like that, Lew. There are other things you could do."

"Not things I *want* to do. And I have the right of first refusal. There are a lot of lives I'm not in the least interested in living, and as long as I keep this troupe together, there isn't any reason I should have to live them. I still truly believe this whole schmear can get better, Bea—and maybe even really worthwhile."

"With toys?"

"They're transitional."

"To what?"

"Depends."

"But not on you. Then who does it depend on? You never see or hear anybody here; there isn't any direction. What they laughingly call policy just sort of grows, like a fungus. Who's actually in charge, Lew? Who's the man to see when you want to sell your soul?"

"Please, Bea, not the rhetoric."

"Let's go to bed."

Allenstein looked at her.

"Right now," she said.

"That sounds like let's have a cheese sandwich."

"Take my mind off it, shut me up. Do me."

"I don't like that, Bea."

"All right, I'll take an aspirin instead."

But she didn't move, and a clock in another part of the house gave a single quavering stroke.

"Are you at least going to try to make something out of it?" she said.

"Out of what?"

"The toys. Something really ought to be done about them. There are still dolls with inflammable hair and things fingers and toes can get stuck in, or that shoot your eye out. And a lot of them do psychological damage."

"I suppose we'll cover all that. Well sure, if we turn up anything grim . . ."

"It must be worse than grim if they're taking the trouble at all."

"Maybe it is, maybe it is. So we'll fix it, Bea. Okay?"

"At least you won't have to be carrying that dummy around with you."

"No way."

"And how about the other one, that Fancy Dan you were telling me about?"

Allenstein frowned. "Tufton? I don't see what his interest could possibly be." He pushed up his glasses and rubbed his eyes. "I need some new clothes. Nineteen sixty-five professorial isn't exactly what you'd call eye-catching."

"Remember what happened with the emperor, Lewis."

"I remember, helpmate." Allenstein yawned. "No," he said, "I can't see where Tufton would fit into this new thing, but if we can just keep our noses clean and get on *his* team . . ."

"He's a someone who can make a difference, is that it? He's one of those people things depend on."

"More than on Prippet or Stirby."

"Oh God," she cried, "why don't we just go to bed?"

This time Allenstein didn't look at his wife, and the unanswered question hung until it was like a veil dividing the room. They sat on separate sides of it, both looking drawn and overtuned even in the soft lamplight.

Frank Prippet stood in his pajamas and tried to peer through the streaked and pebbled glass of his dining-room windows, but all he could see of the capital was a few faint, wavering lights. He sighed and went into the bedroom, where his wife was already settled in one of the twin beds reading a gardening magazine. Her hair was held back by an elastic band and her face filmed by a cleansing lotion which gave her skin the dull coarse look of an untanned hide.

"Still raining," Prippet said.

"It's been a miserable day."

"The paper said it would let up tomorrow . . . for all they ever know."

"It would be nice if it did."

"I hope the weekend's clear."

She turned another page, then put the magazine down and looked over at him. "I'm still not very comfortable about that," she said. "Going away with people we don't know. Mrs. Bascule sounded very nice on the phone, but I wish we'd at least met them at a party or something."

"They don't stay here permanently," Prippet said. "I think you'll agree it will do us both good to get away for a little while, Betty."

"Of course it will. But if the Bascules are friends of the MacFarlanes, I don't see why they weren't asked along too, to help break the ice."

"God save us from a long weekend with Gloria." He made a face. "I understand they also know the Hollingheads in Philadelphia."

"Well I wouldn't say that we did, Frank. I don't think we'd even call the Hollingheads acquaintances."

"Since they aren't coming along either, we won't have to worry what to call them. I don't see why all this matters so much. This is probably not strictly a pleasure trip, Betty, though I'm sure we'll have a very good time. There are a few things Bascule and I should talk over."

"But if you don't know him . . . ?"

"We know *of* each other." Prippet's smile was sly. "Did she say Virginia Beach?"

"It's too early for Virginia Beach. Nothing less than Sea Isle, Georgia . . . and by private plane. They must be very well off."

"I can assure you there's money available to them. It's about goddamn time—for us to be moving in that kind of company, I mean. When I think of all those other sons of bitches who've been getting theirs all along . . ."

"I wish you wouldn't get yourself so upset."

"I'm sorry. But you've got to admit we've been taken advantage of."

"You've worked very hard, dear."

"For everybody else. But things are going to be different from now on." His mouth set in a sullen down-curve. "They're not going to be able to use Prippet any more. They can find another sucker to do all the dirty work for a bunch of worthless IOU's. It won't be long before it's 'Will you support this and that, *Mr.* Prippet' . . . or Congressman. Wait and see how easy they'll find it to say 'please' then. And I know enough about some of those bastards . . . Forgive me, Betty, but I know where a body or two is buried. They'll sweat, I can tell you."

"Frank, you really shouldn't."

There was perspiration in the creases of Prippet's forehead, and his eyes looked slightly out of focus. "They'll know who we are then," he said.

"Nobody deserves recognition more than you do."

"We'll both have it. All these years when they've treated us like washouts, like some kind of hick comedy team."

"It hasn't mattered, dear."

"Don't think I don't know what you've had to put up with. And Krug, too . . . he's worse than any of the others. Wait till he comes crawling around. I know what the women in this town are like . . . and you've had to drag that fat-mouth Gloria around with you everywhere. One of the first things we'll do is move out of here, away from all these goddamned clerks."

"Really, Frank."

"A congressman has an expense account, you know. And I could even put you on my payroll. Everybody does that. You'll see a very different life style, Betty. Better days are coming. The only trouble is they should have been here years ago. But I'll make up for it, you can be sure of that, and this is only the *start.*"

Prippet's wife slipped out of her bed, sat next to him on his and took one of his hands in both of hers. "It hasn't mattered, dear," she said. "And it doesn't now. But it's sweet of you to want things for me." She made an awkward move to stroke his head and only succeeded in mussing his hair.

He gave her a cross look and patted it back into place. "I want them for both of us," he said. "We're not going to be like those zeros who come and go here without ever leaving a mark. We haven't been playing the game this long just to leave a blank on the scoreboard." He forced a smile. "We're entitled to our tin watches after all these years of service, but if I have my way, yours will be something more like gold and diamonds."

Her eyes turned soft with surprise, and her·whole face went so slack there were lines of what might have been grief around her mouth. "Why, Frank, that's very—"

"It's not going to stop with a crummy congressional district," he said. "I've seen enough of these elected people come and go. They think getting here is all that matters, but they're wrong. Getting here is easy; it's *staying* that counts. They don't know how to hang on, they haven't got the stuff. We'll show them what it takes to get on top and stay there. We'll show them what fifteen years of experience is worth."

"Yes we *will.*"

"And we'll enjoy ourselves every minute of it, Betty . . . starting with this weekend. A private plane. That's more like it. The last time . . . The Air Force flew that special group of us to a golf outing, remember? And it's a remarkable coincidence because that was to Georgia too. Imagine. Maybe it's more an omen than a coincidence. Should I bring my clubs this weekend? Probably not. If she didn't mention it I'd look pushy. But I ought to get them out. I'm going to get back into shape." Prippet got up and stood barefoot on the rug, stroking an invisible putter. "Where are they?" he said.

"Why, I think they're in the storeroom."

"I suppose I could rent a set down there if Bascule wanted to play."

"Very likely."

He took a final shot, made a clicking sound like a ball falling into a cup, then sat on the bed again. He took his wife's hand. "You'll see, Betty."

"I'm very glad for you, dear. And I'm sure things are going to turn out just the way you want them to."

"For us, sweetheart."

"That's *right*." She touched him briefly on the cheek. "It's very late. Don't you think we should turn in now?"

Prippet yawned. "It's been a long day. And there are going to be more of them. I'm really going to stay on top of this new project, I can tell you. No more pussyfooting around—they'd better be ready to hop."

Prippet's wife turned down the covers of his bed and he got in. She settled herself and put out the light.

There was another yawn in the darkness. "Look for those clubs tomorrow, will you?"

"I know where they are."

"I might need a new set."

"Whatever you think, dear."

"Well, goodnight."

"Goodnight, Frank."

There was the rustle of sheets, and shortly thereafter deep breathing. Prippet's wife tossed a few times, then gave up and lay very still while she looked at the shadows playing on the bedroom window and listened to the rain dripping from the trees.

The Prippets' light was the last one in Aquarelle to go out, and now the complex was dark except for the security lamps ringing its base and casting a flood of acid-colored light which seemed to be eating at the stone, threatening to topple the overhang of staggered terraces. An inner-belt highway wound beyond the barrier of trees, its globes tinting the rain amber. The highway verged on a stretch of bent, glistening swamp grass slowly being smothered by a tide of garbage fill topped with a thin layer of earth. There was a cluster of shacks at the edge of the dump, then a few frame houses, then the real beginnings of the slum which reached nearly into the heart of the city.

Cleaning crews were moving through the massive buildings of state, and the isolated rows of lighted windows made an intricate and senseless pattern of dashes interspersed with a rare dot. There was no movement in the streets. Washington didn't look so much abandoned as settled into a nighttime attitude of defense, an effect heightened when a searchlight from one of the nearby military installations raked the low ceiling, its beam bouncing unevenly and encountering nothing.

The city seemed to be waiting and slightly fearful, but not of an attack by its own citizenry, and not of a threat from present or future weapons, but from something out of time— perhaps an uncontrollable plague distilled from all the years of neglect and obfuscation and venality—and in spite of the statues and monuments and other manifestations of still-raw history, in spite of the glass and aluminum designed to give a sense of the immediate, the capital at night had the look of a city under seige, a city which was perhaps beginning to crumble.

About the Author

WILLIAM STEVENS was born in New York City, served in the Air Force, and at intervals has worked as a guided-missile technician, junkyard scout, industrial purchasing agent, bank teller, hotel manager, bartender, teacher and car salesman. The author of three previous novels, *The Peddler, The Gunner,* and *The Cannibal Isle,* he now lives in Barcelona, Spain, with his wife and five children.